PRAISE FOR *THE*

"[An] impressive psychological thriller . . . Banner keeps the reader guessing to the end."

—*Publishers Weekly*

"[A] sharply written and taut psychological thriller."

—*Seattle Times*

PRAISE FOR *AFTER NIGHTFALL*

"[A] gripping psychological thriller . . . Well-laid clues allow the reader to sleuth along."

—*Publishers Weekly*

"[A] compelling psychological suspense with a strong Pacific Northwest setting."

—*Seattle Times*

"An elegant and ⬛⬛⬛⬛⬛⬛⬛⬛⬛⬛⬛⬛⬛⬛⬛⬛⬛⬛⬛ on the edge of their seat until the final page."

—*Authorlink*

"*After Nightfall* is a chilling drama . . . Well-fleshed-out characters keep the reader wondering just what is going on."

—*New York Journal of Books*

PRAISE FOR *THE TWILIGHT WIFE*

"[A] harrowing plot that reveals memory to be both unreliable and impossible to fully wash away."

—Publishers Weekly

PRAISE FOR *THE GOOD NEIGHBOR*

"Could be the next *Gone Girl*."

—Harper's Bazaar

"Thrilling."

—First for Women

"Packed with mystery and suspense . . . the final destination is a total surprise. Well done."

—New York Journal of Books

"Breathtaking and suspenseful . . . unique and highly entertaining."

—Fresh Fiction

IN

ANOTHER

LIGHT

ALSO BY A.J. BANNER

The Good Neighbor
The Twilight Wife
After Nightfall
The Poison Garden

IN ANOTHER LIGHT

A. J. BANNER

LAKE UNION
PUBLISHING

Text copyright © 2021 by Anjali Writes LLC
All rights reserved.

Published by Lake Union Publishing, Seattle

www.apub.com

Amazon, the Amazon logo, and Lake Union Publishing are trademarks of Amazon.com, Inc., or its affiliates.

ISBN-13: 9781542031103
ISBN-10: 1542031109

Cover design by Rex Bonomelli

Printed in the United States of America

Some of you say, "Joy is greater than sorrow,"
and others say, "Nay, sorrow is the greater."
But I say unto you, they are inseparable.
Together they come, and when one sits alone
with you at your board, remember that the other
is asleep upon your bed.

—*Kahlil Gibran,* The Prophet

PROLOGUE

Phoebe steals up the winding, forested driveway, her hoodie drawn tight against the cold. The house looms into view, its solid front door locked. She circles around to the back, crouches outside the kitchen window, eavesdropping on another family's life.

No, not another family's—what should have been hers all along but was taken from her. A diffuse light falls from the window and reaches out into the open air, casting the grass in an ethereal silver glow. Each blade a motionless sculpture.

Only the twilight watches her now. There is something glittering and hopeful about the vast, darkening sky—as if loss and grief cannot survive there. In this evening of possibility, she can turn back time, start anew.

Voices emanate from inside the house, casual conversation, a word here and there, the rise and fall of laughter. Her pocket vibrates, and she pulls out her mobile phone, cups the screen with her hand to view a text from Renee. Don't do this. Come home. You are not yourself.

She has not been herself for some time now. Gone is the once-carefree woman who gave her all to a world that has not been kind, that has kept its secrets from her.

She deletes the message—it was never there. Craning her neck, she peers up over the windowsill, certain of what is inside—figures seated at a dining table, pretending their lives are normal, pretending they belong together. Soon, she will find a way inside.

CHAPTER ONE

Eleven Days Earlier

Phoebe tucks small spiked caps inside Mr. Parker's eyelids to make him look like he still has eyes. Then she slips cotton puffs beneath the lids to keep them closed, just so. No sutures required, although she had to glue his lips together, had to stuff cotton into his mouth and nose, which would've killed him if he'd still been breathing.

But she's only doing her job to restore his features for his wife. Mandy wants to view him one last time, to remember him the way he was. But if she could bear to see him in his natural condition, she would know that he has expired, kicked the bucket, bought the farm. Elvis has left the building.

Literally. His name was Elvis Parker. The town's last old-time barber, he worked out of a narrow shop on the waterfront in which he wielded his shiny blade, administering close shaves and buzz cuts, his customers ensconced in vintage vinyl barbershop chairs.

The shop existed on the cold shores of Puget Sound for time immemorial, and for all anyone knows, Elvis Parker owned the place since its inception. To Phoebe, he seemed ageless, indestructible. Now here he is, nothing but a shriveled shell.

Not that she is any better looking. When she glances in the mirror, she sees a wraith with hollow cheekbones and eyes that absorb light, no longer emitting any illumination of their own. Her brows grow untended, the bones defined beneath the flesh, as if they're slowly dissolving the surrounding tissue. It has been this way since the accident. She is gradually disappearing.

But Elvis made her feel visible. He acknowledged her, waving at her on their daily walks along the waterfront. She can still hear him calling out, *Top o' the morning, Phoebe!* as she passed in the opposite direction. When he greeted her, he seemed to see the old Phoebe, the hopeful woman she had once been. For this, she was grateful.

Now she is a mere ghost of herself, and Elvis lives only in memory. His hands will never wave again. They're folded across his abdomen, his fingers superglued together, his thumbs held in place with a ponytail tie that Phoebe borrowed from her assistant, Renee.

"You look spiffy now," Phoebe tells him. "Renee has good fashion sense, doesn't she? She always did. I would've picked a tuxedo, but you look much better in your pinstripe suit. She was right."

And Renee was savvy enough to button his shirt to the top, obscuring a tattoo of a winged heart bearing his ex-wife's name—a tattoo that reminds Phoebe of the one she saw on her own husband's cell phone a few years ago.

Mandy knew about her husband's tattoo, of course. She was married to him for forty-one years. But better not to display the reminder. The service will be difficult enough. Afterward, she will go home to face the rest of her life without him. Days, months, years will stretch ahead without a glimpse of his wry smile, ever again.

But painful reminders will keep popping up: mail arriving in his name, a cuff link left in a drawer, a forgotten slipper protruding from under the couch. She will hide photographs of him, because looking at his image will be too much to bear.

There's a tentative knock on the door. Phoebe stands motionless, hardly daring to breathe, hoping the intruder will go away. A soft, guttural voice says, "Phoebe? Are you in there?"

It's Mike Rivera, the new removal technician. Again. First thing Monday morning. Last Friday, he asked where he could find the infant-removal pouches. Thursday, he needed directions to the property room. As if he couldn't ask someone else. He should be out doing his job, picking up bodies in the mortuary's nondescript white van, the one with blacked-out windows designed to shield the public from death.

"I'm on deadline for a viewing!" she calls out, although this is not strictly true—she has time to finish preparing Elvis, but she does not want to talk to anyone.

"It'll only take a minute," he says, his shadow unmoving beneath the door.

"All right, come in," she says, awarding him extra points for persistence.

The knob turns, and he steps inside, tilting his head, his blond hair shiny beneath the stark fluorescent light. In his blue uniform and steel-toed boots, he's a strange-looking man with a longish face and slightly lopsided, prominent features. He reminds her of that movie star who drives fast cars and plays a bounty hunter chasing androids. The outside corners of his eyelids droop a little, giving him a sad look, although she supposes her perpetual frown and grayish, pinched visage aren't exactly Miss America material.

She doesn't usually care what she looks like to others, not anymore, so it irritates her that she's wiping her forehead with the back of her gloved hand, patting her hair, and smoothing the front of her smock. Mike makes her self-conscious, especially when he gives her that crooked smile.

She doesn't return the favor. He doesn't need any encouragement. His gaze flits around the room. Something is off about him this morning. He is usually relaxed, confident, but today he bites his lip nervously.

5

"Jeez, is that Elvis Parker?" He runs his fingers through his hair, making the strands stick straight up. "Last time I saw him, he was coughing, but I thought he had the flu."

"Try cancer," she replies. "He lived a long time, considering. Seventy-eight isn't bad when your lungs are mush."

"Guess I should quit," Mike says, patting the pack of cigarettes bulging in his breast pocket.

She gives him a strained smile. "Did you come here to discuss your vices, or is there something else I can do for you?" There she goes again with the acerbic tongue. She can't help herself.

"I'm heading out on a pickup," he says. "There's an unusual transfer coming from the coroner. You might want to avoid this one."

She laughs dryly. "Whatever it is, I can handle it." Mike has worked here only two weeks. He doesn't know her, doesn't understand that she has seen everything from bodies arriving in pieces to bloated green "floaters" pulled from the waters of Puget Sound.

"Trust me," he says. "This one might freak you out."

"Nothing freaks me out anymore."

"Suit yourself. But don't say I didn't warn you."

"If that's all—"

"Uh . . . one more thing. Renee wants you to come out with us tonight."

"On a Monday?"

He shrugs. "Monday's like any other day. I got called in for a pickup yesterday. We're 24-7, right?"

"Thank you for the invitation, but I'll pass." Phoebe hasn't gone out with any of her colleagues in three years. She hasn't gone out much at all except for solitary walks, necessary shopping, occasional forays to the library for a new stack of escapist mystery novels. She much prefers books to people.

"We're going to that new pub on Main Street, the Rusty Salmon. You should come. Renee thought you would want company, since today is, you know . . ."

Phoebe's face flushes, the heat rising in her cheeks. Her fingers itch to strangle Renee, who obviously told him that today is the third anniversary of the accident. "Thank you, but I would rather poke out my eye with a trocar." She doesn't mean to be rude, but she's only telling the truth.

Mike remains undeterred. His grin widens to reveal nicotine-stained teeth. "Good one. A trocar," he says, although he may not understand the reference, unless he transfers bodies to traditional mortuaries where embalming is still performed, where the sharp surgical tool is still used to drain fluids from the dead.

"I'd love to keep chatting," Phoebe lies, gesturing toward Elvis. "But I should get back to it before he starts to stink."

"Right, you're on deadline." Mike turns and leaves the room, the door shutting after him with a whoosh. As the air rushes through the vents, she catches the edge of the recurring nightmare, the pelting snow, the flash of metal as the car flies through the blizzard, flipping over and over.

Her hand trembles as she picks up the makeup brush off the floor. She didn't even notice dropping it. Deep breaths, steady as she goes. She must focus on Elvis, on highlighting the appropriate areas of his face: the frontal eminences, the zygomatic arches. She darkens the temples, the orbits, the root of the nose.

The challenge will be filling out his sunken cheeks. Working on the dead requires special skill. No amount of training as a sculptor prepared her for the human face, which is not made of clay.

She is so immersed in her task that when the alarm bell rings, she nearly jumps. The plastic desktop timer shaped like a small human skull reminds her to take lunch breaks, but she often forgets it's there. The entire morning has passed her by.

She presses the button to turn off the alarm, removes her smock and white lab coat, although the protection is overkill. Dead bodies aren't usually dangerous unless they contaminate the drinking water supply or carry the plague or typhus and also harbor the fleas or lice that transmit the diseases.

Little chance of that here.

Still, out of habit, she washes her hands in a Betadine solution. As she scrubs beneath her fingernails, she gazes out the window at a young couple strolling through the eco-friendly burial forest, where grave sites are marked with discreet, natural headstones. Barry Severson, as the owner of Fair Winds, keeps a map of the burial plots in his office in case families or the authorities ever ask him to quickly locate remains. But nothing much will be left behind in the ground—except maybe a few scattered bones, gold fillings, artificial metal hip joints. At Fair Winds, belongings are not buried with the dead. No clothing or cars or motorcycles or musical instruments.

Phoebe turns away from the window, dries her chapped hands on a paper towel. "Stay spiffy," she tells Elvis. She switches off the light and leaves the room, retreating down the hall into the comfort of her office, her cocoon with its entire wall of books. It was generous of Barry to cede her this space when he bought Logan's half of the business. She did not mind stepping back into the shadows, staying on in a narrowed capacity, hiding out in the preparation rooms, content to work on faces.

Well, maybe *content* isn't the proper word. She prefers to remain in limbo, to act as if she, too, has died. She walks the earth, but she might as well be a phantom flitting through her life unnoticed, disturbing the air but barely registering her presence.

A car rumbles into the parking lot outside, where underground tree roots push up through cracks in the concrete. In that empty spot at the corner, the signpost, now half-covered in moss, still reads RESERVED FOR OWNER, although Barry won't park there out of respect for Phoebe. Logan always chose that spot, parking the car at a slight angle, never straight. She does not use that parking space, as she generally walks the mile or so to work.

Mike's warning plays back through her mind, about the transfer coming from the coroner. *You might want to avoid this one.* He has sparked her curiosity. She glances out the window. No sign of the white van in the parking lot. He must still be out on the pickup.

Turning back toward the room, she empties her thermos of water into the potted winter camellia vibrant with brilliant red blooms, a recent gift from a grateful customer. The accompanying note read:

Dear Phoebe,

Thank you for your compassion when we lost Mom last month.

Lost, as if dead people can be found again. Phoebe merely restored Mom's face, scraping off bacteria like a layer of pond scum.

You did a beautiful job with her hair.

Renee did the honors, wielding her Supercuts skills from yesteryear.

And her smile.

Well, Mom wasn't smiling before Phoebe worked on her. She was dead. The dead don't smile, a complex expression requiring numerous facial muscles.

Her green burial was perfect. She loved her flower garden, and she always wanted to nurture the earth whence she came.

With love and appreciation, Muriel Watson

Who writes whence *anymore?* Phoebe wonders.

Muriel and her sister, Miranda—that's who. They're quite a pair, both archaic in their use of the English language.

But the letter reminds Phoebe of her calling to protect the bereaved from the necessary messiness of death. She creates the impression of slumber, protecting grief-stricken families from the truth: smashed-in faces, bodies in advanced stages of decay or arriving in damaged pieces.

When Muriel Watson touched her dead mother's cheek, mouthing the words *sleep well,* Phoebe knew she had done her job, even though the cheek was mostly made of wax. She had waved her wand and conjured a comforting illusion.

Her job looks so easy, but nobody knows how many years of practice were required to hone her skills, how many classes, how many times she messed up while learning to create wax ears or noses or chins.

These days, she is proud of her work, even though sometimes a sudden realization hits her: that she creates art from the shell of a person who used to be alive. Who once laughed, loved, hated, cried, who once had thoughts. She is constructing only a vague approximation of life. She is not fooling anyone.

But her misgivings quickly pass, and she keeps going. *After all,* she thinks, *don't we all lie to each other? To ourselves? We pretend to listen, nodding our heads, when we're thinking of what to make for dinner. When people ask how we are, we say we're fine, which is what I will say next time anyone asks.*

Like Renee, for example. Maybe she thinks that on this anniversary of the accident, Phoebe will flip the switch and jump into the cremation chamber. But dying in flames would not be a dignified way to go—certainly not painless, either. It would be far easier to simply fall asleep and never wake.

Which is perhaps what she has already done. She moves through life in a mechanical way, as if sleepwalking. Every day at this time, as she is doing now, she opens the bottom drawer of her desk and removes her brown paper lunch bag, wrinkled and softened from multiple uses. She lays out her usual hummus-and-avocado sandwich, organic apple, and bottle of chamomile tea on the desk in front of her, everything arranged symmetrically.

Then she unwraps her sandwich and chews on the empty future as she flips through her pile of mail, which includes Barry's new brochure advertising the revamped "green" funeral home. The cover page reads, WELCOME TO FAIR WINDS. He slapped a sticky note on the front: *PLEASE REVIEW AND APPROVE.*

The interior pages feature photographs of each staff member along with short biographies. Beside Phoebe's picture, which notably shows her maiden name, Glassman, the biography reads: *Ms. Glassman is an expert at styling and cosmetology. Educated at the University of Washington, she is a former artist and sculptor. She will beautify your loved one . . .*

Beautify . . .

All right, she could go with that description, but the word *former* gives her pause. She is still an artist. The headshot is four years old, from happier days, when her dark hair tumbled past her shoulders, her cheeks were filled out and glowing, and her brown eyes shone.

Now Phoebe is adrift, ephemeral, her skin stretched over her bones, her hair cut short for convenience. Nobody would recognize her from the photograph. Maybe this is as it should be.

She scrawls *approved* on the brochure, suspecting that Barry also emailed her the file, but she avoids the internet as much as possible to protect herself from alarming news—anything that might trigger a traumatic memory.

At the bottom of her pile of mail, she finds the new mortuary-supply catalog. She doesn't know why the catalogs still end up on her desk. Maybe because they're often addressed to Logan McClary, and she is his surviving spouse.

She flips through the numerous ads for embalming fluids, formulated to achieve maximum restoration for "natural" elasticity, as well as products to solve every possible problem from jaundice to edema, as if these diseases of the dead can be cured. Next thing, she imagines, they will offer a new product, "reanimator," for achieving maximum resurrection and return to actual life.

These noxious substances are relics of the Civil War, when embalming evolved as a way to preserve the bodies of fallen soldiers so they wouldn't stink on the long journey home on the train. Eventually, they always did. Start to stink, that is. Bodies decay. It's what they do. Pickling and preserving them will only delay the process.

At Fair Winds, embalming is no longer offered, and most clients don't demand facial reconstructions, either. But a few outliers, like Mandy Parker, insist on viewings, on gazing upon the faces of their loved ones in repose. And thus, Phoebe's artistic skills come into play, aided by solvents, glues, powders, and brush-on sealants to create the illusion of a "second skin" over incisions and wounds that will never heal.

For the patients on Phoebe's table, there will be no recovery, no waking up. The dead will be interred—ironically, in an eco-friendly burial forest—some of them still caked in chemicals and waxes.

As she turns the pages, her fading, chipped nail polish catches the light, and she is reminded of how she used to take better care of herself. Before. These nails are so unlike the glittery press-on ones that she wore on her wedding day. At the reception, while she was making a toast to Logan, her fake thumbnail fell off and plopped into his glass of champagne, making everyone laugh. She expected to enjoy such mirth, endless anniversaries and toasts, for decades. She was wrong.

Instead, she is flipping through images of tiny caskets, "removal pouches" in a variety of festive colors, "miscarriage kits," vaults, metal and wood caskets in small sizes. All displayed like party favors. She carefully rips out the pages, tears them apart, and quietly hides the crumpled bits of paper in the recycling bin beneath her desk.

She looks up to see the white van pulling into the far corner of the parking lot. Mike and another technician unload a body, an adult in a large cadaver pouch. They hurry the stretcher in through a side door, looking around in a furtive way, nearly tripping over themselves.

After they disappear from view, Phoebe quickly finishes her lunch. She should work on Elvis, but she needs to see what Mike is up to. She is halfway down the hall when a text pops up on her cell phone from Renee. Come to prep room two. Don't let anyone see you.

Serendipity—I'm almost there, Phoebe thinks, her fingers hovering over the screen. Maybe the "unusual transfer" from the coroner is freaking out Renee. She was always squeamish, even in grade school. And this is not her normal profession, nothing much like fashion retail.

On my way, Phoebe texts back.

When she opens the door to the prep room, Renee whips around, her cheeks flushed, the clip at the back of her head barely restraining her luxurious reddish hair. She looks refined in layered New York street style—black ankle boots, wide-leg pants, and a patterned turtleneck sweater to add a touch of the bohemian. She has always had a natural, unique sense of style that Phoebe could never match. Even the freckles on her face seem placed there to enhance her beauty. She presses a finger to her lips, rushes past Phoebe to shut the door.

"What's going on?" Phoebe asks. The faint, putrid odor of death wafts through the air. The stark fluorescent bulb leaches all warmth and color from the room. Everything appears gray, metallic, lifeless.

Renee has gone pale, her eyes wide. "Barry said not to show you."

"Mike warned me, too. What gives?"

"You should take a look. But brace yourself."

"I'm fine," Phoebe says with confidence. She approaches the body, folds back the sheet to reveal the face of the decedent on the table. The dead woman is slim, her unruly hair a dull brown. Her skin looks pale beneath the unsparing light, which is much harsher than the gentle pink lights installed in the family viewing rooms.

"Phoebe . . . I'll get in trouble," Renee says softly. "You can't tell Barry I showed you—"

"I'll take responsibility," Phoebe says, moving in closer to examine the telltale signs of a partial autopsy—the cut lines on the woman's forehead, barely hidden by the hairline, the vertical line of sutures at the top of the sternum, above the sheet, which reveals only her shoulders, neck, and head. Her skin has darkened in some areas, bruised by lividity, from her blood settling due to gravity. There is no way to know what color her eyes were in life. They've sunk into recessed clouds. Her mouth yawns open, a natural occurrence after death.

The woman was young, nobody Phoebe recognizes. But as she gazes at the woman's face, her nerve endings catch fire. The woman's chin, her high forehead, her oval face, the shape of her nose, streamlined except for a small bump halfway down.

"Holy crap," Phoebe says, stepping backward, slammed by what she is seeing.

"I shouldn't have shown you," Renee says, rushing to yank up the sheet, but Phoebe grabs her arm and says, "Leave it." Her breathing comes in fast, shallow gasps.

Keep it together, Phoebe tells herself. *You're used to this. You've done this before.*

"Here, sit down," Renee says, pulling up a chair, but Phoebe waves her arm dismissively, unable to tear her gaze from the woman on the table. She is a younger version of Phoebe, nearly her exact double.

CHAPTER TWO

As Phoebe takes in the mirrorlike image, the woman's features shimmer and blur as if viewed through heat waves on a blistering day. It's not right that someone so young has passed on, but Phoebe has come to understand that a long life is never guaranteed. People go at any age, sometimes a minute after they're born.

Every life has its natural span, until the Lord calls you home, Mandy Parker told her at the memorial service after the accident. Or perhaps someone else spoke those words—there were so many of them, and none of them a comfort. The aphorisms wounded Phoebe's soul, the pain dulled only by the heavy drugs in her brain. She drifted above the mourners like a weather system created by benzodiazepines.

But now, her mind is clear, this dead woman real on her table. *Get a grip,* she tells herself. She draws a deep breath, trying to center her thoughts. This has happened before, a body arriving that resembles someone she knows, but then the differences emerge, the divergences, and she realizes it's a relative or merely a coincidental resemblance. But she has never seen a near-exact replica of *herself* on the table, at least, never a young woman who looks *so* much like her.

This woman was likely in her early thirties, perhaps a decade younger than Phoebe, who is forty-three. The body has been washed, the skin still damp, the hair wet, and there's a steady drip of water from the faucet, a distant rush down the pipes extending back into the wall. The plumbing forms a complex network of conduits, ducts, and fittings, octopus-like tentacles reaching beneath the preparation tables and into a filtering drainage system. It wouldn't do to contaminate the freshwater supply.

A droplet glistens on the woman's shoulder like a forgotten tear. But she looks peaceful, not sad, no frown lines on her forehead. She no longer suffers. Phoebe almost envies her.

"Are you okay?" Renee asks.

"I'm fine," Phoebe says, taking a deep breath. "You weren't supposed to show me this body because she looks exactly like me, right?"

Renee nods. "Barry and Mike didn't want you to freak out, I guess. She looks like your twin."

But there are differences, Phoebe thinks. The young woman's hair is light brown, her fingernails manicured, not short, and she was thicker, more robust than Phoebe. *Curvier.* "How old was she exactly?"

"Thirty-two."

"Too young," Phoebe says with a heavy heart. "Who was she?" The ankle tag reads PAULINE STEELE. The name does not ring a bell.

"Your long-lost cousin or maybe a sister?" Renee says.

"I would've known about her. My parents would've told me."

"Are you sure? I mean, what if they didn't?"

"What are you thinking? My mom had a kid with another man? That would've been impossible to hide. I would've been ten years old. I would've seen her walking around with a giant belly."

"Could you ask her? We could call the Willows right now—"

"She barely remembers my name. I wouldn't want to upset her. But no, there's no chance."

"What about your dad? I mean, could he have had an affair?"

Phoebe wishes she could ask him. She can hardly believe he's been gone six years. "My dad was Mr. Shy. He stuttered around strangers.

Seriously?" His preferred pastime was grading his students' English papers.

"No, I guess not. He was always a reserved nerd."

"That's an understatement." Professor Raja Glassman was unassuming to others, but to Phoebe, he was a loving parent, her steady support during her mother's many absences to dig up ancient cities in faraway countries. She can't remember her father ever looking at a woman other than his wife. "The resemblance is a coincidence."

"You're right," Renee says, her shoulders relaxing. "It happens, right? People have doubles."

"Yes, exactly. Where's the paperwork?"

"It's in Barry's office."

"What happened to her?" Phoebe reaches out but stops short of touching Pauline's hair.

"A jogger found her in her car at Waterfront Park. Opioid overdose."

"So sad. Another one. Accident or . . . ?"

"Inconclusive, I believe, but probably accidental." Renee plays nervously with her bracelets.

"What about family?"

"Only her mom in California. She just had surgery, can't travel yet. We're supposed to send the remains—"

"No father? Spouse? Siblings?"

"Apparently not."

Phoebe steps back farther, putting a little distance between herself and the body. "How did it all play out? I'm assuming Don called from the coroner's office?"

"Yeah, he spoke to Barry, and then Barry sent Mike on the pickup."

"They kept me out of the loop," Phoebe says, her voice tight with resentment. "In my fragile condition, I could so easily fall apart, seeing my doppelgänger lying there, right? Because maybe that's where I secretly want to be, dead on the mortuary table." She laughs at the absurdity of the efforts to shield her. "They could've sent her to Haven of Repose."

"Haven of Repose has flood damage from the storm last week."

How serendipitous, Phoebe thinks, *that this doppelgänger should end up right here, under my nose.* "Do we know what Pauline Steele was doing in Bayport?"

"No idea. She lived in Portland, I think."

"Oregon, seriously?"

"Go figure," Renee says.

"So strange," Phoebe says. "Could you give me a minute with her?"

Renee hesitates, fusses with her hair. "I don't know—maybe you should take a break, get some air."

"I don't need any air," Phoebe snaps. She's not breakable. To withstand what she has been through, she has hardened herself, grown stronger.

Renee lowers her voice to an urgent whisper. "What if I piss off Barry? I need this job. I can't go back to New York. *We* can't go back."

Phoebe knows what Renee means. Her return to Bayport was hasty—she fled her husband, bringing her young son, Vik, clear across the country. But better not to ask too many questions. "I got you the job," Phoebe whispers. "I won't let you lose it."

"It's like I'm still on probation," Renee whispers back. "Even after six months. Barry thinks I suck at this kind of work."

Which you sometimes do, Phoebe wants to say. *This is not your calling.* "Don't worry," she says instead. "I'll be quick. I just want a closer look. Two minutes."

"Okay, but I'm holding you to that." Renee sighs and leaves the room.

Phoebe looks down at the body. "What happened to you? How did you end up here? Who were you?" She folds back the sheet covering the shoulders, aware of the inertness of the body on the table, of the congealed blood in collapsed veins. And there, on Pauline's right arm, just above the elbow, is a familiar tattoo, a unique and intricate motif in black and white, so carefully designed. There is no mistaking it. Very distinct. The butterfly in flight, and on one side, the wings dissolving into many tinier butterflies taking off, becoming flower petals as they fly, smaller and smaller, on the cusp of life and death. Phoebe has seen this tattoo before, on her husband's cell phone screen.

CHAPTER THREE

The air expands in her lungs, transforming into a gaseous poison. *Okay, stay calm. Don't jump to conclusions.*

But this is no coincidence. Pauline might have come here searching for Logan's widow to make amends for an affair. She must've known he was dead. But she came here three years after his funeral.

Phoebe pulls her cell phone from her pocket, snaps a few photographs of the tattoo, then she folds down the sheet to Pauline's navel and scans her torso and arms for signs of trauma, for any obvious cause of death. Nothing. Pauline could have simply fallen asleep and never woken up.

Phoebe starts to pull the sheet farther down but stops. *I can't do this.* She's accustomed to seeing the dead in all forms—battered, disease ridden, clothed or unclothed. But this is different. She doesn't want to see the whole body. Doesn't want the image in her head of a woman who might have been screwing her husband.

Phoebe pulls the sheet back up, accusations crowding her mind. She longs to resurrect Pauline from the dead, interrogate her about how well she knew Logan and why she was in town. But Phoebe already knows the answers. She would be naive not to. She *was* naive, back then. Naive and willfully blind.

Perhaps this is not the same tattoo she saw on his cell phone screen. But there can't be many dissolving butterflies in the world in exactly these colors, on a woman who resembles her.

She scrolls through the camera roll on her phone, all the way back three years, six months. She has not dared to look at those happy days. Gritting her teeth, she swipes past the pictures of joy, past the life that is no longer hers.

Her fingers tremble, her breathing shallow. There it is: the butterfly on his home screen. She snapped a picture of his phone with her phone when he was asleep, when her antennae had already begun to quiver. When she had nothing but hunches. When she needed concrete evidence.

His phone is long gone now, but the night Phoebe saw the tattoo remains vivid in her mind. Cinematic. She can replay the details. She remembers Logan pulling his arm out from under her, turning over in bed, his back to her. The moon was bright, almost full, reflecting off his dark hair. The antique clock on the nightstand ticked loudly, and she wondered how anyone could have slept with that noise a hundred years earlier.

But Logan snored through everything. He'd brought the clock as a gift, another collectible to add to the clutter. At least he'd thought of her while he'd been away. She felt some relief, now that he was home, even though he'd arrived late, claiming to have been slowed by traffic on the highway from Portland. An accident, an overturned semi, racing too fast in the rain, had stopped the cars for miles, he'd said.

She'd told him he was away too much. She needed him to stick around, and he'd promised he would. *I'm working on our future,* he'd said. *You'll love it, wait and see.*

But she wondered about Fair Winds. Barry was left to run the business without his partner, and when Logan returned from trade shows, she could sometimes hear the two of them arguing in Barry's office. She felt slighted. Logan had promised her that he would make her a partial owner of the business. She was smart, talented. She had good ideas. But he'd begun to shut her out.

He'd changed in other subtle ways, too. His touch was distracted, perfunctory. And he smelled different. Sometimes, the odor of a nightclub clung to him, the faint scents of tobacco and alcohol tingeing his skin. But he said he'd been in meetings during the day, in his hotel room at night.

He'd come back from Portland yawning, claiming to have worked so hard, he needed to sleep. Even though she'd worn a new, practically transparent negligee. It wasn't the first time he'd made an excuse. He seemed foreign to her, like some stranger sleeping in the berth next to her on a train.

When he began snoring again, she slipped out of bed and tiptoed to the bureau, lit by the moon. On top, he had emptied the contents of his pockets. Coins, crumpled bills, a folded receipt. His wallet. His keys. His phone.

She grabbed the phone and went out into the hallway, tapped the home button. The screen lit up. He had changed the image. It was no longer a photograph of their lush garden in summer. Instead, there was an arm bearing an intricate tattoo. A woman's slim but shapely, tanned upper arm. Close up, an intimate shot.

Phoebe's insides congealed, a sinking sensation in her gut. She didn't want this to be happening. She wanted to see his eyes filled with love, as they had been when he'd recited their wedding vows. They had planned the ceremony together, had laid out all the travel brochures, the honeymoon options. And so much more. How could he do this?

Or was she paranoid?

She had seen hundreds of tattoos, but never one like this.

No, she was not paranoid, and it wasn't only the tattoo. His behavioral changes had accumulated over time to form a single word: *unfaithful*.

No, don't go there, she admonished herself. Desperate for an inno-cent explanation, she reached for unlikely scenarios. He was learning to become a tattoo artist. He was going to surprise her with the news. She thought all this even as she punched in his four-digit passcode. If she could get into his phone, maybe she could find emails, texts, more photographs. Evidence. And she would know for sure.

She must have made a mistake. The code did not work. She tried again. No luck. She didn't want to risk trying a third time. His phone might lock up, and he would know she'd been snooping.

If she were to ask him about the new code on his phone, he would give her a casually composed, plausible explanation. He would say the phone had prompted him to change the passcode or he'd been prompted to upgrade the operating system, and in the process, he'd chosen a new code.

She wanted to stomp back into the bedroom, shake him awake, hit him in the head with the phone. Demand to know who the woman was and why her tattooed arm was on his cell phone screen.

But Phoebe had other considerations, other reasons for remaining quiet. She didn't want to argue now. Or anytime. It would be useless. She knew even then that he would not admit to having an affair.

And she was so tired. The kind of tired that pressed into her bones, compressed her lungs. She did not have the strength to fight with him, to counter his magical explanations designed to pacify her.

She went back to bed and fell into a shallow, restless sleep. In the morning, when she snapped awake, he was already up. His side of the bed was empty. She found him sipping coffee and reading the newspa-per at the kitchen table. His phone sat on the countertop. When she surreptitiously tapped the screen, the familiar, colorful garden photo-graph appeared. The butterfly tattoo was gone.

In the end, she asked him about it. And he said without blinking that he'd seen the tattoo on a stranger and thought he might want one someday. In fact, he said, they should get matching tattoos, he and Phoebe, of two butterflies.

She sensed that he'd made up his answer on the spot. He insisted that he didn't know the tattooed woman, and weren't there countless people in the world with skin art? Hadn't they seen enough of those people at the mortuary?

She had to concede this was true, although a warning light blinked in the back of her mind. She pressed him a few more times. His answer never changed, and he gave his perfectly plausible reason for the new passcode: he'd upgraded the operating system.

Now, three and a half years later, Phoebe's stomach roils. She is surprised at herself, at her desperate need for an alternate explanation, even now. She longs to exonerate Logan, to remember him as a saint. But he was a deceiver, a philanderer. *Pauline probably fucked my husband.* Maybe she came here . . . for forgiveness. Now. After all this time.

Perhaps this is a leap, Phoebe thinks. Her mind is jumping ahead, making assumptions based on a simple image of a tattoo. But it wasn't just the tattoo. She remembers his hushed phone calls in his home office behind the closed door, his long trips during which he sometimes didn't answer his phone, his sometimes-distant expression. The way he lied about small things. And Phoebe relies on her gut, on her intuition, after years of intimacy with him. Yes, she knew, she understood, that Pauline's tattoo was the tip of a much deeper proverbial iceberg.

I'm glad you're dead, Pauline Steele, Phoebe thinks, but then in horror, she yanks back her hatred. She didn't mean it. Poor Pauline. Maybe the naive girl never knew about Logan's other life. He probably duped her the way he duped Phoebe. But again, somehow Pauline showed up here now, not three years ago.

Back in her office, Phoebe calls Don's cell phone. His message blares in her ear, his voice deep, with a nasal twang: *You have reached Donald Westfield at the county coroner's office. Please leave a message . . .*

"I need to talk to you about Pauline Steele," she says briskly, trying to sound businesslike. "Call me as soon as you can."

Then she powers up the computer, googles Pauline Steele. The young woman's Facebook and Instagram accounts pop up, private and locked. Her profile photo shows her face gazing into the sun. She's smiling, her hazel eyes bright and alive. Animated. *This is a difference between us,* Phoebe thinks. *My eyes are brown.*

A few of Pauline's Facebook posts are marked "public." Mountain vistas, trees, books in a library, clichés in handwriting. She liked folk bands, Netflix shows. She listed her location as Portland, Oregon. All the details that make up a life. Wish me luck on my journey, she wrote in one post, showing a path leading into a misty wood. And then: Help me solve the mystery.

Phoebe scrolls through the comments. One comes from a sharp-featured woman named Xia Page, her cropped hair blonde, streaked with purple. The guy has a habit of disappearing. He's an asshole.

Did she mean Logan? That would be a stretch, but still. Phoebe clicks through to Xia Page's profile. More of her information is public, unprotected by her privacy settings. She works at a restaurant called Forever Vegan. Phoebe scrolls back through images of her hikes in the mountains, outings with friends and family, and there is a photograph of her and Pauline, cheek to cheek over a spaghetti meal in what appears to be a dining room. Besties and housemates forever.

So Pauline and Xia were roommates. Phoebe lingers over Xia's profile, then jots down as much information as she can. Xia's name, her place of work. If necessary, it should be easy to find Pauline's most recent address in Portland, which might still be Xia's address.

There are no online images of Pauline's specific butterfly tattoo. Phoebe tries a variety of search terms and clicks through hundreds of internet photographs until her shoulders hurt from hunching over, her vision blurring.

When she stands and stretches, the day is almost gone. She knows little more than she did when she first saw Pauline on the table. Don has not returned her call. How busy can a coroner be?

Fine, if he won't give her more answers, she will seek them on her own. Phoebe slinks down the hall and unlocks the door to the property room, which holds decedents' personal effects. Dust motes shimmer in the air, caught in the winter sunlight streaming in through a single window. This room is a cemetery of sorts, a temporary burial place for the effects of the dead, held until families show up to claim them. An almost-forgotten space.

A few boxes have been here for months, some for a year. The unclaimed effects are paired with matching cremated human remains, which are kept in a separate storage unit. She peruses the labeled boxes, finds Pauline's on the middle shelf, right in front.

She spirits the box back to her office. It's against the rules to riffle through others' belongings. But she is only borrowing these items before they're sent off to the next of kin. If anyone asks, she will say she is doing her duty, taking the required inventory, documenting every detail.

Inside the box, the printed inventory list sits on top, signed and dated by Renee in her flowery handwriting. Phoebe sets aside the list and pulls out Pauline's belongings, one by one. Blue cotton bikini underpants, jeans one size up from hers. Socks, boots. Waterproof lace-ups. Also one size up.

Underneath a knit scarf, she finds a black handbag containing pink lipstick, a small hairbrush, a travel-size bottle of lotion, lip balm, moisturizing eye drops. A key ring holding nail clippers, a tiny flashlight, and a few keys. A dead iPhone similar to hers, but her charging cable doesn't seem to work.

She finds a wallet with a driver's license listing an address in Oregon, takes a picture with her phone. Pauline weighed 120 pounds, ten pounds more than Phoebe. Eyes: hazel. Hair: brown. Height: five feet, six inches. Two inches taller than Phoebe. No credit cards.

But there is a roll of antacid tablets, a red-coated pill, a penny. Numerous business cards and pocket photos in Pauline's wallet. It takes some time for Phoebe to look through all of them. Stuck to the back of a business card is a faded photograph, creased and ripped on one side. It's only half a color picture. At first, she doesn't quite comprehend what she is seeing. The hair, the smile, the clothing. She recognizes the shirt, the background crowd at Pike Place Market in downtown Seattle. Her hands tremble, a cloud passing through the room. Invisible, cold fingers press on her throat. It can't be true, but it is. In Pauline Steele's purse, Phoebe has found a photograph of herself.

CHAPTER FOUR

The floor tilts, nausea rising in her throat. She sits back, draws a deep breath, looks at the photograph closely beneath the light of her desk lamp. The picture was taken seven years ago, she estimates. Her skin was tanned, smooth, no sign of grief or pain in her eyes. No inkling of the future. She can barely remember the way she felt in that former life: still full of happiness and hope at thirty-six. And she remembers the person she was then, too—carefree, adventurous. She and Logan backpacked through Olympic National Park, making love in meadows beneath the moonlight, swimming in clear pools fed by waterfalls from snowmelt. In those days, anything was possible, and she felt invincible, immortal, her heart open.

The photograph was taken when she and Logan were visiting Seattle early in their relationship, when they were giddy in love, hardly aware of anyone else, infatuated with each other. Leaving a wake of failed relationships behind them. He had been married once back east, while Phoebe's longtime boyfriend had never wanted to commit to marriage.

She looks good in the image, flushed and healthy. Logan had been there in the other half of the photograph, the missing half. She can remember the way he looked, too. Handsome, as if he'd been lifted from the cover of *GQ* magazine with his piercing, dark eyes, his James Bond expression, his dark hair windswept, a slight cleft in his chin. At other angles, in other light, he could look haunted. Not in this picture. In this image, he looked open, smiling, caught in an unguarded moment. But someone ripped him away, obliterated him. There she is, alone in the past.

That day, she and Logan walked from the ferry landing all the way to Pike Street. In the background, there's a sign for an underground bookstore and the fuzzy shape of the woman who painted her entire body green and dressed up as the Statue of Liberty. The sun was shining, people passing in a blur. The produce stands displayed colorful fruits and vegetables in pyramids.

Logan is absent from the image, but his arm is still there around Phoebe, disconnected from his missing body, in the mauve sweater Phoebe had given him. She wore a pink winter coat to match her cold nose.

This picture was one of their favorites. They were both so happy. They checked into a hotel that night, and Logan called in sick the next morning. He'd never missed a day of work in his life, until then. Phoebe corrupted him.

Now, she sees her past self as a distant stranger. She has a strong urge to tear the photograph into tiny strips of confetti, but she needs the evidence that Pauline must've known who she was, must've known Logan was gone. A simple internet search would've yielded the information. Surely she would've visited Phoebe at work or at home.

Voices approach in the hall. Phoebe's office darkens. The wind picks up, bending the spindly trees outside. The whole day seems brittle, easily broken.

She tucks the photograph into her pocket. The voices recede down the hall. The sun hangs at a low angle in the sky, nearly dropping below the horizon.

Don Westfield might have come across the photograph, or perhaps he simply missed it, since there are so many cards and pictures in Pauline's wallet. He may know who Pauline was.

He knew Logan, after all. The two were friends. They might've confided in each other. Men did that, kept each other's secrets.

Phoebe holds on to the photograph, returns the rest of Pauline's effects to the property room, then paces in her office, staring at the picture, trying to decide what to do. The mortuary has gone quiet. Most everyone seems to have left for the day, and she hasn't yet seen the death certificate. She hurries down the hall to Barry's office, finds the door locked. She must have just missed him. She doesn't have time to go to his house—she needs to visit her mother tonight at the Willows.

CHAPTER FIVE

On her usual walk home, Phoebe strides past the waterfront shops, the library, the fire station. Her breath condenses into puffs of cloud in the cold. At twilight the town glows, shadows elongating. She climbs the hill into her quiet neighborhood, and when her Craftsman-style bungalow comes into view, half-hidden by the wild front garden, the wind picks up, swirling dead leaves through the dead grass and the dead stalks of flowering plants that she should have cut back in the autumn.

She grabs a meager stack of mail from the box, doesn't even bother to look through the envelopes. She only ever receives fundraising demands, shopping catalogs, coupons for local grocery stores. Bills.

On the porch, her worn welcome mat reads WIPE YOUR PAWS, but nobody ever visits anymore. She should get the porch railing fixed; the wood is beginning to rot in the damp northwest climate, and she imagines the carpenter ants and subterranean termites tunneling in, taking over the house and evicting her.

There was a time when she hosted fundraisers here for the forest reserve, a network of wooded trails she worked to protect for future generations. The volunteers met twice a month for dinner, often hosted by Phoebe. And she had started two local book clubs, but she has lost track of them now. She can't focus on reading anymore, can't smile or laugh or socialize with those whose lives are easy.

Inside the house, the past exerts its own gravity, the air heavy with dust and memories. Logan's belongings remain, although Phoebe told her therapist, Dr. Ogawa, that they'd been packed up and donated to the homeless shelter. But on the antique coatrack in the entryway, Logan's parkas, pullovers, and Seattle Seahawks hoodies still hang on hooks. In the closet, she shoved extra boots and shoes all the way to the back. The past crowds into the present, the ancient books and figurines on the shelves, antique desks, and side tables jostling for space between the sagging couch and the vintage armchairs.

Medicine bottles from bygone eras catch the light, delicate crystal vases glinting on the coffee table, no longer at risk of being knocked over by Phoebe's gray tabby, Remington, who passed away last Christmas at age twenty-two. He slipped through her fingers like sand, blew away in the wind, and with him he took what little remained of her heart.

She navigates the obstacle course of piled-up junk into the kitchen, tosses the stack of mail onto the countertop, throws off her shoes, lets out her breath. The answering machine blinks insistently. Before she checks the messages, anything is possible. Logan might be calling to say it was all a mistake, he didn't have an affair. He always loved only her. He didn't get into the car that night. Nobody took the winding, icy road out of town a little too fast. Nobody lost control of the car. Nobody spun off the road on the way to Bayport Pizza. She had it all wrong, he would remind her.

Or, oh no, it could be someone from the Willows, calling to say her mother fell and hit her head or wandered off the property. But to Phoebe's relief, it's only a marketing call dictated by a computerized voice, trying to get her to buy life insurance. The Willows would call her cell phone number. They know she's coming by tonight.

Phoebe hits the "Delete" button, goes down the hall to take a shower. Beneath the rushing hot water, she scrubs off her day, all the lingering wax and glue and mortuary makeup.

She dresses in comfortable jeans and a sweater and drives through town to the Willows, a sprawling one-story building in a clearing surrounded by gardens and forest.

As usual, the foyer smells like disinfectant and stale coffee. She signs in on the guest sheet in the reception room furnished with soft blue couches, printed carpets, and leafy indoor plants. She makes her way through a labyrinth of hallways to her mother's apartment. The door is propped open. For as long as Phoebe can remember, Lidia Glassman has hated enclosed spaces. Perhaps someone locked her in a closet when she was a child. She suffered a panic attack once in the car when the door got stuck. The lock didn't pop up. While Phoebe's father reached over to help, she climbed into the back seat, flung open the door, and stumbled out, gasping into the open air.

This is how Lidia treated her family, too: like a car from which she needed to periodically escape. And thus she disappeared on archaeological expeditions, absent for months at a time. When she returned home, she seemed to appreciate her husband and daughter, perhaps because she had enjoyed a little freedom.

A year or so after she moved into the Willows, she started wandering off the property now and then, but she has not done so in the last few months. Phoebe finds her in a chair by the window, knitting. Phoebe sits beside her. "How are you, Mom?"

"Enjoying this beautiful evening," Lidia says, and Phoebe smiles, relieved that her mother does not remember much about the recent past. For her, the accident never occurred. "Where is that husband of yours?"

"He's busy tonight," Phoebe says, taking her mother's hand. *Busy being dead.*

"You look peaked."

"It has been a strange day. Someone showed up on the mortuary table who looks like me . . . She had a picture of me, so I guess it's not a coincidence."

Her mother stares off through the window. The outlines of the trees melt into her faint gray-haired reflection. "Mortuary," she echoes. "What are you doing in that place?"

"Just . . . visiting," Phoebe says, sighing. *It's better this way,* she thinks. Better that her mother remembers so little. Maybe, like Phoebe, she blocks out the worst horrors of her past so that she can go on living.

"Today is an anniversary," Lidia says, looking at the large calendar on the wall. The nurse has penciled in various events, including visiting musicians and actors, authors who sometimes read from their books in the common room.

No, I don't want you to remember, Phoebe thinks, her heart palpitating. She wants to snatch the calendar off the wall. "Yes, it's a special day," she says, forcing a smile.

Her mother blinks slowly at her, as if trying to retrieve a memory. "Not your wedding anniversary, surely. You two are not still married, are you?"

"We never got a divorce," Phoebe says. That much is true.

"It's only a matter of time before you're done with that man."

"And why is that?" Phoebe tries to keep her voice steady.

Lidia sets aside her knitting, a square of silvery wool that might become anything at all. It's still tabula rasa. "I only want you to be happy. I don't want you following in our footsteps."

"What do you mean, Mom?" Phoebe goes to the kitchenette, which takes up one wall, and opens the small refrigerator. Takes out a bottle of water.

"I was never done with your father. I should've been, but—well, he should've been done with me, I suppose."

"Why? What are you saying?"

"We had our moments. But we've been through this before."

"Dad was a good guy. You loved him—"

"Of course I loved him. But he didn't want me there in the end."

"He was in a coma. He probably didn't even know we were there." Phoebe pours the water into a glass from the cabinet, takes a long drink.

"I'm sure he did," Lidia says. "Your father was still in there." She circles back to this every few weeks, reliving the last days of her husband's life, when she even remembers he is gone.

"I know," Phoebe says, sighing. A desperate hollow space opens inside her. If only she could talk to her mother the way she did as a child. They chatted while Lidia performed her rituals—unpacking or packing her suitcase, coming or going. She took her time, choosing lightweight shirts for a tropical environment, waterproof pants for rainy islands, foldable, wide-brimmed sun hats.

When she was very small, Phoebe imagined stowing away in her mother's luggage, jumping out and surprising her in New Delhi, Rabat, or Mexico City, or wherever she was going.

But as she grew older, she merely wanted to convince her father to go, too, to buy plane tickets for all three of them, but he agreed to accompany her mother only twice, to London and to the Caribbean, the only trips they took as a family.

And now, she can't upset her mother, can't tell her the details about Pauline, about the photograph, about the tattoo.

"Has Logan gone off on that damned errand?" her mother asks, looking toward the door.

"Yes," Phoebe says shakily. "I sent him to the store. You know how he loves grocery shopping." She sits next to her mother, sets the water glass on a side table, the liquid inside catching the light.

"No, not that errand. The one Raja sent him off on, and don't think I didn't know. Don't think I didn't hear everything they said. They thought I wasn't there listening, but I was."

"Listening to what?" Phoebe's stomach twists into knots. She hates it when her mother seems so confused.

"He asked me to leave the room. Leave the room! But that was the day before. Is today the day your father—"

"No, Dad died in April."

"We were married in June," her mother says. "We thought it would be the best month, but it was raining cats and dogs."

"It was raining on our wedding day, too, and we were sure the chance of rain would be zero in July."

"You looked so beautiful, honey."

An instant image brightens in Phoebe's mind, of Logan gazing down into her eyes, gripping her hand too tightly, whispering, *I love you*. She couldn't wait to be alone with him. "Not half as beautiful as you looked when you and Dad were married," she says. "Your photos are stunning." She picks up her glass again, finishes the water.

"You're too kind to an old lady," her mother says.

"You're only eighty-one. Not that old, right? I was going to ask what you want to do for your birthday. It's coming up."

Her mother's brow furrows. "How do you know how old I am? How do you know when my birthday is, young lady?"

"Because I'm . . . because you told me." Phoebe's heart drops. She looks at her mother as if through a clouded window.

"I didn't tell you any such thing," her mother says, looking around. Her gaze flits from the photographs on the shelves to the sliding glass doors reflecting her own shadowy, ghostlike face. She is trying to get her bearings, Phoebe knows, trying to remember where she is and who she is, but she does not want to reveal her confusion. She has learned to hide what she doesn't know.

"You must've forgotten," Phoebe says, getting up with the empty water glass in hand. The space between her and Lidia grows, a continent expanding between them. "But you did tell me." She puts the glass in the sink. Such a small receptacle compared to the large sink in the house she grew up in across town. She has not been back there since her mother sold the place and moved out. Now Lidia's life is compressed, everything packed into one room.

"Well, maybe I did. I can't keep track of everything. Anyway, I'm sorry you can't stay for dinner. I've got a date."

"I'm glad to hear it," Phoebe says, the tears stinging her eyes. "I have a date, too." *With sorrow and a frozen dinner.*

"I appreciate the visit," her mother says in a formal voice. "Will you see yourself out?"

"Yes, I know the way." Phoebe heads for the door, a pressure on her heart. She lingers to look at old pictures of happier times. Phoebe and her father skiing, her mother on a dig in Honduras, the three of them at Christmas opening presents under their living evergreen tree, which her father always replanted in the garden after the holidays. And there is Phoebe at her tenth birthday party in Bayport Park, in the warmth of August, blowing out candles on her lemon cake while her father looks on. Renee stands next to Phoebe, grinning at the cake. There are other people milling about in the background. There is something disconcerting about the image, something that nags at Phoebe. Maybe it's the absence of her mother. Lidia was away in Paris.

"I'll be back again soon," Phoebe says. "Have a good dinner."

"Thank you for coming," her mother says politely. "Oh, if you see my daughter on the way out, could you tell her I'll be in the cafeteria?"

CHAPTER SIX

Back home and weary, Phoebe throws a frozen dinner into the microwave. Long ago, it seems, she and Logan gleefully flipped through gourmet cookbooks in search of an unusual recipe, an exotic dish to conjure for the forest trail committee or for Phoebe's mom or for the book club. Quite often their meal preparation devolved into a wild lovemaking session on the kitchen floor. But now, there is no sign that a marriage once flourished here.

Phoebe sets the timer for four minutes, hits the "Start" button, and heads down the hall past the locked room, the storage space of lost dreams she can't bear to enter. She wishes, for a moment, to lose her memory like her mother. Just enough.

But no, for Phoebe it is better to remember. *Better to have loved and lost . . .* or however the saying goes. Still, she can't go into the room. Renee suggested she pack everything up, sell the house, start again. But Renee had an easier time leaving. After high school, she took off, traveled the world before returning to New York, working her way through boyfriends before settling down, getting married, and having a son. Now, she has come back to Bayport, but she might stay only long enough to formulate another plan.

But Phoebe has no plans. There is no point in making them—it is all she can do to tread water to keep from drowning.

She retreats down the hall to her studio. The earthy smell of clay greets her, the half-formed face in progress, the ones she has already made lined up on the shelves. She's sculpting the features of a child, a girl of five going on six. Every evening, Phoebe loses herself in remaking the cheekbones, reshaping the eyes, the nose, the mouth, and chin out of clay, returning to her roots as an artist.

When she fell in love with Logan, she abandoned her career as a sculptor. He convinced her to attend mortuary school, where she learned to reconstruct entire faces from photographs. The classes challenged her. Her first wax head looked nothing like the person in the picture, Logan, whose face she should have known. She had touched his cheeks, his nose, his chin often enough. But still, she couldn't do it. The instructor praised her for a "nice first effort," but the face was too stylized. "Keep practicing," he said, and over time, her technique improved. She is now skilled at restoring most faces without allowing artistic license to intrude.

Here in her studio, she uses clay, returning to her own imagination, and yet tonight she is distracted. The forehead is too broad, the nose too prominent. The face of Pauline Steele keeps disrupting her thoughts. The tattoo, the photograph of Phoebe in Pike Place Market. Her mother's rantings.

She gives up on her sculpture and returns to the kitchen, sits alone at the breakfast nook, and consumes the prepackaged, microwaved lasagna right out of the plastic container. She has no energy to cook a meal from scratch. No use in buying fresh produce, which inevitably becomes a science experiment, growing a fur of white mold in the fridge.

She tries to imagine her mother on a date with another resident of the Willows. Or maybe she made up a story. It doesn't matter, anyway. She was always gone, always doing her own thing. *I shouldn't have gone there*, Phoebe thinks. *She can't help me anymore. I'm the one who should be helping her.*

Phoebe had invited her mother to live with her, but Lidia did not want to leave the Willows. And Phoebe can't handle her mother's bouts of anger, her disorientation when she temporarily forgets where she is, *who* she is.

I should just go to bed, Phoebe thinks, *pop a sleeping pill, start fresh in the morning.* But she finds herself heading for Logan's study, which is exactly the way he left it. In a briefcase beneath the desk, he packed gold watches, a rare pen, a coveted baseball card. Perhaps he planned to sell or trade his most valuable possessions, preparing to make a great escape to a secret rendezvous point with Pauline Steele.

His computer sits on top of the desk next to his printer. After he died, Phoebe logged in, hoping for some insight into his thoughts and activities in his last days, but his Google searches yielded nothing, and she found no unusual files on his hard drive. He hardly ever used email, and he had no social media profiles (neither does she). His entire persona belonged to Fair Winds, as far as she could tell.

But there's the origami. His favorite hobby, his escape. When he grew restless, he stepped up the paper folding. In the days before his death, he left origami cranes everywhere, twenty of them on the shelves, on the windowsill, on his desk.

Phoebe left everything as it was, hoping for a clue. Or maybe she kept the room the same to keep Logan the same. He would remain unchanged in the lingering smell of his soap, in his subtle cologne, in the hint of the cigar he sometimes smoked with the window wide open, as if she wouldn't notice.

She flips off the light, leaves the museum of his office, and in the master bedroom, she hesitates before opening the closet. So many times, she has brushed her face against his hanging shirts, sniffing the fabric, inhaling the memory of him. She has not washed his clothes. The scents of sweat and cologne have faded but have not disappeared altogether.

She checks the pockets of his jackets and pants again. She did this three years ago, recalls finding nothing unusual—at least, nothing to which she paid much attention.

She finds lint, a coin, a rubber band, nothing of much interest until she rechecks the pocket of a jacket he rarely wore and pulls out a crumpled receipt for dinner at a restaurant in Portland, Oregon. At Forever Vegan. Why does that name sound familiar? Pauline's housemate, Xia Page, works there. But did Xia work there just over three years ago, when the receipt is dated?

Phoebe flattens the receipt on her dressing table. There is Logan's signature, a rushed, illegible squiggle, as always. Dinner for one, takeout. This is why she didn't flag the receipt when she found it before. She figured he was carrying dinner back to his hotel room.

Her cell phone rings shrilly. Maybe it's Don returning her call. But no, it's Renee. "You okay? How was your visit with your mom?"

"She knew me for a bit," Phoebe says, collapsing onto the master bed. Over the phone, she hears people laughing in the background, glasses clinking.

"I'm at the Rusty Salmon," Renee says. "It's hopping for a Monday night. We were hoping you would join us, but I've got to go home. The babysitter can't stay past nine. Mike just stepped out for a smoke, but he'll stick around here if you want to come down."

"Right, okay," Phoebe says. "I lost track of the time."

"Listen, I'm sorry about your mom. I'm sorry I haven't been out to visit her lately."

"It's okay," Phoebe says. "I know you've got your hands full."

"Is she worse?"

"She's often confused. But she has periods of lucidity. The light shines in her eyes, like someone opened the curtains and gave her a clear view of her life. But then the lights go out again."

"I know that makes it so much harder to take," Renee says, her voice full of sympathy. "Your mom was always so sharp and independent. Remember she used to cook for us when she was around? Those spicy recipes she learned on her travels. What was that Ethiopian vegetable stew?"

"*Gomen*," Phoebe says. "Collard greens."

"Yeah. That was good stuff. We have happy memories. Hang on to those."

"I'm trying." Phoebe blinks away tears, her grip tightening on her phone. "There's something else . . . I can't stop thinking about it. I'm pretty sure Logan was having an affair—"

"With Pauline? I knew something was off. I could see it in your face."

"Yeah, and I think she was coming to see me."

"That's quite a leap, isn't it?"

"Why would it be? He had her tattoo on his phone a few years ago, and here she is."

"Well, maybe," Renee says doubtfully. "Maybe not."

"I need to understand why she was here, and if she was here to see me, then why now?"

Renee breathes into the phone, then says cautiously, "He's dead, Phoebe. You know that, right? And now she's dead, too, so . . ."

"Wouldn't you want to know the truth?"

"Maybe, or I might want to just move on."

"Would you really?"

"I was thinking about something . . . from when we were young. Wasn't your mom gone for like a long time on one of her archaeology trips?"

"Her longest dig was in France," Phoebe says.

"Yeah . . . she was gone awhile. Was it longer than nine months?"

"She was supposed to be gone a year, but she came back early."

"Like how early?" There's more laughter in the background.

"I know what you're thinking, but you're wrong. My mother did not have a baby in France," Phoebe says. "She was only gone about four months."

"Are you sure?"

"You're still on some trip about Pauline being related to me. She's not."

"I know. It's just so strange."

"You said yourself that people have doubles. If Logan was with her . . . maybe he was drawn to her because she looked like me."

"You don't know he was with her," Renee says.

"I went through the checklist of 'how to know your spouse is cheating on you,' and he fit almost every warning on that list. But I was blind."

"All right," Renee says, still sounding doubtful.

"Maybe he saw her through a window and thought she was me at first. He went in and started talking to her—"

"And slept with her? Just following your line of thought here. If you're right, he was an asshole. A dead asshole. Sorry."

"It's okay. You're right. Wherever he is now, in some purgatory, maybe Pauline is with him. I need to know more about how she died. Don must've been first on the scene—"

"No, he wasn't," Renee says. "Mike Rivera was."

CHAPTER SEVEN

When Phoebe enters the Rusty Salmon, the warm glow envelops her, the conversation muted, pale-blue light reflecting off bottles behind the bar. Everywhere, polished wood gleams, the smells of alcohol and perfume in the air. Renee's words echo in her head. *Mike Rivera was.* And yet, he did not say a word. She is eager to question him.

She's jumpy, too, no longer accustomed to noisy crowds. She tries to push aside her memories of this place, from when it was a Mexican restaurant. She and Logan came here often, but there are no reminders of its former incarnation. Blue walls have replaced the festive yellow and orange. There is nothing left of her happy past in this space.

And there is no sign of anyone from work, which fills her with sudden panic. What if she missed Mike? Renee said he would be here. Maybe everyone left. Phoebe feels silly now, dressed up in a black turtleneck and slacks and made up in hastily applied eyeliner and lipstick. Heads are turning. Perhaps people recognize her from the news three years ago. She is a circus attraction, the survivor—step right up, everyone, see the woman who lost everything, so tragic, poor thing, wonder how she's holding up.

She is about to leave when she hears someone call out, "Phoebe! Over here!"

It's Mike. She breathes a sigh of relief. When she reaches his corner booth near the window, she finds him in a soft plaid shirt, jeans, blue sneakers. His dark-blue eyes reflect the candlelight flickering on the table.

"Have a seat," he says. "You look . . . nice."

Whatever that means. Maybe he noticed that she cleaned up, that she is not always in a smock and lab coat. "You look different," she says. She can't say he looks handsome, exactly. But there is something about him.

"I'll take that as a compliment."

"Thanks for hanging around. I know it's late. Almost ten."

"Renee said you would make it. I'm a night owl, anyway. I was reading." He lifts a book onto the table. He marked his spot with a paper bookmark from the Bayport Book Stop, the only bookstore in town, and she feels an instant stab of regret. She has ventured into the bookstore only once since the accident. She should go in again, but the pain of loss is too great—the Book Stop was one of Logan's favorite destinations.

"*Flowers for Algernon*," she says. "I read it in high school, I think, about a guy who becomes smart and then loses it all again?"

"Damn, you spoiled it for me."

"It's not like it's a big secret. Everyone knows what happens."

"Not everyone. Now there's no point in reading to the end."

"But there's no twist like the ending of *The Sixth Sense*. We never find out that the guy has been a ghost all along. It's more about asking if we're better off enlightened, then losing what we once had, or never having had it? Sorry, I shouldn't have told you."

He breaks into a wide grin. "I'm kidding. I know what happens. I'm messing with you."

"Now I feel stupid." Her cheeks flush.

"You're far from stupid. I've seen the books in your office. Astronomy, theoretical physics. Have you read all of them?"

"Most of them. What were you doing in my office?"

"I was talking to Renee. She was heading in there with your mail. Barry has her doing shit like that."

"So she's the one assaulting my inbox with catalogs. I'll tell her to give them to Barry next time." Phoebe reaches for the laminated drink menu propped behind the flickering candle.

"She's not too happy about doing grunt work." Mike puts the book back on the seat next to him.

"Well, she didn't go to mortuary school," Phoebe says. "She's trying to get her life back on track. We've been friends forever. She was my neighbor in first grade, and she was always a little easily distracted."

"How so?"

"She's creative, you know? Always wanted to start her own clothing design business, but she's also impulsive. Gets herself into trouble . . ."

"We all do that on occasion."

"Once, when we were about fifteen, she wanted to keep walking on the beach even though the tide was rising. We got trapped in an inlet and had to climb a cliff to get out of there. We ended up in someone's backyard in the dark. A dog chased us all the way to the road. We were lucky we weren't stranded or bitten."

"Sounds like an adventure."

"Yeah, it was, actually," Phoebe says. "I guess I was a thrill seeker back then, too." She peruses the drink menu. Moscow mule, mojito, whiskey sour, spritz.

"What's your poison tonight? Let me buy you a drink." He waves at the waitress. She heads toward them.

"I can buy my own," Phoebe says. "What were you drinking?"

"Ginger ale," he says, gesturing to his empty glass.

"I need something stronger." She orders a gin and tonic. The waitress nods and walks off.

"Going straight for the hard liquor tonight, huh?" Mike says.

"Drowning my sorrows. You know, third anniversary of the accident and all."

"Don't blame you. I might do the same when I finish reading this book if it's so depressing."

"Do you always read in bars?"

"I grew up in a big family. Five boys, four girls. I hid inside books."

"My family was small, just the three of us." *Some of the time,* she thinks, *when Mom was home.* "My parents were determined not to have children, I think. They didn't want to focus on anyone other than themselves. I think I was a late accident, an inconvenience."

"That sucks," Mike says. "Every kid should be a miracle. Nurtured, you know?"

"My mom and dad came around, eventually. They nurtured me as best they could. What about you?"

"Our parents tried to nurture us, but it was hard to do with so many kids."

"You were one of nine, seriously?"

"Catholic. We multiply like rabbits."

"Well, *you* don't, obviously," she says, glancing at his fingers, no rings. "Unless you have a wife and kids stashed away?" He must be close to her age, she thinks, in his forties. In the short time she has known him, he has been a man without a past, but now he takes on a new dimension, a wake of invisible history behind him.

"Nope, I'm single, and I'm a lapsed Catholic, much to my parents' chagrin," he says. "They would like me to be a true believer. But I'm jaded, I guess."

"How so?"

"I see too many deaths that don't make sense, you know? Too many bad things happening to good people."

"Some would say everything happens for a reason, but we just don't know what it is."

"You believe that?" he says.

"I don't know what I believe." Phoebe swallows the dryness in her throat, focuses on the waitress, who is returning to refill Mike's ginger ale, the fizzing bubbles of carbon dioxide rising to the top like divers needing air. She plunks a gin and tonic on the table and rushes off.

"So you're an atheist now?" Mike asks.

"I don't know. I want to believe in a heaven," Phoebe replies wistfully. The gin leaves a strange, spicy taste on her tongue, of juniper and the tang of lime. "It would make everything so much easier, to imagine the people I love going to some beautiful place for eternity."

"Yeah, me too."

The drink burns her throat, her stomach, but she likes the pain, her brain cells dying one by one, marinated in alcohol.

"So where are you from?" he asks, gulping his ginger ale.

"Here," she says.

"Originally."

"My dad was half-English, half-Indian. My mother is Greek. A while back, she flew to Greece to dig up *her* mother's bones a few years after the burial. They do that, you know, exhume the bones to make room for other bodies. There's not enough burial space in Greece."

"I read about that," he says. "People are buried with their socks on so the families can tell where the skeletons end, and then they put all the bones in boxes in sheds."

"I'm not going to do that with my parents. They will stay buried."

"So you're not keeping up the tradition. Have you been to Greece?"

"Farthest I've gone is San Francisco to study art. I used to work in clay."

"I know," he says.

"What?" She swallows another mouthful of poison. The pub acquires an ethereal glow. "How do you know? Did Renee tell you?"

"You still have art at the co-op gallery on Main Street. The link is on your website."

"I forgot I still had a website," she says. Her tongue thickens, aided and abetted by gin. "The gallery is supposed to contact me if they sell something."

"Then they should contact you. I bought a piece yesterday. The one with the girl's face on the bowl."

She nearly chokes on her drink. "Thank you, I think."

"I'm interested in your art, that's all. Shit, you don't . . ."

"Are you stalking me? You waited for me tonight."

"Renee said you were coming, but I didn't expect you to knock back the gin. I pictured you as the herbal tea type."

"I am. But tonight is different."

"You should slow down. That gin is potent. That brand in particular."

"And you know this because—"

"I used to be a bartender, among other things. The one you're drinking has added botanical essences, like rose petal and cucumber."

"Thought I tasted something weird." She looks at her glass of clear liquid, which could be mistaken for water, but maybe that's the whole point. "You said 'among other things.'"

"I worked as a medical assistant for a while, phlebotomist. Drawing blood, that kind of thing."

"What made you become a medic?"

"I always wanted to help people," he says. "Runs in the family. My brother became a firefighter. My grandfather was a cop. One of my sisters is a doctor in Florida. Another one works for a lab that tests blood, DNA, stuff like that."

"I bet you all get together for the holidays," Phoebe says.

"Yeah, when we can. We're all pretty tight. But I'm here and they're all over the country."

"At least you have them," Phoebe says, downing the rest of her gin.

"Whoa, slow down," Mike says. "Maybe try the ginger ale. They brew their own batches here."

But she sticks with gin. The more she drinks, the calmer her thoughts become. The sad memories recede. The past disappears, her anxieties quieted. It would be so easy to do this every night, to silence the voices, kill the pain. She wonders if this is what Pauline Steele did, overdosed on pills to numb herself.

"So what about Pauline?" she asks him.

"Excuse me?" he says.

"Must've been difficult to find her and not be able to save her. She was so young."

"How did you know I found her?" he says, sipping his ginger ale, not missing a beat.

"Renee told me. She said you were first on the scene. She said you're a part-time paramedic. Did you try to revive her?"

"It was way too late."

"How long had she been dead?"

"I couldn't tell you. I'm not the expert."

"Was she in the driver's seat? Did it look like suicide to you?" She leans forward, skewering him with her gaze.

"That's not for me to say," he says, swigging his ginger ale. His brows furrow. "You should talk to Don."

"He's avoiding me. He's not returning my calls."

Mike sits back. "So you came here to grill me instead."

"Sorry, but you have to understand my interest. The resemblance between me and Pauline is uncanny. And you found her. Exactly when was this?"

"Two nights ago. Around ten p.m."

"Do you know why she was in town? Did Don say anything? Did you find anything unusual in the car?"

"I have no idea; no he didn't; and no I didn't, aside from the pill bottle."

"There was a bottle," she says.

"With her name on it, a prescription. She must've needed pain medication."

"Why would she overdose on it?"

"Why do you care?"

"Sorry," she says, realizing he knows nothing about her past with Logan.

"Seriously, you might want to slow down with that stuff," he says, gesturing toward her glass.

"Thanks for the unwanted advice." She lifts the glass and takes another sip.

"So, you came here to interrogate me," he says. "Not because you like me."

"I do like you. We were having a normal conversation, weren't we?"

"I thought so."

"You never told me where *you're* from."

"LA," he says. "My parents are still there."

"I'm still here because my mom is at the Willows, here in town. She's . . . in the early stages of dementia."

"Oh shit. I'm sorry."

"Don't be. She recognizes me sometimes." But even as she says this, a weight presses on her chest. "She receives good care there. She has a view of the woods. She chose to move there when my dad died, and she started losing her memory not long after."

His expression softens. "That's got to be hard. You got other family?"

"I don't need anyone."

"Really? I do. Gets lonely not having anyone around."

"What would you know about that?"

"My fiancée left me two years ago. Married her dentist. They live in Vegas now." He runs his fingers through his hair, gazes into the flickering candle.

"Oh, I'm sorry. You haven't dated anyone since then?"

He tilts his head, looking at her. "Depends what you mean by 'dated.' The short answer is no. Nothing serious."

"I'm sorry." The gin is making her woozy.

"She was an artist, watercolor," he says. "But it was a hobby for her. It wasn't a profession like it was for you. Why don't you make art anymore?"

"I guess restoring real faces takes all my energy now." She sees no point in telling him that she still remakes the girl's face in a variety of expressions, at a variety of ages. But her newest creations are not for sale. "When I met my husband, he steered me toward Fair Winds. I kind of fell into the profession."

"You should keep up the sculpture. You're good at it."

"I am keeping it up. Did you see my work on Elvis today?"

"Yeah, you made him look like he's having a good dream. You would never know what killed him."

"Thank you," she says. "What about Pauline? What killed her? In your opinion, did she overdose on purpose, or was it an accident?"

"We're back to that," he says, and laughs. "You can't let it go."

"If you were like, the coroner, what would you say?"

"I'm not the coroner. Don Westfield is the coroner."

"But if you were, would you say she was taking the pills to kill the pain from some injury she had? Or was she an addict? Or what?"

"Maybe she did take the pills for pain, at one time," Mike says, letting out his breath. "Who the hell knows? But in my unprofessional opinion, based on the way she was sitting in the car, leaning back, no sign of anyone else around, I would say she definitely did it on purpose. But there's a third option, too."

"What is that?" Phoebe says.

He downs the last of his ginger ale. "The car doors were unlocked. For all we know, someone else was in there with her."

CHAPTER EIGHT

Phoebe wakes at home in bed, or on it, barely beneath the top cover. Dawn is spreading across the sky. She is still clothed except for her shoes. She sits up quickly, an invisible hammer slamming into her skull. Her tongue swells, her throat sticky, the night blank behind her.

Well, not entirely blank. She remembers grilling Mike, not noticing how much alcohol she was imbibing. He didn't know if anyone else was around when Pauline expired. It was all conjecture.

She drank herself into a stupor, and she doesn't know how she returned home. She must have walked. She didn't sleep with Mike. Or so she hopes. She couldn't have. She did not undress and certainly did not brush her teeth. Her mouth tastes like an animal died on her tongue. Her bra cuts into her rib cage like a corset from a bygone era. Her first hangover in twenty years. She is nauseated, too old for this, and her workweek has only just begun.

On the first anniversary of the accident, she locked herself in her room and took too many sleeping pills. Hoped not to wake up. But she did wake up with a massive stomachache.

On the second anniversary, she went to bed early and cried herself to sleep. She has made it through the third anniversary but no better off.

The floor creaks in the living room. The squeaky board near the kitchen. The clink of cutlery. A drawer sliding open and closed. Logan must be here. He was never gone. Or a burglar has moved into her house, expecting no protest from her. Or a ghost. Or her mother. Lidia might have escaped from the Willows—not that she is imprisoned there. No, that's ridiculous. The Willows is ten miles away.

Phoebe squints against the morning light, looks around the room. If a stranger has broken into her house, she's out of luck. She doesn't own a gun or a baseball bat or anything to use as a weapon. She grabs a large hardcover book, a biography of Leonardo da Vinci, and staggers out into the kitchen.

"Mike!" She drops the book on the table. "What are you doing here?"

He's in the clothes he wore last night, his shirt rumpled now, his hair sticking straight up. He's brewing coffee in her ancient pot. "Good morning," he says. "I wanted to make an omelet, but you don't have eggs. Or cooking oil. Or onions. But you have a lot of dishes."

Now she vaguely remembers asking for a ride home, the smell of cinnamon in his car. He drove slowly so she wouldn't throw up. When they got here, the house was too dark, too full of silence. She couldn't bear to be alone. She asked him to sleep on the couch, and he agreed. She feels ashamed now, stripped of her defenses. Only the effects of alcohol would allow her to reveal her vulnerability.

"I didn't realize you couldn't hold your liquor," he says, "or I would've made you stop after two drinks."

"You can't make anyone do anything," she says, the heat climbing in her cheeks. "I take responsibility."

"You drank way more than you should have."

"I can't remember everything I said. But I remember you said Pauline's car doors were unlocked."

He shakes his head and grins. "You're stuck on that, aren't you? I told you all I know."

"Yeah, thanks." She rubs her throbbing forehead. "And thank you for making coffee. But I probably need to be alone. This is all weird."

"No problem. For the record, nothing happened between us." He heads for the front coatrack, where he hung his coat on top of one of Logan's jackets.

"I didn't mean to imply," she says, following him.

"No worries." He looks around the living room, points to the old black Remington Noiseless typewriter on a table by the window. "You have some cool stuff in here. My grandma had a typewriter like that. She was a journalist."

Phoebe looks at the typewriter, which has been gathering dust since the accident. She once typed letters on the antique contraption, marveling at its muted sound. "It's been a long time since I thought of anything in here as cool," she says.

"I was looking through your books. You've got some rare editions. My grandma collected the classics. She left them to me when she died."

"You had an interesting grandmother." A shaft of sunlight illuminates the bookshelf next to the typewriter. *I forgot about my love for rare books,* Phoebe thinks. "I collected them, in case I ever wanted to open . . ." She bites her lip. No use in telling him about plans that will never come to fruition.

"What, an antiques shop?" Mike asks.

"Something like that. It was a fantasy I had once . . . just a silly dream," she says.

"You could do it." He opens the door and steps out onto the porch, shrugging on his coat. Tiny droplets of moisture float around in the cold air.

"I haven't thought about it in years," she says.

"Yes, you have. You mentioned it last night when you were drunk," he says. "You said you had this idea to open a shop for all your junk."

"I used that word, *junk*?"

"Yeah, but nothing in your house is junky," he says.

"I hope I didn't say anything else compromising," she says, walking to the door. "I really don't remember much. You must've taken off my shoes and put me into bed."

"It wasn't hard, once I figured out where the master bedroom was . . ."

"Thank you." The cold air dulls her hangover headache. She wishes for a freeze, for piles and piles of snow. "I hope I wasn't babbling."

"You were talking quite a bit, but it's okay."

"I hope I didn't get, you know, too personal."

"If you're asking if you talked about your dead husband, then yeah, you did."

"Damn," she says, losing her breath, the mist swirling. "Anything else?"

"Yeah," he says, his eyes sad, and she knows she slipped up, burdened him, told him in her drunken stupor what she hasn't even been able to tell herself.

"I apologize for bending your ear."

"Anytime, Phoebe. If you remember what you said, and you want to talk about it, I'm here. Bend my ear anytime. But most of what you told me, I already knew."

"Knew what?" she says. Time seems to stop, the mist suspended in the air.

"I knew your little girl died in the accident, too."

CHAPTER NINE

Of course he knew. Everyone knows. If he has been living anywhere near Bayport, and if he reads the newspapers, he knew three years ago. But she has no idea how long he has been in town or how long he has known or who might've briefed him. His brows seem to droop more than usual. Perhaps this is his look of sympathy.

He comes closer to her, lifts the locket on her necklace, containing a small vial of ashes. She wears the necklace all the time, usually hidden beneath her blouse. "Is this . . . ?"

"Her ashes. Mixed with Logan's. A little of each." The tiny vessel has become a part of her, so much so that she has barely noticed it these past several weeks—until now.

He lets go of the locket and steps back. "What was her name? You didn't tell me last night."

"Ava," she says, her throat dry. In speaking the word, she has conjured the past, stirred it up like silver dust coalescing into the shape of a smiling little girl. "My husband liked old movies. She was named after Ava Gardner." She splits off from her body and hovers somewhere far away.

"What was she like?"

"She was . . ." Needles of ice sting her face. "She was beautiful." She's pulling in air, her lungs expanding, but her ribs won't budge. Every memory rises to the surface—Ava's infectious giggles, her pudgy fingers reaching to grab Phoebe's hair, pulling so hard she yanked out strands at the roots, smiling all the while.

"Are you okay? No, I don't guess you are," he says.

"I hate myself," she says in a rush. "I killed her." A fist clenches in her stomach.

"What?" He blinks, rubs at his chin in apparent surprise. "I thought she died in an accident."

"She did, but there were times when I was so frazzled, I wished she would be quiet."

"That's not the same as killing her."

"They say your thoughts make reality. She could be so sweet, but she was also a more terrible two than any other two-year-old ever, and—"

"Sounds like most of my siblings," he says.

"She never slept, and I couldn't console her, couldn't keep her occupied. I was so tired. I couldn't even sing her to sleep. Why am I telling you this?"

"Because you need to?" he says, his brows rising. "Listen, I'll go on over to the store and buy some things to make you an omelet. You don't have any food."

"I appreciate the offer," she says, backing away. "But there's somewhere I need to go this morning."

"Yeah, right," he says, his face falling. But he doesn't argue. He honors her request and turns away. As he heads down the driveway to his car, he disappears into the mist.

She turns back toward the living room, sees the interior of her house the way he must've seen it. Cluttered with the past. Constipated with junk. But he didn't judge. Instead, he complimented her, admired her antiques. For this, she feels a soft rush of gratitude.

She walks down the hall, an impossible distance to the closed room. She hesitates, takes a deep breath, goes inside. Everything is the same. A child's room furnished in white and yellow, arrested in time. A play of light and darkness on the walls, shadows of the evergreens outside the window. She curls up on Ava's bed, pulls up the musty covers. Closes her eyes. She remembers now. Ava hiccuped when she laughed. Sucked her thumb. She liked to draw with crayons, her tongue sticking out.

Phoebe has not opened the white chest of drawers, has not taken down the mobile from the ceiling. Has not removed anything from this room. When she closes her eyes, she sees Ava the way she would be now, at almost six years old. She will always be here, growing older, her black hair longer, that prominent chin jutting out when she's acting stubborn. Phoebe knows what she would look like. She has been sculpting Ava's face in her studio down the hall, re-creating her daughter's features, imagining the way she would grow up, the way she would look today.

CHAPTER TEN

Before the accident, Phoebe rarely parsed her time into rigid segments. Somehow she managed to balance all that she needed to do, taking Ava with her to the trail volunteer meetings, to fundraisers, to book club meetings. It was only when Logan began to disappear that Phoebe found herself sometimes at a loss, staring into space, forgetting what she was supposed to be doing.

Today, she hurries through her morning routine, mapped into manageable segments of time: ten-minute shower, two minutes to cry in the bathroom, twenty minutes to dress in sensible shoes, slacks, and a sweater. A minute to tie back her hair. No makeup, no earrings, no rings on her fingers.

She takes the car and bypasses work, having left a message for Barry. She drives up the hill to the outskirts of town, where the remodeled county coroner's office with its cedar siding and slanted metal roof sits behind a swath of forest, hidden so that local residents can pretend it isn't there. They go about their daily lives, carrying on as if death does not exist, as if they will defy the odds and be the first ones to live forever.

Perhaps she should've stopped by Fair Winds to examine the body of Pauline one more time before the cremation, which might happen this morning. There isn't much room in the refrigeration unit, and more bodies will soon arrive.

It would also be polite to offer condolences to Elvis Parker's family, but she has done her job, has restored him to his former glory. Everyone will be gathering for his memorial service. Nobody will miss her.

She's sweaty and nervous as she pulls into the nearly empty parking lot at the coroner's office. There are never many cars here. *Who would stop by the morgue for a casual visit?* She left another message for Don, warning him that she was on her way. Still no response.

She walks up to the entrance, but before her fingers touch the buzzer, the door swings open, and Don Westfield gazes sternly down at her. He must've been watching on a video monitor. He's decked out in a blue, fitted suit; shiny dress shoes; and a pale-pink shirt. Mauve silk tie. He might be meeting with a grieving family or has just met with one.

He lets her into a foyer painted gray and layered with industrial brown carpet, the only splash of color an unobtrusive painting of an ocean against a tentative, dimming sky.

"You are one persistent woman. What can I do for you?"

"You know exactly what you can do for me. You've been avoiding my calls."

"Not avoiding. I've been busy." He looks past her. "You're here now. Let's make it fast." He ushers her into a conference room, an oblong table in the middle taking up most of the room, the pewter walls bare, a whiteboard along one side. Two tall tinted windows overlook the parking lot. Surrounding the table are swiveling office chairs. She wonders what he tells the anguished families when they come in here. Coroners rarely, if ever, summon next of kin to view the bodies of their loved ones. In real life, bodies are identified by their surroundings, the ID cards found with them. Don identified Logan and Ava that way, by the context, the car, their clothing, identification.

He motions to a chair. She sinks back against the too-high cushion, and he sits across from her, the table separating them. The room is deceptively bland, but she knows what lies beyond the doors in other rooms, where the carpet gives way to concrete and tile floors, from which blood and other body fluids are easily washed away. Metal cabinets hold DNA samples on slides; stainless steel refrigerators store blood in vials for transfer to laboratories; a locked evidence room holds various body organs vacuum packed in formalin. Spleens, hearts, livers—whatever the forensic pathologist, who performs autopsies, determines might be future evidence in a criminal case.

A cooler entered through a wide metal door stores unclaimed bodies or those waiting for transfer to mortuaries, for every suspicious or accidental death in the county comes to the coroner. Don presided over the deaths of his friend Logan and little Ava. He tended the bodies, transferred them into Barry's care for cremation. Phoebe was in no condition to help.

Don taps the long fingers of his left hand on the table, the flat gold wedding band like a miniature reflecting mirror. "What's going on?"

"Pauline Steele's death was an overdose," she says. "I know all that. I know she had an affair with Logan. But I need more information. I need to know everything about her." As she slides the photograph across the table, the blood drains from his face.

"What is this?" he says.

"I found it in her wallet."

He frowns. "We have strict protocols regarding the handling of personal effects."

"Tell me you recognize the picture."

He hesitates, and then his shoulders slump. "This is you."

"And you must remember," she says, looking at him. That day in Seattle becomes sharper now, like a foggy window slowly clearing. "You were there. All of us were. You and Wendy, before you two had kids. And Logan and me. You took the picture."

"Wow, yeah, I remember now," Don says, his eyes misting. "You found this in Pauline Steele's effects? We must've missed it."

"Must've," she says, not quite believing him. "Why did she have this? I gave this picture to Logan for Christmas, in a frame."

Don purses his lips, his face closing, the muscles suddenly tight. "I have no idea."

"You were his friend."

He sits back. "Yeah, but I don't know anything about—"

"Pauline? He knew her. He was involved with her, wasn't he?"

Don laughs nervously. "I don't know. I do know that he loved you and Ava."

"He had Pauline's tattoo on his phone for a short time, then he removed it." She watches Don's face, wondering what he knows. "She looked like me. And you knew it. I need to know why she was here in town."

He scratches his chin with the backs of his fingers. "Are you sure you want to pursue this? Logan is gone. Ava is gone. They're not coming back."

"Thanks for reminding me," she says bitterly. "Because, you know, I'd forgotten."

"Hey, I'm sorry." He reaches across the table, but she keeps her hands in her lap. He withdraws his hand.

"You recognized the resemblance between Pauline and me," she says. "And the tattoo. That was why you didn't want me to see the body. If Renee had not called me into the prep room, I might never have known. Barry would've cremated the body, and nobody would've told me. Did Pauline think Logan was still here? She must've known he was dead. And if she knew about me—"

"Don't read too much into this. Let it go. This is a dead end, pardon the pun. Going over and over all of this. It doesn't help."

"Don't tell me what helps and what doesn't help."

"We all need to move on, Phoebe."

She stands abruptly, nearly knocking over the chair. "I'm going to find out what's going on, no matter what you say."

"There's nothing going on." He sits back, and she can see by his expression that something very much is going on. He has never been a good liar. She can read his expressions when he sends over a decedent. She knows when a death is suicide or murder or unusual in some way. She can read it in his face. In the twitch of his lips, a tick in his right eyelid.

"You can tell me," she says, "or I'll find out on my own."

"You know what might happen if you run with this."

"What?" she snaps, anger bubbling up inside her. "Are you warning me about something? Is this a threat?"

"No, no." He ducks his head, raises his hands, palms forward. Then he looks up at her. "You might not believe this, but I care about you. I want you to be okay."

"Are you patronizing me?"

"I'm only saying this can't lead anywhere good."

"Whatever I find out," she says, heading for the door, "it will be the truth. And I have a right to the truth, don't I? I'm going to call Pauline's mom."

"She's in mourning, Phoebe."

"So am I." She flings open the door.

"Wait," he says.

She turns to glare at him.

"Don't bother her mother. I'll tell you what I know. You're right about Logan, that he was . . . I don't know how to tell you this."

"Spill it," she says. The tendons are tight in her neck. "I can take it. I've survived this long."

"I was as shocked as you were," he says. "I'd never met Pauline until the morning before she died, when she came here to see me."

CHAPTER ELEVEN

"What? She came to the morgue?" Phoebe sits across from him again, her body in a deep freeze. "Pauline Steele came here."

Don slides a tattered business card across the table. With his name on it, his contact information. "She lost her job, and she was moving out of her apartment in Portland. When she was shifting furniture around in the apartment, she found a few things, including this. She said it had fallen behind the bureau."

"She found *your* business card in her apartment. How did it get there? Did you know her? Was she your friend or something?"

"I'd never met her before she showed up here, like I said."

"How did it end up behind her bureau?"

"Logan dropped some things, apparently."

"Logan. *Logan.*"

He pulls the business card back toward him, tucks it into his pocket. "She showed up here distraught. She couldn't keep still. I thought she was high." His eyes glaze, as if he is seeing Pauline Steele now, superimposed on Phoebe. "She was looking for him."

"But she must've known he was dead."

"No, she didn't. She never knew him as Logan. She knew him under a different name, Michael Longman."

"What?" Phoebe can barely choke out the word. "You're making this up. That's impossible."

"I would never lie to you."

"But you kept things from me. Important things."

"I told you—I did not know all this."

The air becomes a slow-moving glacier, a cloud of ice. "A fake name. How convenient for him."

"Logan left the card in her apartment by mistake. And the picture of you, I'm guessing. Must've happened three years ago. The cards must've fallen out of his wallet. They must've been sitting behind the bureau in her bedroom all this time."

"How often did Logan stay with her? How long were they having an affair?" Phoebe is far away, trying to trace back time, trying to understand his absences, the lies he told her.

"Off and on, she said. But I couldn't pin her down. I'm sorry, Phoebe."

Off and on, like a light bulb, a switch easily flipped from fidelity to infidelity, from love to betrayal. "I shouldn't have rushed into marrying him," she says, her voice shaking. "I should've taken more time before—"

"You can't blame yourself for trusting him."

"I got pregnant. I barely knew him. But I thought I did."

"It could've happened to anyone," Don says softly, sympathetically—the way he must speak to grieving families to pacify them.

"What if she hadn't decided to move?" Phoebe says half to herself. "Maybe she wouldn't have ever come here. She never would've looked for you. She had no idea who I was."

"No, she didn't. I was her first stop, her first clue."

"Did she know Logan, or this *Michael*, was married with a child?"

"She had no idea where Michael Longman lived until she found what he'd left behind. She had a picture of you but not his real name, not your name, either. She was looking for Michael Longman when she came here."

"Then how did you know she was talking about Logan?" Phoebe says. "Maybe this was all a mistake. She was looking for someone else."

"She had the photo of you, and she showed me pictures of the two of them on her phone. Her and Logan."

Her lips go numb, a terrible pressure on her chest. "Did you know before? Did he confide in you? You were friends. He never once gave you a hint?"

"I had my suspicions. But he was cagey."

"You never told me about these . . . suspicions."

"What was I going to say, Phoebe? I had no evidence. You two were so in love—you were completely smitten. I could never have convinced you anyway. I wasn't even sure myself."

"You never met her? Pauline? Did she go on trips with him?"

"Not as far as I know." Don looks down at his hands, then up at her. Does she see regret in his eyes, or subterfuge? "I confronted him about my suspicions. He denied everything. He never spilled. He always made up a story."

"Like he did with me."

"I was trying to figure this all out, I swear. I was trying to decide how to tell you. You remembered Logan as a good guy. So did I."

"I had strong doubts," she says. "You sent Pauline's body over to Fair Winds, and you told everyone not to fill me in." Her voice trembles with anger.

"I was only trying to protect you. I was worried you would . . . harm yourself."

"It's not your job to protect me."

"But what happened right after the accident—"

"That's over now," she snaps. "Why won't you leave it alone? Why won't *anyone* leave it alone?"

"Okay, I'm sorry. I will. It's forgotten." Don reaches across the table again. His eyes are full of sympathy.

She stiffens, her hands in her lap. "What did she think happened to this Michael Longman after he disappeared three years ago?"

Don withdraws his hand, lays it flat on the table. "She looked him up, dead end. No address. She thought he had abandoned her. She seemed to believe he planned to start a new life with her. She thought he was trying to untangle himself from a clingy, psychotic girlfriend. That was what he told her. Everything seemed okay when she left. She thanked me for talking to her, said she appreciated the information. I thought she was heading back to California, moving on with her life. But I underestimated her obsession with him. Her attachment to him."

"Why would Logan—I mean *Michael*—abandon her?" Phoebe says. "If they were so much in love, how did she explain that away?"

Don rubs his face and sighs. "She thought he'd changed his mind and gone back to his girlfriend. She suspected he'd lied to her, since she couldn't find him. But it wasn't out of character for him. There were times when he dropped off the map."

Dropped off the map. In some other city, in some other life, Pauline suspected her fiancé of lying. She thought she was the only one missing him, but while Logan was with her, Phoebe was burping her baby, feeding her, cradling her, carrying her all night, struggling to keep her eyes open, to keep her child quiet. All alone for so many nights, wanting him to come home.

"I should've known," Phoebe says through gritted teeth. "The bastard." Spots dance in front of her eyes. She pushes back her chair, bends forward to let the blood rush back into her head. She's aware of a car rumbling into the parking lot, the murmur of voices out in the foyer. *Michael Longman, Michael Longman.*

She can't bear the thought that Logan might have been planning to leave her and Ava, start a new life with Pauline under his new name. The origami takes on new meaning now. She thought he was just nervous, folding paper over and over again, but he once told her that in Japanese culture origami cranes are a symbol of hope and healing, that if one could fold one thousand origami cranes, one's wish would come true. She thought he'd been wishing for a long, happy life with her and Ava, but perhaps she had been wrong.

Her teeth are chattering. "It's so cold in here."

"You're in shock," Don says. "I shouldn't have told you. Not this way."

"Yes, you should have. I needed to know everything. Pauline was still hoping he would return to her, even after three years." She tries not to imagine Logan showing up on Pauline's doorstep, carrying a bouquet of roses, the way he would sometimes come home with flowers or gifts. Guilt gifts, she realizes now. How many times did he slide into bed beside her after sleeping with Pauline? The thought brings nausea to her throat, makes her feel defiled, contaminated all over again.

"She was in shock, too," Don says. "She hid it well when she walked out of here. But her calmness was likely because she'd settled on a plan."

"You think she committed suicide," Phoebe says. "But you ruled her death accidental. Her car doors were unlocked. Anyone could've been there with her."

Don looks startled. "How do you know that?"

"Doesn't matter."

"Someone must have told you. Who was it?"

"Nobody told me," she says, giving him a defiant look. "But I'm right, aren't I?"

"There was no sign of a struggle. We can't prove suicide or foul play. When I talked to her mother, she said Pauline had been in and out of rehab, that she took it pretty hard when Michael stopped showing up."

"Michael!" She still can't get used to that name.

"When she left here, she was quiet and seemed calm. But what I told her must've sent her into a downward spiral."

"You didn't send her," Phoebe says. "Logan sent her. She sent herself."

"She must've driven to the park and taken the pills. She had a prescription for pain meds for a fall off a deck a while back. She broke both her ankles, had pins in them for a while. Her mother told me. She must've had some real pain issues. She became dependent on the opioids."

"Forgive me if I can't summon any sympathy for her."

"Remember, she didn't know he was married. She thought he had an unstable girlfriend."

"Or so she said. She might not have known his real name, but what if she did know he was married? That never seems to stop anyone."

"No, it doesn't," Don says regretfully.

"I wonder," she says, a sour taste on her tongue. "Was he planning to leave his own baby daughter?"

"He loved Ava more than his own life."

"You think he was going to steal her from me. Take off with her."

"Honestly, I don't know." Don holds up his hands again. "She said they talked about moving to Paris."

"Paris!" She remembers a newfound obsession he had with learning French, reading French authors. But he never suggested to Phoebe that they fly to Paris. She hates him now, more than ever.

"They were learning French together," Don goes on. "But he didn't tell Pauline he had a kid. That part seemed to shock her. Maybe he would've just shown up with Ava. Who knows?"

The taste of something rotten spills across her tongue. "Will you excuse me?" She gets up and dashes down the hall to the women's restroom. She barely makes it to the toilet before vomiting into the bowl.

CHAPTER TWELVE

Phoebe conducted an internet search for Michael Longman, but she could not find an image of Logan. She found mortgage specialists, doctors, real estate agents, photographs of men named Michael Longman, but they were not him. Under his fake name, he didn't exist. Evidence of him under his real name, Logan McClary, extended back to his childhood, to his parents, to the town where he had grown up. So he had created the fake name for Pauline, to shield his other life, to keep her from showing up in Bayport to talk to his wife.

Phoebe tore his home office to shreds but found no more secret receipts, tickets, or plans. She unfolded the origami cranes, flattened out the creases, looked for secret messages inside. Nothing. That's all they are, the cranes he created. Illusions. Nothing but blank sheets of paper.

She boxed up his books. Labeled them for charity. How easy it is now to scrub him away, to pack him up. Knowing for sure that he lied to her. Somehow, what she had suspected about him did not seem real until now. She has no problem yanking his clothes from the bedroom closet, cutting up his fancy suits.

When she has calmed down a bit, she brings out the family photo albums, flips through the pictures of their vacations from the days before Ava was born. In their adventures in Arizona, Canada, California, and New Mexico, she now tries to detect some proof of deception, some sign of the man who lied and cheated. She tries to find evidence in his expression, in an unguarded moment, but he was the same person in all photographs, although more disheveled in one, groomed in another.

She even braves flipping through the photo albums of the three of them, of Logan, Phoebe, and Ava. Joy filled his eyes when he looked at his daughter, carried her on his shoulders, swung her around, hauled her in a sling on hikes. He loved trying to feed her in her high chair, but she was stubborn and picky, and most of her food ended up on her bib or on the floor. She delighted in splashing in the kiddie swimming pool in her diaper, Logan carrying her around, pretending to be a dolphin.

Phoebe told him that children whose fathers read to them from an early age became more literate and successful than children whose mothers read to them, or who didn't have anyone read to them at all. Every night, he read to Ava from a picture book. She was enraptured. With her tiny, chubby fingers, she reached out to grab the pages and turn them, and sometimes she babbled as if reading, or she pounded on the page, whacked the book and sometimes threw it to the ground, indicating her displeasure with Logan's choice of reading material.

All or part of their family life might not have been real. Logan might have been acting the whole time, but he was supportive when Phoebe's father passed away. Her mother, devastated by her husband's death—despite her long, independent career and her many solo travels—couldn't stand rattling around the big house alone. So she focused on selling the place and moving into a retirement community.

Logan was steady, Phoebe's rock the whole time. He helped with all the funeral arrangements for her dad, staying by her side.

But that was in the beginning. She first met him in the gallery downtown, where she worked part-time and showed her clay sculptures. He seemed so sincere.

"You make a living with your art. I'm impressed," he said.

"I'm not sure I would call it a living, but I get by."

Why had he become a mortician? she wanted to know. His father had been in the business when Logan was little. Logan had never considered such a career until a rare liver condition had almost killed him. He'd had a sudden revelation, a desire to help people through the darkest days of their lives. He bought into Fair Winds to work with Barry, his friend.

Was all this true? Was anything true? Phoebe took him at his word. On their first disastrous dinner date, when the rain dumped on them, Logan turned on the charm. He picked her up and drove her to a fancy Italian restaurant, parked across the street. They ran through the rain to the door, but the restaurant was closed. They dashed back to his car and took refuge inside, both of them laughing.

"We'll find another restaurant," he said. "I'm sorry about this."

"It's fun," she said, grinning at him. "I love surprises."

He turned the key in the ignition, but the car didn't start.

"Double whammy!" she said, shivering but also laughing. "I need to take off these wet clothes." She blew on her numb hands to warm them.

"I have a blanket in the back seat. Help yourself."

She climbed into the back seat, made pretzels of her limbs to peel off the wet clothes, wrapped herself in the blanket. She laid her clothes on the seat next to her.

"Glad your seats are vinyl," she said, still shivering.

He looked over his shoulder at her. "You warmer now?"

"Feels like a camping adventure without the tent."

They stayed in the car, chatting until the rain stopped, then Logan got out and tinkered with the engine while she watched, staring at the raised hood. Occasionally he peered around at her, and she waved at him, smiling, aware of how absurd it was that she was sitting naked in a strange man's back seat, wrapped in his blanket. She had imagined a romantic, candlelit dinner, but somehow this unplanned side trip excited her.

She doesn't remember how he managed to start the car. But when he finally succeeded, he drove her to her rented cottage, walked her to the door. She still had the blanket wrapped around her. He was carrying her bundle of wet clothing. She invited him in. He seemed not to notice his own damp clothing.

"Nice place," he said, placing her wet clothes on the foyer table. And it *was* a nice place back then, mirroring Phoebe's love of art and nature. Sculptures, books, and plants adorned her space—everything colorful and full of life. He petted her cat, who purred and wove around Logan's legs. "Fluffy dude."

"His name is Remington," she said. "Sorry about the mess—I wasn't expecting company. But hey."

"I love all the books," he said. "Listen, sorry I fucked up our first date."

"That implies a second date," she said, gripping the blanket, feeling its soft fibers against her skin. The faint scent of aftershave or soap emanated from the fabric.

He shifted from foot to foot as if suddenly bashful. Remington leaped onto the couch, tail swishing. Logan jabbed his thumb backward over his shoulder. "I should head out. I'll call you—"

"Leaving so soon?"

His eyes widened. "I figured you might be cold . . ."

"Only hungry," she said, dropping the blanket on the floor. The seconds ticked by. He looked at her, his cheeks flushing. She expected him to pull her into his arms. But he didn't, although she could see the lust in his eyes. Outside, the rain pattered down in rhythm with her heartbeat.

Remington jumped down off the couch and left the room.

Logan smiled, whistled softly, and said, "Phoebe. I . . . Let's take it slow."

"You're a guy, and you're saying 'take it slow.' I could fall in love with you." She grabbed the blanket, wrapped it around herself again. Goose bumps were rising on her skin.

"Yeah, get dressed. I can wait. I'm taking you out for some food."

And her dream of a candlelit dinner came true. He courted her, sent her love notes, brought her flowers. He preferred to call instead of sending a text. She grew to love the sound of his voice, its raspy, guttural edge. The slight East Coast accent, barely discernible. Every time his name popped up on her cell phone screen, her heart flipped.

He seemed gallant, ethical, willing to wait. Loyal to a fault. She fell for him even before they made love for the first time at his bachelor pad, a tidy, sparsely furnished rental near Fair Winds. He lit candles, bought her a dozen roses, ran a bubble bath, the works. *It was all too good to be true,* she thinks now, but back then, she ignored or explained away the anomalies. She was so naive.

She was blind even after they were married. Like the night she found him in the backyard, sitting on the swing, staring into the forest. They were in the new house, the house in which she still lives.

He turned to her, his eyes shining, and said, "Do you ever feel like you belong in another life?"

"No," she whispered, trying not to wake Ava. The baby was asleep in her arms.

"I'm going to sign up for classes. Branch out, learn something new." His eyes shone with a feverish excitement.

She laughed. "Mortuary school wasn't challenging enough for you?"

He stared off into the distance, as if seeing some longed-for destination. "I thought I wanted to settle down, but the way we're going, we'll never be rich enough to fulfill our dreams."

"Rich! I don't need to be rich," she said. "I didn't think you did, either. Where is this coming from?"

"We could start a whole new life. We'll have it made."

"We can do what we want without being rich," she said.

A. J. Banner

"But life would be easier," he said. "I have to be away . . . to take the classes. On investing, starting a business from the ground up."

"I don't understand, Logan. We need you here, Ava and I."

"I know. And I'm here. I will be."

"Okay, fine. Do whatever you need to do." She got up and went inside, lacking the energy to argue. She was bone-tired from taking care of Ava. She hoped he was only fantasizing, but as it turned out, he made good on his plan. Gradually—she can't put her finger on exactly when it began—he faded, in and out of view, always leaving. He always returned to her, but she felt that he had left behind a part of himself in the place where he'd been. The truth was, she never knew him at all.

CHAPTER THIRTEEN

In the morning, at Fair Winds, Barry's office is locked again. Normally punctual, he has been showing up late now and then, these last few months. She will have to wait to see Pauline Steele's death certificate.

She heads for the cooler. Pauline's body is gone.

"Barry had the cremation done already," Renee says behind her. "He said he needed to move things along."

"He could have waited," Phoebe says, irritated. She turns around.

"You know how he is. He doesn't like this room to get too crowded." Renee is in jeans and a sweater today, but as always, she makes the mundane into something extraordinary. The jeans feature impressionistic floral images, like a painting of Monet's garden. And the silvery turtleneck shimmers in the light. When she entered the fashion show in high school—she knitted her own pullovers, stitched her own slacks—Phoebe envied her talent for design.

"You could've given me a heads-up."

"Hey, I didn't know you were so interested," Renee says, frowning. "Don't you think it's better this way? You can forget about it now. The body is gone."

Before I could get another look, Phoebe thinks, gritting her teeth. Maybe Renee is right—she should let this one go. But she can't. "I need to talk to Barry," she says.

"He should be in soon. Look, I need to tell you something, before you hear it from someone else." Renee smooths down her sweater, won't meet Phoebe's gaze. "I'm grateful for what you've done for me since I came back here. But I'm applying for a sales position in California. Near where my sister lives in Monterey."

"Okay," Phoebe says, feeling a stab of loss, although she knew this was coming.

"Darin's been asking me about this job. He might want custody of Vik. That scares the hell out of me."

Darin, the ex-husband. When Renee and Vik came back to town, Phoebe didn't ask questions. But she started to suspect that Darin had been controlling, even physically abusive. Renee had given up a high-profile fashion retail position, her plans to start her own line of designer clothing. She used her savings to move back across the country, to rent a house. She left behind her entire life in New York to pick up the slack in a funeral home.

"Don't worry so much," Phoebe says. "There's nothing wrong with this job. Everyone needs funeral homes. Everyone wants their loved ones taken care of."

"Tell him that. He thinks it's morbid. He doesn't want Vik exposed to dead people."

Phoebe laughs—a hollow, mirthless sound. "Vik never even comes here."

"I know, but I don't want Darin to get custody. There can't even be the possibility. I don't want to lose everything." Her hand flies up to cover her mouth, her eyes widening. "I'm sorry. I didn't mean it that way. I mean, I know . . ."

That I have lost everything. "Don't worry about it," Phoebe says briskly, although a boulder sinks in her stomach. "You're a good mom, Renee . . ."

"I try to be, but there is so much more that I want, too, and I don't want to lose Vik on the way," Renee says, a fierce longing in her eyes.

Phoebe knows, remembers Renee fantasizing about creating her own line of fashion.

"Darin doesn't deserve custody," she says. "He couldn't actually succeed, could he?"

"I don't think so," Renee says tentatively. "But you never know. I need to quit this place. I'm not even qualified to do much here. I'm answering the phone, cleaning up, washing bodies. Filling in the gaps. I don't have your training. I don't want to be a mortician. No offense."

"None taken," Phoebe says. "I can't blame you. This was always temporary for you. We both knew that."

Renee reaches over and gives Phoebe's hand a squeeze. Her fingers are warm, her grip firm. "Why don't you come with me? Just get the hell out of this place?"

"Barry said I can keep working on restorations as long as I want. I belong here." She can't imagine what else she would do.

"You belonged here when it was you and Logan. But now it's just you, and you're punishing yourself. How long are you going to do this? You need to forgive yourself."

"Maybe some things can't be forgiven." Phoebe barely manages to choke out the words. Tears sting her eyes, but she won't let them fall.

"So you stay here and do what, pay penance? It takes a certain stamina to work here. People are always asking why. Why do their loved ones die? Why do we have to grieve? And you never have the answers."

"You're right," Phoebe says. "That's why I don't deal with people anymore. The living ones."

Renee closes her eyes, moves her mouth as if reciting a prayer to calm herself. Then she opens them, her eyes bright with hope. "We could just go. You and I and Vik. We could drive to California, stay with my sister. You could look for work. Make your art. There's so much you could do."

"I can't just up and leave. I have to find out about Pauline, and Logan was—"

"Logan!" Renee spits his name. "What you're doing is a dead end, an excuse. For not moving on. Whatever people did, it's over now."

"People. Who are *people*? You, are you one of the people?" It occurs to her, in a sudden flash, that maybe, just maybe, Renee and Logan . . . *No, don't go there.*

"Why would I be one of the people?" Renee says, tapping her foot. "Okay, yes, I am. I stayed with Darin too long. Like you're staying here too long."

"Who are you to judge me? Or anyone?" Phoebe is hyperventilating now, her face hot, breaking out in a sweat.

Renee blinks, steps back, her mouth slightly open in an expression of shock. "Phoebe, I—"

"Excuse me." Phoebe strides past Renee, down the hall to Barry's office, her body shaking. Yet part of her longs to turn around and apologize to Renee, to the friend who helped her through the most difficult time of her life.

Barry's office door is ajar. Phoebe shoves it open. His office is neat and tidy, no pictures of his family. He used to keep framed photos of his wife and two sons on his desk, but they've all vanished. He's on the phone, his solid shape turned toward the window, his thinning hair almost translucent in the light. He's in a slightly loose blue suit. He swivels in his chair to give Phoebe a brief smile. "Yes, sure," he says to the person on the phone.

She takes a deep breath to compose herself and gestures toward his desk. He nods slightly, distracted, giving her unwitting permission to look through the files as he turns back toward the window. "Uh-huh, yes. We do have wicker caskets," he's saying. "Completely biodegradable, like I said."

She sifts through the death certificates, her hands still trembling a little, picks up the file for Pauline Steele. She died of an opioid overdose just as Don said. No indication of an ongoing investigation. Case closed. She checks the accompanying police report. First responders were Mike Rivera and his partner. She jots down the phone number for Pauline's mother, Darlene Steele. She might know why Pauline was visiting Bayport, whether or not someone was with her.

CHAPTER FOURTEEN

As Phoebe drives a rental car through rural Modesto, following the GPS directions, she feels oddly buoyant, alive, on a mission to solve a mysterious death. Even though she might be the only one who considers Pauline's death a mystery. To everyone else, the young woman was simply another casualty of the opioid epidemic. But Phoebe suspects otherwise.

She hadn't traveled in three years, barely left the house, and yet, this Thursday morning, she strapped herself into an airplane seat, gazed through the window in awe at the majestic, snowcapped peak of Mount Rainier, the blasted top of Mount Saint Helens, and the varied and stunning terrain all down the West Coast. She felt unfettered, gliding thirty thousand feet above the planet, where nothing earthbound could touch her.

But now, she's facing a meeting with a grieving mother, and she's unsure what to say. As Phoebe spoke on the phone, Mrs. Steele listened quietly, and then she burst into tears. *I can't believe what you're saying . . . My daughter was involved with your husband? But he said he wasn't married. And then he up and disappeared! You look like her? Please come to California. We need to meet face-to-face.*

Phoebe agreed, and now here she is, parking in front of a white bungalow surrounded by rolling fields and solid blue sky. She pushes open a white, painted gate and navigates a series of garden statuary to the porch.

Before she even knocks, Darlene Steele answers the door. As if she has been watching out the window from behind a curtain. She appears fragile, smaller than her daughter, her features delicate. Her fine hair, the color of a yellowing autumn leaf, is tied back in a clip. Grief seems to have rubbed part of her away, leaving a faint imprint like a pencil drawing. A fluffy white cat weaves around her feet.

She stares at Phoebe. "It's like I'm seeing a ghost," she says softly. "You look so much like Pauline."

And you do not, Phoebe thinks, taking in Darlene's light-gray eyes, her angular features. *She must've taken after her father.* "The resemblance did spook me," she replies.

"I wanted to come up to see her, but I just had hernia surgery." Darlene steps back to invite Phoebe inside, then closes the door. Then she hugs Phoebe tightly, as if trying to squeeze out her daughter. She smells mildly of something earthy, like a mossy rock. Another background scent hovers in the air, of pastries baking.

"I hope you're recovering well?" Phoebe says.

"As well as I can, but everything slows down as you get older," Darlene says, pressing her hand to her abdomen briefly, as if she has only just remembered to feel a stab of pain. "I should fly up there to get her remains and her belongings . . ."

"Don't worry about all that," Phoebe says. "I believe we're mailing everything to you."

"Thank you. That does help." Darlene leads Phoebe into a small living room, the decor a time machine of 1970s kitsch: a bright-green couch, shiny oil paintings on the walls, a record player with a large vinyl collection, small ceramic figurines all along the mantel, interspersed with photographs of Pauline as a child, growing up, graduating from high school. A black cat sits atop a bookshelf, regarding Phoebe through sleepy green eyes. And on an armchair, an orange tabby stretches luxuri-ously and licks its forepaw.

Darlene gestures to the couch, and Phoebe sits. The orange cat promptly curls up in her lap, making her miss her old cat, Remington.

The white, fluffy cat follows Darlene to her armchair. "I wish I'd known what was going on in her head," she says shakily. "I thought she was over the worst of her addictions. But, you know, she never got over what happened. She was so little . . ."

"What happened?" Phoebe says, a shiver running through her.

"Her parents died in a plane crash when she was four years old. Frank Tyler, her dad, was the pilot. He flew small aircraft, mostly. He took Pauline's mom with him sometimes. Her birth mom, I mean. Her name was Marianne. She was my best friend." Her voice falters.

The words *her birth mom* reverberate through the room. "So Marianne was Pauline's biological mother? That means you're her . . ."

"Well, I adopted Pauline. I'm her mother now," Darlene says briskly. "I helped take care of her almost from the beginning. Marianne made me promise to always be there for the child. It was in their wills, you know . . . Frank's and Marianne's. I was to raise Pauline if anything ever happened to them."

"I see," Phoebe says. "That was good of you."

Darlene's shoulders relax a little. "Yes," she says faintly. "Lucky they left Pauline with me that day, on their anniversary. Frank took Marianne up in the plane. It was a blessing that the child was not with them. She was saved." Her hands have begun to tremble.

"I'm sorry if I've brought up even more difficult memories," Phoebe says.

"Oh no, it's not you. The past catches up with us sometimes." Darlene squares her shoulders, draws in a deep breath and exhales.

"So you adopted Pauline on your own?" Phoebe asks. She knows she is prying.

"I was divorced." Darlene's face sours. "Pauline and I made a good team. She didn't need another father."

"You two were close, then," Phoebe says.

"Most of the time. Last month, she moved back here, into her old room." Darlene gestures toward the hall. "The house feels empty without her now. Sometimes I don't know how I'll make it through the day."

"I understand completely." Phoebe pets the cat, a knot of discomfort tightening inside her, a memory of how she, too, often could barely get out of bed in the morning.

"She was going to interview for a new job," Darlene goes on, her voice tremulous. "I thought that was why she went to Washington. I had no idea about your husband."

"Neither did I," Phoebe says. *At least, not at first.*

"It must have been quite a shock to you as well. How did you know?" Darlene leans forward now, seeming to hold her breath, waiting.

"I didn't know who the woman was, but I suspected he was having an affair. I saw her tattoo on his cell phone screen. A long time ago now. I had almost forgotten, to be honest. It all came back to me when her body arrived at Fair Winds. It was such a shock to see her lying on the table. Forgive me for mentioning it. She had gone to Bayport to see my husband's friend, the coroner."

Darlene mouths, *Oh*, tears filling her eyes. "I wish she would have confided in me. She must have been devastated. I mean, I knew she loved a man a few years ago. I did meet him. Michael Longman. Then he left her. He just . . . disappeared. She was inconsolable. She searched for him everywhere."

There it was, that name again, *Michael Longman*. "She never would've found him if he hadn't accidentally left behind clues," Phoebe says. "He gave her a fake name. His real name was Logan McClary."

Darlene looks as if she has just been slammed by a bus. She presses her hand to her chest. "My word."

"Maybe I shouldn't have told you all this. You've suffered such a terrible loss."

"Oh, I would rather know than not know." Darlene takes a few deep breaths, gets up, holding on to the back of the chair. "I've got cookies in the oven, and would you like some tea as well?" Her voice is strained, as if her vocal cords might snap.

"That would be nice, if it's not too much trouble." Phoebe keeps petting the orange cat, warm and purring on her lap.

Darlene walks stiffly into the kitchen with the fluffy, white cat in tow. The oven door squeaks open and shut, and the mouthwatering smell of cookies grows stronger. Perhaps Darlene Steele soothes her sadness by baking.

Like Renee, who flew back to Bayport after the accident and cooked lasagnas in a frenzy, bringing them over every day, too much food for Phoebe. Too much food for ten people.

Phoebe gently places the orange cat on the cushion next to her and gets up to peer closely at the family photographs. Here and there, hooks are still embedded in the wall, but the pictures have been removed, leaving gaps like missing teeth. Pauline smiles out from the remaining photographs—as a little girl, a sullen adolescent, and as a teenager in a cap and gown, smiling with a younger Darlene beside her, a proud mother.

In another image, as a toddler, Pauline sits on a young woman's lap. Not Darlene's. The woman looks familiar. Something about her hair, her nose, the broad cheekbones, the curve of the jaw. She must be Pauline's birth mother, Marianne Tyler. She cuddles her daughter cheek to cheek, lifting Pauline's pudgy hand to wave at the photographer.

"Sugar or honey?" Darlene says behind Phoebe.

"Nothing, thanks," Phoebe says, whipping around. Darlene's gaze flits to the photograph, her expression veiled. She hands Phoebe a mug of tea and nods toward the photograph. "That's Marianne. She was scared when she found out she was pregnant. She didn't know how lucky she was."

"Looks like she loved her daughter," Phoebe says.

"As well as she could. But she was never sure about being a mother. I couldn't understand her ambivalence. I always wanted . . . Well, never mind now."

Always wanted what? Children of your own? Phoebe wants to ask. "Do you have pictures of Frank Tyler?" she asks instead. "The pilot." She takes a seat on the couch again, next to the cat.

"Let me look. I think so. He and Marianne were joined at the hip." Darlene opens a drawer and produces a picture of the family of three. Pauline's father is holding her, gazing at her lovingly. He looks so young, not older than twenty-five, his hair slicked back, sleeves rolled up. In baggy canvas slacks and loafers. Pauline's mother looks on, her hand on her baby's arm. "He was more in love with Pauline than Marianne was," Darlene says. "Frank adored his little girl. But he picked the wrong profession. I warned him not to fly that day. The fog was too thick. But he thought he was invincible."

"What a profound loss," Phoebe says, handing back the picture.

Darlene's face is pinched with misery. "Pauline vowed never to have children of her own. She said she didn't want to be tied down. Didn't want to take care of a child. But I think she feared abandonment. The kid would grow up and leave her, like her parents did."

Phoebe nods thoughtfully. "I can understand that feeling." She sips her fruity tea, bites into a coconut cookie.

"Pauline had a lot of trouble when people left her. She took it hard when Michael disappeared."

"Did she ever hint that she knew he was married?"

Darlene's hand trembles as she places her cup on the table. She picks up the fluffy, white cat and cradles him. "He fooled both of us. You know, this is all a shock." Suddenly, she looks too brittle to handle such information, as if the new knowledge of her daughter's obsession with a liar and a cheat, the married father of a child, has broken her. "I'm still trying to process all of this."

Phoebe shows her the photograph of herself in Pike Place Market. "This was in her wallet."

Darlene holds the photo close to her face, her hands still trembling. "Why did she have this?"

"I believe this was what prompted her to come to Bayport, along with the coroner's business card. He was a friend of Logan's. Of Michael's. You never saw the picture? Logan was in the other half."

"I've never seen this." Darlene hands back the photograph. "How long were you married?"

"About four years. We had a baby . . ."

"A baby!" Darlene's mouth drops open. "I never would've guessed. Michael never mentioned such a thing. He was charming. But there was something underneath, and I told her so. He was always checking his phone. Now I know why. He was married to you. And he had a baby. Imagine that. But it all makes sense now."

"He died," Phoebe says. "That was why he disappeared. He died along with our daughter. Ava was two years old."

"Oh, I'm so sorry." Darlene presses her hand to her chest, red blotches on her neck.

"There was no way you could know."

Darlene wipes her eyes and blows her nose, as if expelling her grief. "I don't believe our loved ones are ever truly gone. They are always still alive in us."

"I suppose they are," Phoebe says, although often she feels Ava slipping away. The details of her face grow fuzzy, slowly disappearing until Phoebe's hands begin to work the clay again, conjuring a likeness of her daughter.

"Do you have a picture of your husband?" Darlene says. "What was his name, Logan? I wonder if he was really Pauline's Michael."

Phoebe pulls out of her wallet a small wedding photo, one she has kept all this time, taken in front of the arboretum in Wright Park. She's in her simple gauzy dress, elbow-length sleeves, no train. Uncomplicated elegance. Logan is dashing in a tuxedo.

Darlene frowns, peering closely. "You look so beautiful. That's him?"

"Is he the same person you knew as Michael?"

"Michael dressed differently. He was clean shaven."

"That's right. Logan shaved off his beard and mustache soon after we were married. I've got more recent pictures on my phone." Phoebe scrolls back three years again.

"Yes, yes," Darlene says, swiping through the images. "That's him. How strange to see him with you and your little daughter. He was a shape-shifter. I'm so sorry about what you have been through. And sorry for my daughter." She wipes more tears from the corners of her eyes.

Phoebe tucks the wedding picture back into her wallet, drops her phone into her pocket. "Would you mind if I see her room? I won't disturb anything."

"Follow me." Darlene gets up, still stiff, and leads Phoebe down the hall. "I can't go in. It's too overwhelming . . . but you go ahead. I'll just take some mail over to the neighbor." Phoebe waits until she hears the front door squeak open and closed. She glances out the window. Darlene Steele presses her cell phone to her ear as she descends the driveway, envelopes in her other hand.

There isn't much time to search Pauline's room, a teenager's space arrested in time, decorated in brooding grays and black. Gray bedspread, black bookshelves, an old guitar propped against the wall, a string missing. Phoebe checks in the closet but finds nothing unusual—only a few sweaters on shelves, a couple of hanging shirts, a lonely pair of old white sneakers on the floor. There is nothing in the desk drawers, only high school textbooks on the bookshelves. Nothing unusual, no obvious clues.

She slips down the hall, into the nearest bathroom. On the countertop, she finds scented lotion, makeup, eyeliner, a hairbrush, toothbrush.

Things Pauline must've left behind. Duplicates of the overnight gear in the property room at Fair Winds. A couple of magazines sit on the toilet tank. She picks one up, and a photograph falls out, showing part of a house and a playground in the background, barely visible through the trees.

On the back, someone has scrawled in round handwriting, *24 Cameo Lane, Wappenish, WA. A possibility?*

Wappenish, a small agricultural town on the east side of the Cascade Mountains, a few hours' drive from Bayport. Was Pauline planning to visit the middle of nowhere, and if so, why? A possibility of what? Phoebe pulls out her cell phone and snaps a few shots of the front and back of the picture.

"Did you find anything?" Darlene says anxiously, meeting Phoebe in the living room. Her eyes are bloodshot from crying.

"I found this," Phoebe says, handing over the picture. "Did she ever mention a town called Wappenish?"

Darlene looks at the photo and frowns, flips it over. "I've never heard of this place."

"She never said a word about going there?"

"Nothing, unless she was applying for a job there. She was applying all over the place."

"Why would she have taken this photo?"

"Perhaps she knew someone there?"

"Do you mind if I keep it?" Phoebe asks.

Darlene, in a sleight of hand, has already pocketed the photograph. "I'd rather hang on to it," she says sadly. "I know Pauline has no use for it now, but it is a little piece of her that I can hold on to."

CHAPTER FIFTEEN

At the Willows the next morning, the hallways are quiet. Several of the residents have taken the transport bus to the local library on a field trip, but Lidia Glassman did not want to go. She is propped on pillows in bed, looking at the picture on Phoebe's cell phone, the one of the address in Wappenish and the words *A possibility.* Phoebe has related to her mother the story of her visit to Darlene. She's not sure how much her mother retains. She seems to be far away.

Lidia rests her lightweight hand on Phoebe's, the same hand that made bag lunches, drew pictures to help her daughter with homework, patted her arm to comfort her before a test at school. "What is this place? It looks like a nice family home."

"It's in a town that Pauline might have visited, or maybe she meant to visit. Maybe there's nothing important there. But I want to check it out, because . . ." Phoebe takes a deep breath. She couldn't help unloading her thoughts, although she knows it's wishful thinking to expect her mother to follow along. *My heart can't let go of the mom you once were,* Phoebe thinks, tightness in her chest. She longs for her coherent, brilliant mother back, the mother who sometimes still appears but inconsistently, erratically. The mother who never failed to offer a wise tidbit of advice. The mother who will eventually disappear forever.

"You're looking for someone," her mother says.

There it is, a glimmer of the wisdom. "I think it was Pauline who was looking for someone," Phoebe says. "For Logan, for me . . . she had that picture of me. But I don't know who or what is in Wappenish. I don't know what she meant when she wrote, 'A possibility.'"

Lidia's hand slips off Phoebe's arm and reaches up to pat her own silver hair. She looks out the window. "It's a lovely sunny day. The daffodils will be springing up soon. Your father liked them." She is fading again.

Dad found comfort in his garden when you were away, Phoebe thinks. "He did love his flowers." She gazes at the picture on the nightstand of her parents crouched among dozens of blooming daffodils. Her father is kissing the top of Lidia's head. The two of them were deeply in love, although they might not have seemed like a good match. Phoebe's father, mild mannered and professorial, complete with round, retro spectacles, was handsome in a square, straightforward way, counterpoint to his carefree, gorgeous, and jet-setting wife.

While Lidia enjoyed dancing, he enjoyed reading, but she let him read to her from the classics, as he read to Phoebe when she was a child.

"Checkers?" Lidia says, her eyes brightening.

"One game." Phoebe brings out the old board game, helps her mother to the table. Lays out the pieces. She usually lets her mother win, only because she does not want to upset her, and today her mother is calm. Phoebe does not want to ask if Lidia remembers anything she said.

"I should have told you," her mother says as they play. "But it was better not to." She does not look up at her daughter.

"Told me about what?" Phoebe asks.

"We wanted you to have a happy childhood."

"I did, Mom. You were a good role model, an independent, ambitious mom."

92

"Well, there's that, I suppose."

"I wanted to check in on you, make sure you're okay before I go away for a bit."

"Why wouldn't I be? Raja will be home tomorrow."

Phoebe's heart drops. It has been months since her mother has thought of him as alive. "Dad won't be back for a while, Mom."

"He's Professor Glassman to you," her mother snaps. "Don't overstep."

"Right," Phoebe says, hollow inside. "Professor Glassman." There are many kinds of loss, she has come to understand.

Her mother picks up a checker and places it on the board, skipping over several of Phoebe's pieces. "I'm going to win again," Lidia says. "Perhaps I should let you have a game."

"That's okay. It's fun just to play."

"You're sad. I understand." She pats Phoebe's hand.

"I'm okay. I just wanted to see you before my journey. Don't be lonely while I'm away, okay?"

"That's all right. My daughter comes by."

"Oh, Mom, I'm sorry." Phoebe doesn't know exactly what she is sorry for. That she can't care for her mother, that she can't save her, that she can't bring back her memory or her husband.

"You should go," her mother says, when she has won the game.

"Push me out of here, why don't you?"

As Phoebe pulls on her coat, her mother says, "If you're looking for her there . . . Perhaps it's a mistake. After all this time."

"Looking for whom, Mom?"

Her mother places the checkers pieces back on the board. "I think I'll play against myself. That's always fun."

"Whom would I be looking for? Someone in Wappenish?"

"Wappenish? Where is that?"

"Why would it be a mistake?"

"What are you going on about, sweetie?" her mother says, returning to her checkers board.

Phoebe wants to press her, but she can see that her mother is far away again. She bends down to kiss her on the cheek. "I'll let you know what I find out. Don't be lonely."

"I won't be," her mother says. "My daughter will be here soon."

CHAPTER SIXTEEN

The drive east across the mountains, the same Friday afternoon, affords Phoebe stunning views of snowy peaks, valleys, and lakes. The farther she travels from Bayport, the easier it is to grapple with her mother's condition. *I'm alone now,* Phoebe thinks as she descends into Wappenish. *One day, she will forget me for good. I have to accept this fact.*

The quaint town, surrounded by orchards, sprawls against the backdrop of the Cascade Mountains. The sky is a crisp, painted blue, the air cold and dry. She parks in front of the house at 24 Cameo Lane, in a modest middle-class neighborhood.

She double-checks her phone. This is the correct address. The handwriting on the postcard is round and clear. But how can this be the house? The Craftsman-style cottage is uninhabited, a For Sale sign swinging in the wind. The windows lack shades and the garden is overgrown.

She parks across the street at the curb, gets out of the car, and strides up to the front entrance, cupping her hands to peer in through the vertical window next to the door. Inside, the house is unfurnished, full of light, the walls newly painted in a cream color, the oak floors polished.

She retrieves a brochure from the receptacle attached to the For Sale sign and calls the real estate agent, a woman named Dee Percenti. She answers almost immediately, with simply a friendly, "Dee here!"

"I've fallen in love with the place," Phoebe says, only half a lie.

"You and a million other people," Dee says with glee. "Isn't it just darling?"

"Is there a sale pending?" Phoebe says, feigning disappointment.

"We've had a lot of interest."

But no firm offer yet, Phoebe thinks.

"Why don't you hang on?" Dee says. "I'll be right there."

She shows up in a red Mazda five minutes later, pulling up behind Phoebe and hurrying from her car, carrying a clipboard and a large ring of keys. Her solid white dome of hair forms a helmet on her head, her red pantsuit fitted like skin.

"So what brings you to Wappenish?" she says, ushering Phoebe up the walkway in a haze of heavy perfume.

"Change of pace," Phoebe says. "I'm looking to move to a quiet area, with more of a sense of community."

"You'll find that here in spades," Dee says, clopping in spiked heels up to the porch. "Community is what we're all about." She finds the correct key, opens the door, and shows Phoebe through the house. "New kitchen, perfect home for a family."

Phoebe murmurs her approval. "You say you have other interest? I mean, I'm interested. Just wondering."

Dee's face lights up. "Well, we do have a few parties ready to make an offer."

"It is definitely a family home," Phoebe says, heading down the hall toward the bedrooms.

"This is perfect for a kid's room," Dee says, showing Phoebe a bedroom with blue walls. "How many children do you have?"

"Only one. So far. A girl."

"One of our interested parties also has a little girl!"

"Oh, how old is she?"

"Maybe six, seven? There's another room if you want to have more kids. It's the guest room, but you could make it whatever you want."

"Lovely. You know, a friend told me about this house." Her heart pounds as she follows Dee out onto the back deck. The wind is colder now. "She was thinking of buying. Her name is Pauline. Do you know her?"

"I don't recall a Pauline, but we've had a lot of people come through here." Dee strides out into the garden. "We had an open house last weekend. Maybe she came through then?"

"That must've been it. She looks a lot like me, actually."

"I don't recall, but I took over this listing only last week. We had another agent on the job, but she's on maternity leave."

"Oh, I see," Phoebe says, her heart falling.

"Lots of room for family gatherings." Dee is tottering in her heels now, toward the back of the property. The distant sound of children's laughter drifts into Phoebe's ears. Barely visible through the trees is a playground, just as shown in the photograph.

"This is lovely," Phoebe says. "A great place for kids."

As they traipse back around to the front yard, Dee says, "I've got another appointment, but here, take my card. I'll be happy to answer any questions."

"Thank you so much," Phoebe says. "I'll be in touch."

Back in her car, she sits for a minute, wondering if she has hit a dead end. Renee's voice echoes in her head. *He's dead, Phoebe. You know that, right? And now she's dead, too, so . . .*

So what does any of this matter? Renee would tell her to go home and get on with her life. But she finds herself driving around to the playground, teeming with young children. They're playing in a castle made of tunnels and steps and cubbyholes. And surrounding the paradise of play structures, parents, nannies, guardians sit on benches, watching, smiling and laughing and talking, pushing their hair out of their eyes and squinting in the sunlight. The day is cold but sunny.

Phoebe parks across the road by the curb, feeling like a voyeur watching happiness in which she will never again participate. She tries to hold the memories at bay, of Ava laughing, grasping everything in sight, running on her fat little legs.

What was Pauline hoping to find here in Wappenish? *There is something here,* Phoebe thinks, *but I don't know what.*

She leaves the playground and checks into the Wappenish Motel. She has called in sick to Fair Winds. She needs time to investigate. It was a relief not to speak to Barry directly. The new receptionist promised to give him the message.

In her small motel room, the bed is surprisingly comfortable, the covers printed in the solid, bold patterns of northwest native art. The lampshade matches the bedspread and the framed print on the wall above the flat-screen television. The room is otherwise drab, unremarkable. The tile is cracked and yellow in the bathroom, but the tiny motel soap smells pleasant, floral.

After a long shower, she sleeps deeply, waking with a vague memory of a dream in which she was pacing in a blue room, restless and trapped, surrounded by shadows, occasionally glancing out through the window toward manicured gardens. But she's not trapped, and the motel room walls are not blue but a bland off-white. *I'm in the motel,* she reminds herself. *It's Saturday morning.* Today, she is scheduled to go into Fair Winds for a few hours, but she calls in again, and this time the call goes through to Barry. She's surprised to hear him answer—he must be catching up on work.

"You okay?" he asks, sounding worried.

"I didn't realize how tired I was."

"Take the time you need." Papers shuffle in the background. The phone is ringing. As usual, he sounds distracted. "Feel better. Keep me posted." He abruptly hangs up.

She whiles away the morning driving through town. In the afternoon, when the sun comes out, she parks across from the playground, the one that was barely visible in the photograph. Through the trees, she can see the roof of the house for sale on Cameo Lane.

She gets out of the car, strides across the road, pops on sunglasses. It's nearly dinnertime. The cold wind wafts over her. She keeps watching the children in the sunlight, more of them out playing now, birds twittering in the nearby forest, the mountains capped by soft clouds in the background.

A young woman, perhaps too young to be a mother, is watching a little girl playing on the climbing bars. The child is five or six, hard to tell, her hair a deep black color, long and wild. She keeps running, never slowing, pushing her hair out of her eyes. Something about her draws Phoebe's attention. The child is wiry, frenetic, impatient, while her mother or nanny keeps watch, a long sweatshirt pulled down over her hips. She was reading a book, which now sits open, upside down on a backpack on the bench. Her hair is pulled into a ponytail.

"Mel, get over here," she calls out, exasperated. The girl ignores her, runs faster to the slide, pulling up her red corduroy pants, and races up the ladder as if her life depends on it. Then she flings herself down the slide.

"I'm going to call your dad," the young woman says.

Is she the mother, then? They're getting younger and younger these days, and Phoebe supposes she was older than most when she had a baby. She imagines herself in the woman's skin, racing to bring Ava home, saying, *Playtime is over, time to wash your hands, time to sit down.* No, she would never do that again, if given one more chance. She would let Ava play forever, let her stay dirty and never have to take a bath, only when she wants to play in the bubbles for hours until her fingers wrinkle. Her whole childhood would be one long indulgence. Bedtime stories, ice cream, cake.

"My daddy won't worry!" the child, Mel, shouts back.

"We have to go," the woman says crossly.

What is it about these two, when everyone else on the playground weaves around them, children calling out, parents laughing? But Mel and her guardian—mother or nanny or babysitter—are captivating.

"No, we don't have to go," Mel says, now running to the castle, disappearing into a tunnel.

"If I were your mom, I would whip you," the woman mutters. Mel, in the tunnel, seems not to have heard. She reappears at the other end, shooting out as if catapulted. She knows exactly how to elude the nanny.

"I'll make your favorite dinner," the nanny says, standing at the bottom of the slide. Her voice is edged with panic. Mel stands at the top, hands on her hips. She is stubborn. So was Ava. She insisted on trying to lift her head early, on sitting up, on running almost before she could walk, walking before she could crawl.

This child, Mel, pulls down her sweater, jutting out her chin, her hair backlit by the sun, her face in shadow.

"You're lying," she says. "We're having liver and onions. Yuck!"

"No, we're not," the nanny says.

"I saw liver in the fridge. I'm not going."

Phoebe imagines the house in which this child, Mel, lives, and wonders if she has a mother, either working or inattentive or incapacitated. Or maybe her mother is dead. There are so many things that can break apart a family.

Phoebe remembers the conversation she had with Logan, when she had grown large and bloated from the pregnancy, and she couldn't sleep, couldn't lie on her side or bend over to tie her own shoelaces. When she felt so tired, she thought she could sink into a thousand pillows and sleep for years. *I can't wait to get this baby out of me. I can't wait to go back to work.* She was on bed rest in those last weeks, her mind spinning when she wasn't passed out, and in moments that weren't always fleeting, she wondered if she even wanted a child, wondered if it was all worth it and if she was cut out for the years that lay ahead. *You don't really mean that,* Logan said. *We both want her. We're both going to love her.*

You didn't feel that way when I broke the news, Phoebe yelled at him. *You walked away.*

I know—that was wrong.

She loses her breath, reminded that he did not want a baby at first. Only after Ava was born, his fear and reticence gave way to fierce love, protectiveness. Or so it seemed.

The nanny stamps her foot, Mel slides down in slow motion, and when she reaches the bottom, the nanny grabs her hand. "Honey, we can come back, but right now we have to go." As they walk back toward the bench, Mel drags her feet.

The sunlight wanes, slanting through the trees, casting elongated shadows like motionless people. The skipping girl turns to look toward Phoebe, only a glance, and Phoebe whips off her sunglasses to see the child in the natural light. *I'm dreaming—imagining.* The glasses fall to the ground. She crouches to pick them up, and as she stands again, her throat catches. She almost calls out to the girl. *No, stop, this can't be happening.* It's all she can do not to race to the child, grab her hand, hold on to her. Spirit her home.

I have to keep it together.

This girl, Mel, lives with another family in another life, and yet. Her chin, the pout, the black hair. The expression in her dark, wide eyes, the sound of her high-pitched, determined voice. *I know you, little girl,* Phoebe thinks. *I always have.*

CHAPTER SEVENTEEN

Phoebe furtively snaps a quick photo of the child, puts on her sunglasses again, the world darkening to a rose-tinted hue. She rushes to the car, head spinning. In the driver's seat, she is breathing fast, in a sweat. She whips off her shades, swipes through the pictures she has taken of her sculptures. The faces of Ava. She compares the sculptures to her photograph of Mel. The images match. She even created the long hair, and if she had painted the sculptures, the strands would've been black, the eyes dark brown. If her figurines were to come to life, they would turn into a stubborn, determined, carefree little girl. They would be Mel.

Other children will look like Ava, Phoebe tells herself. *Or the way I imagine she would look now.*

It wouldn't be the first time. Grief can do that, make a person see things. Make a person hope. She is shaking all over, her ribs tight.

She hits speed dial for Dr. Ogawa, gets voice mail, does not leave a message. She hasn't spoken to her therapist in months. Phoebe crosses her arms over her chest, squeezes her eyes shut. *Breathe. This is not possible.*

She can't trust herself to drive. But she must. Hands on the wheel, key in the ignition. She pulls out into the road, drives to the corner, turns left, in the direction she saw the nanny walk with the child as the two of them left the playground.

Seeing this child is a stinging reminder of all the days and years gone, the precious moments she expected to share with her daughter. Seeing her off on the school bus for the first time, making her lunch. First Halloween trick-or-treating on her own. First complete sentences. Phoebe has imagined it all, has grieved the loss of every moment.

There they are, the nanny and the child crossing the road, skipping along. *I can't drive past them. I'll lose them.* Phoebe pulls over, pretends to rummage in her purse, lets them move far enough ahead. It's all she can do not to dash from the car, grab the girl, and steal her away.

She must keep herself together. *She can't be Ava, you know she can't be.*

Phoebe picks up her phone again from the passenger seat, her left hand gripping the steering wheel. She can hardly hold the thing. Fingers trembling, she presses the "9." Then the "1." Only one more digit. What would she say to the emergency operator? *My daughter is alive. She died with my husband in a car accident, only the thing is, she didn't die, not really.*

A fantasy, and yet all she wants to do is follow the little girl, snatch her up, and hold her, never let her go. Sniff her hair, kiss her cheeks.

A young couple passes the car, glances at her, then they turn to each other and whisper, and she realizes how disheveled she must look. Her eyes in the rearview mirror are bright and shiny and . . . feral.

She throws the phone back on the seat. If she follows the child home, knocks on the door, who will answer? The ghost of Logan? *Ridiculous, impossible.*

She dials Renee's number, hangs up, dials again.

"Phoebe," Renee says, sounding distracted, noise in the background—a television or a radio. The clanking of dishes.

"I saw a little girl," Phoebe spills. "She looks exactly like Ava."

"What are you talking about?"

"I mean, this girl is probably six, seven years old. Her name is Mel, but she is exactly like Ava."

"What? Take a deep breath. That girl is not your daughter."

"I know, but the likeness."

"Where are you?"

"Mom!" Vik shouts in the background, at the other end of the line. A spear of jealousy pierces Phoebe in the chest. Renee has always had her son. *I should be happy for her,* Phoebe thinks, but she's drifting further from her friend. No matter what Renee ever did to help, she never understood, not really. She would have to lose Vik to truly know.

"Doesn't matter," Phoebe says.

"Hang on," Renee says, then covers the phone. Her muffled voice comes through: *We'll talk about it in a minute, okay?* She comes back on the line. "Listen, we need to talk later, okay? Call me back. Promise."

"But—" Phoebe says, but Renee has already hung up.

Phoebe takes a deep breath and pulls away from the curb. In what direction were they walking? Right turn here. The sky is dimming. The traffic is picking up.

This is not coincidence, Phoebe thinks, that she spotted this child. It can't be. There they are, still strolling along, Mel holding on to the hand of her nanny, or babysitter. They're turning up a winding, wooded driveway.

Phoebe pulls over to the curb again. Her heart is about to burst out of her. She is barely contained inside her skin. What a wonder is the universe to have brought her here, to have made this child visible. She tries to calm her breathing. Perhaps she was meant to fly to Modesto, to talk to Darlene, to find the postcard, to end up here.

Mel and the nanny are halfway up the driveway now. Phoebe opens the car door, gets out, looks around. A young couple is strolling up the road, laughing, walking a shaggy sheepdog.

Phoebe gets back into the car and closes the door, ducks her head, pretending to look for something in the glove compartment. The couple is laughing as they pass by, disappearing around the corner.

She looks up again. *Don't run up to the house—you don't know what you will find.* She should leave now, take a breather, gather her wits. *You can come back.*

On the mailbox at the bottom of the driveway, a small sign reads GARAGE SALE, SUNDAY ONLY.

Today is Saturday. She has waited this long. She can wait one more day.

But she gets out of the car, steals up the driveway. The house is larger than others in the neighborhood, but not a mansion. The nanny and Mel are still outside, their silhouettes dark against the twilight sky. Laughter drifts through the air. They walk around to the back of the house. A door squeaks shut.

Phoebe weaves her way up behind the trees. There are no lights on outside. She sprints to a side window, stands on tiptoes to peer inside, and there is the child, seated at a low table. She is coloring with crayons, and through the slightly open window, through the screen, Phoebe can hear the girl humming, the way Ava hums in her dreams.

Phoebe crouches in shadows. She is so close. She could pull off the screen, reach in, grab the girl, and take her home.

"I don't want milk," Mel says crossly.

The nanny hands her a glass of milk. "You need protein, hon. You've been playing outside all day."

"I said, I don't like milk." That little determined voice. Ava never liked milk, either.

She tries to slow her breathing, tries not to let anticipation run away with her. This girl. The likeness is profound, breathtaking. Ava loved to draw with her little crayons, circles and crude shapes. Her tongue protruded from her mouth in exactly the same way.

Think about what you're doing. Spying. Sitting here in the cold.

Phoebe moves away from the window. Her knees are stiff. Texts pop up on her phone from Renee, asking where she is.

Phoebe wants to reply, but she can't, not yet. She turns off the phone. Her hands are going numb as she peers inside again, taking in that soft chin, the determined pout, those eyebrows, bushy like Logan's. The way Mel swings her right foot and taps her heel against the leg of the chair—so familiar. Phoebe does that, too.

There is no good reason to knock on the door, not before the garage sale, but Phoebe needs to talk to the child alone. To hold her.

She leans back against the house, shivering, and takes in the garden illuminated strangely by the light of the moon. Don's voice echoes in her head, warning her about what could happen.

But she imagines the garden at home, the way it should look. Not overgrown, neglected, with rusty contraptions scattered about. A falling-down swing set.

No, a blue plastic tricycle should be lying in the grass, a kite tangled in a bush, tiny rain boots on the walkway. A hand-painted rock with a big daisy facing the sun. A kiddie swimming pool, the kind you inflate in summer, small and round and shallow.

Phoebe makes her way back down to the road as headlights sweep around the corner. She ducks her head, pulls up the collar of her coat. The car turns up the driveway, and the shadow of a man gets out. He's tall, maybe six feet, Logan's height. She can't take a risk and go back. Not tonight. Not yet. She needs time to think.

She drives into town in a daze. Returns to the motel, flops onto the bed, her bones heavy as lead. She touches the locket on her necklace. Ashes inside. Cremated remains. She sees Dr. Ogawa's concerned face and imagines what she might say: *Tell me why you're obsessed with someone else's daughter. Let's talk about what this means.*

Don is right, Phoebe thinks. *This can't lead anywhere good. But I can't let it go.*

She turns on her phone. Immediately, it buzzes insistently.

"Where are you?" Renee says. "I'm worried about you. I texted you."

"I know, I've been busy," Phoebe replies.

"Doing what? Should I call someone?"

"Whom would you call?"

"I don't know. Are you okay?"

Phoebe laughs a little hollowly, tells Renee what has just happened. She has known her friend forever. Renee listens, and then she says, "Phoebe. That girl you saw. You don't know that she looks like Ava—or the way Ava would be now. You last saw her when she was two years old."

"I've been sculpting her at every age. You know I can do age progressions."

"Oh my God," Renee says. "How can you even know what Ava would look like? You can't be sure your sculpture is even accurate!"

"I do it every day at work. I reconstruct faces."

"But this is different. Come home, okay?"

"I'm staying here tonight."

"What about work? You have a job."

"Not on Sunday." Phoebe's job feels far away. The prep room, the instruments on the table. The wax and makeup on the rolling cart. The metal slabs on which the decedents lie motionless and desiccated beneath fluorescent lights. "I have to talk to her. I saw her through the window . . ."

"You can't trespass! You can't look in windows. Do you know how much trouble you could get into?"

"You're patronizing me." Phoebe paces on the carpet, her voice rising. She has to stay calm. There are people in the next room, the muffled drone of the television reverberating through the walls.

"Should I call your therapist?" Renee asks.

"No, don't call her," Phoebe says, but she feels herself faltering.

"Don't do this. You know what could happen. Get a grip!"

Phoebe turns to stare at herself in the mirror. She sees in her face, suddenly, that frantic obsessiveness. Her hair sticks up, her face pale, her eyes wild, shiny. Overexcited. "I can't help myself," she breathes into the phone. "What would you do if you lost Vik and then you saw a boy who looks like him again? I feel like I lost Ava only yesterday."

"I know, sweetie," Renee says softly. "You know I love you. You know I'm on your side. But this is not helping. Don't do anything rash, okay?"

"What would I do?" Phoebe knows exactly what she would do. She imagines it over and over again, has been imagining it ever since she left that house. She can't sleep for imagining holding Ava in her arms again. Her little girl.

"Stay away from that house. They could have you arrested if they find you there, and your life would be destroyed."

Phoebe laughs and laughs, crying, then sobbing, collapsing on the bed in the fetal position, drawing her knees up to her chest. "My life, destroyed? Do you even hear yourself? My life was destroyed three years ago."

"There's something you must consider. The kid could be Pauline's. If you say Pauline was going there?"

"I don't know for sure."

"She looked like you. That would produce a kid who looks like you, too."

Phoebe stops moving, the sounds of the motel crowding in. Cars pulling into the parking lot, a voice through the wall, a television. "She didn't have any kids. There was no record of a child."

"Maybe you don't know about the child."

"Darlene Steele would've known. She would have said something!"

"You can't possibly believe that the little girl is actually Ava."

"I . . . I don't know," Phoebe says.

"Then who died in that accident? There were bodies. Barry cremated them at Fair Winds."

"Anything is possible," Phoebe says, her vocal cords tightening. "I'll be back tomorrow, after the garage sale."

"After what garage sale?"

"Goodbye, Renee. I'll see you soon."

CHAPTER EIGHTEEN

The nightmare returns—of pelting snow on the windshield, the screech of brakes, the car spinning out of control, flying into the air, and she lands in the blue room again, white rhododendrons blooming in the garden. *White like tufts of snow,* she thinks. *It all makes sense.* But when she wakes in the motel room, she realizes how absurd the dreams were, how disconnected and illogical.

She showers quickly, makes coffee and a bagel but hardly tastes her breakfast, checks out, and drives into the bright, clear day. She pulls up to the curb behind a line of other cars parked in front of Mel's house for the garage sale.

"The early birds picked through the best ones," the nanny says as Phoebe pretends to look at delicate teacups displayed on a table. Her muscles tense, every molecule alive as she watches Mel sitting cross-legged, playing with an intricate homemade dollhouse, complete with three stories of rooms and tiny, detailed models of furniture, people, even plates of food.

"You've still got plenty of good teacups," Phoebe says, listening to Mel speaking softly under her breath, holding the dolls, a man and a woman, as if the two are conversing. The child's hair falls past her shoulders, shiny and black, and she wears pink pants, a pink shirt, a pink sweater.

"We didn't put everything out," the nanny says, coming up beside Phoebe. "I mean, if there's anything specific you're looking for, I could check in storage."

"Nothing specific," Phoebe says, looking up at the house half-hidden behind the trees. "Beautiful place you've got there."

"I know, but it's not mine," the nanny says, smiling. "I'm just working the sale for the owner. When he bought the place, the previous owner had left a bunch of stuff here in storage. She was like a hundred and two years old. She died and left everything behind. Didn't even have an estate sale or anything. It was like, you buy the house, you buy everything in it. So he did. He's lived here for like, over two years, and he only got around to having a sale now."

"I see," Phoebe says, pretending to look at sets of dinner plates, doing the mental calculation of years in her head. Mel quietly rearranges the tiny kitchen. "What about the lady of the house?" Stupid question. The nanny will start to suspect something.

"Mr. Favre isn't married," she says, smiling at a well-dressed woman who has just walked up to look at furniture. *Favre. Interesting surname,* Phoebe thinks.

It's all she can do not to rush over and scoop the child into her arms. She is only a few yards away. But even as Phoebe watches her play, she falters again, unsure. Renee's words come back to her. An echo of her sessions with Dr. Ogawa, as well. *Grief can play with the mind.*

Mel sits with her knees bent back, her legs double jointed. Phoebe has never been able to do that. But Logan could. *And so can millions of other people,* she reminds herself. *Don't stare at the girl. Keep looking at all these useless kitschy things. All this junk.*

"It's nice of you to do this for him," she says to the nanny. "You know, running his garage sale."

"I take care of Mel, too. She's his daughter." The nanny nods toward the child.

"Mel. That's a nice name. I have a little girl about the same age. Her name is Ava."

She watches the nanny's face for a sign of recognition, but she merely smiles pleasantly. "That's cool. Maybe they could have a playdate. I'm Liv. Short for Olivia." She reaches out to shake Phoebe's hand briefly, her fingers warm and firm.

"A playdate. Sounds perfect. Mel . . . is a lovely girl." Phoebe keeps pretending to shop, picking up vases, turning them around.

"She's a handful," Liv says, nodding toward another couple approaching the sale.

"How old is she? Ava is five. Almost six."

"Mel is almost six, too," Liv says.

Phoebe wants to ask the date of Mel's birthday, for her birth certificate, evidence that she belongs to some other mother. But that would be absurd. "Ava looks like Mel, actually," she says.

"Really? That's cool." Liv starts humming to herself, refolding shirts laid out on a table. The couple calls her over to ask a question, and Phoebe sidles over to Mel, sits next to her. The day shines around them. She can't take her eyes off the little girl. *Don't stare.*

"That's a beautiful dollhouse," Phoebe says. "Is it yours?"

"Yeah," Mel says, rearranging the living room furniture. "It's not for sale."

"Well, you're lucky. I used to have a dollhouse like that one." It's true. Phoebe loved playing with miniature dolls, cars, trees, farms, furniture. Everything small.

"Did you have the people?" Mel asks, holding up a miniature model of a woman in a blue dress.

"I did have people, but they weren't as beautiful as yours. Who is this?"

"Nobody," Mel says, suddenly guarded. "She's just a lady."

I used to wear a blue dress like this one, Phoebe thinks. A sleeveless summer dress that fell just below the knee. She resists the urge to sniff Mel's hair, to call her Ava.

Your daughter is dead—she is nothing but ash in a vial on your neck-lace, a reasoned voice in Phoebe's head tells her. She has a sudden urge to rip off the locket, hurl the horrible thing into oblivion. This is all wrong. She wishes there were no cremated remains inside, only ashes from a fireplace, perhaps, or sand.

Phoebe points at the male doll, the adult in a shirt and tie, because of course it's the man who dressed for the office. "He's the dad, right? And the other one is the mom?"

"There's no mom," Mel says, putting the woman in the kitchen. "She's just a lady."

"No mom! Is that what it's like in your house?" Phoebe says softly. "No mom?" She glances at Liv, who is still talking to the couple.

"I had a mom. But she's gone."

Phoebe wants to say, *No, I'm right here.* She sees baby Ava so clearly, smiling up from the crib, saying, *Ma.* "I'm sorry your mom is gone," she says softly, her voice shaky. Liv glances at them but keeps talking to the couple.

Time to back off. The nanny is on alert. Phoebe smiles pleasantly and stands, picks up a turquoise ceramic vase priced at fifty dollars. "Did your mom go away somewhere?" she asks, turning the vase around, not looking at the child.

"She died when I was little."

"Oh. I'm so sorry."

"It's okay. I don't remember her."

But I'm right here, Phoebe wants to scream. She wants to ask Mel about her father, about who he is, *where* he is now, how long they've lived here, where they lived before. "Liv seems nice," she says instead. "I bet she takes care of you."

"Yeah, but she makes liver and onions. Ew!"

"But you like Liv."

The child nods and looks at Phoebe, and something catches in her eyes. Recognition? "Are you a nanny too?"

"No, I'm not," Phoebe says, squeezing the vase, almost breaking the glass. "But I'm a mom. I have a little girl."

"You do?" Mel looks up at her with interest now. "Could she play with me? What's her name?"

"Her name is Ava," Phoebe says, exhaling, her fingers tingling. She waits for a response.

Mel squints at her. Was that a spark of knowing? "Does she have a dollhouse?"

"Nothing as elaborate as this one. When did you get this one? Were you living in this house?"

Mel shakes her head.

Pull back, stop pushing.

Liv approaches them, her eyes on the vase in Phoebe's hands. She will have to buy this gaudy thing, can't change her mind now. She needs more time with Mel, needs to talk to the father.

Mel gets up and waltzes off. Phoebe wants to chase after her, drill her with questions, but the chance is lost. For now.

"I see you found something," Liv says, grinning. "Isn't the vase gorgeous?"

It's gaudy, Phoebe thinks. "I wish you had five more," she says, surprised at how easily she keeps on lying. "Tax on the fifty?"

"No, just fifty even."

Phoebe hands over the cash, half of what she carries in her wallet. Three twenty-dollar bills. The garage sale is teeming with people now.

"See this chip on the bottom?" Liv says, turning the vase upside down to reveal a tiny ding. "I could take a few dollars off."

"I don't mind," Phoebe says quickly. "Nobody will see it."

Mel returns, talking to the dolls, her hair catching the light.

"Mr. Favre decided to keep the other three vases in the set," Liv says. "They're perfect. Worth a lot without the chips. They're all different colors. All handblown by the same artist. They're rare."

"Oh, really?" Phoebe glances toward the house as Liv tucks the twenty-dollar bills into her metal money box and hands back a ten-dollar bill. "Would he sell them to me, do you think?"

"I don't know. I doubt it."

"Is he home? Maybe I could ask." Phoebe tries to sound casual, but her urgency must show through.

Liv gives her a strange look. "He really loves his art . . . He's been trying to make his own. He's doing all this . . . origami stuff."

"Origami?" Phoebe nearly gasps. The voices around her recede into a rumble. *One thousand origami cranes will make your wish come true.*

"Are you okay? Did I say something? You look pale." Liv's voice comes from far away.

"No, I'm fine," Phoebe says. "It's just . . ."

"You really like that vase, huh?" Liv wraps the thing in newspaper now. "Sorry I don't have Bubble Wrap."

"I'm serious about the other vases. I'm interested." *Origami, origami.*

"I could take your number."

Phoebe hesitates, an irrational, ridiculous part of her thinking, *He will recognize my telephone number, and he will take off with Ava.* But the father is not Logan, and the child is not Ava.

Anyway, Phoebe has a new number now. She whips out her phone, gives Liv her number under the name Anna, and then realizes she will need to change her outgoing message. Instead of saying, "You've reached Phoebe Glassman," she will have to mention only the telephone number.

"I'm sure he'll love to talk art and antiques with you," Liv says.

"Really," Phoebe says. "He loves antiques, too, does he?"

"Yeah, he does get into them when he has time. He works so much."

"So, he's at work on Sunday?" Phoebe says, looking around, also wondering what he could possibly do in Wappenish that would bring in enough income for this house.

"He's traveling all week, left early this morning. He doesn't actually have a workplace so to speak. I mean, he works from home, but he goes to his studio out back. He's on the computer a lot."

Phoebe recalls Logan on his computer, tapping away, lost in another world.

"What does he do?" she asks. "I mean, what profession is he in? I'm thinking of trying to work from home. You know, start my own business."

"He's in software consulting," Liv says. "But don't ask me the details. He has to travel a lot. I stay overnight here with her way too often." She nods toward Mel, shaking her head sadly.

"Where's her mother?" Phoebe says.

"She passed away. Tragic."

"That's terrible. When was that, exactly?"

"Oh, about three years ago? I think he came out here to try to forget."

"Out here. Where were they living before?"

"Somewhere in LA, maybe?" Liv says.

"This is quite a change from LA."

"Yeah, hey, excuse me, will you?"

"Yeah, sure!"

"Let me help you with that!" Liv rushes off toward a woman with a pile of precariously balanced ceramics in her arms.

Phoebe looks around in a panic, then follows Liv. "I meant to ask . . . could I trouble you to use the restroom? I've got a long drive ahead of me. I'm only visiting town."

Liv hesitates, helping the customer transfer the cups to the table.

"Never mind," Phoebe says quickly. "It's okay. I'll find a gas station."

"No, sorry. Why don't you go ahead? I'm sure Ben wouldn't mind."

"Ben."

"I mean Mr. Favre. Go ahead."

"Thank you," Phoebe says. "I'm grateful."

"No problem." Liv is already adding up the cost of the cups on a sheet of paper. "Side door, top of the driveway. Just go through the kitchen and the bathroom is the first door on the right, when you get into the hallway."

Phoebe rushes up the driveway, pretending she hasn't already done so. *What are you doing?* she admonishes herself. *You can't possibly think* . . . There must be photographs of Mel inside the house, pictures of her father, her mother. *What about the accident, the cremations, the service?* She knows she should not go inside. *You're trespassing on someone else's property.* But she pays no heed.

CHAPTER NINETEEN

The side door squeaks, and it sticks halfway when Phoebe tries to pull it closed. She has to yank extra hard. The air in the kitchen seems to draw into itself. Now she's on the inside, looking toward the window, imagining herself crouched out there, where she was last night, looking in.

There is one origami frog on the kitchen counter, a simple crane on a side table. Phoebe's throat goes dry. She glances out the side window, glimpses the garage sale at an angle through the trees. She ventures into the hall. The kitchen door slams behind her. Mel waltzes up next to her, disturbing the air. "I can go pee by myself," she says, sticking out her bottom lip and glaring at Phoebe as she whirs past.

When Phoebe was five years old, she did that, stuck out her lip in exactly that way. She has a photograph to prove it. "You escaped," she says, grinning at Mel. "Good for you."

Liv is on her way up the driveway. Someone is chasing after her, garden sculpture in hand. She stops to talk. There isn't much time.

"I'm not supposed to talk to strangers," Mel says.

"You're also not supposed to leave Liv's sight," Phoebe says. "You should wait for her."

"This is my house."

"Yes it is, Mel."

"My name is Melina."

"Beautiful. Did your mom name you?"

Mel shrugs, opening the bathroom door.

"Do you remember your mom?"

"No," Mel says, pouting. She gives Phoebe an inquisitive look. "You're a mommy."

"Yes," Phoebe breathes. "Yes."

Liv has broken away from the customer.

Mel nods and goes into the bathroom. "I have to pee. There's another bathroom upstairs!" She locks herself inside.

"Okay, thanks," Phoebe says. *There will be time. No rush. You know where she lives now.*

In the spacious foyer, a crystal chandelier hangs from the ceiling. Phoebe climbs the stairs, her heart pounding, and on the second floor, she peers into the master bedroom, a large bed meticulously made, the pillows puffed, the corner of the bedspread turned down. A lace doily sits on top of the antique dresser.

She tiptoes into the room, the floor creaking. An origami instructional book sits on the nightstand. A photograph on the dresser depicts an angular woman with long, wavy blonde hair, high cheekbones, the look of a wispy model. Her right hand touches the thick fabric of her sweater's collar.

Is this Mel's mother? She could be a friend or an aunt. The picture could be from a magazine—if the woman is actually a model. He might not even know her. Phoebe quietly opens the closet, riffles through empty pockets, stands on tiptoes to check the top shelf, for what? For photo albums, some indication of who Mel's father might be. She pulls open drawers, checking through the men's clothing, occasionally glancing out the window, her hands trembling. Everything is neat, unfamiliar. She's unsure what she's looking for. *You're trespassing—stop.* But she can't help herself.

She rushes into the bathroom, sits on the closed toilet lid, and draws deep breaths, her hands clenched. Her brain is humming, the blood thick in her veins. *I'm in here to use the restroom, that's all.*

This bathroom, luxurious and opulent, taunts her with familiarity. The soap is her favorite scent, lavender; the cologne on the countertop is Axiom, Logan's brand. She could almost believe the toothbrush, the toothpaste, the shaving cream all belong to him. Her breath shudders through her. She flushes the toilet, washes her hands. Rushes back out into the hall, but she stops with her hand on the railing at the top of the stairs. *Now is your only chance to investigate, to find out who Mel might be.*

But she knows who Mel is—a child who only looks like Ava. It's coincidence, it has to be. There is no other possibility. Yet Phoebe finds herself peering into other rooms—a bland guest room, a small storage closet, and into the child's room done up in pastel blues and pinks.

She goes inside, edging along like a shadow. The faint scents of baby powder and laundry detergent conjure images of Ava in the nursery, smiling up at the glittering mobile hanging from the ceiling.

Mel's bed is unmade, the striped bedspread a blend of yellow and white, plush pillows on top, printed with pictures of elephants. The walls are painted blue and pink, adorned with watercolor butterflies and hummingbirds. A toy box sits in the corner, overflowing with teddy bears and large picture books. A coloring book sits open on a small activity table, a miniature chair pushed underneath. The dresser is painted sunflower yellow. A few dresses hang in the closet, shoes on the floor.

Phoebe pulls open the top drawer of the dresser, the blood rushing in her ears. The floor creaks—she freezes and glances toward the door. Nobody is there. Must be the house settling. She tiptoes out into the hall bathroom, painted in yellow and orange to match Mel's room. A plush orange bath mat sits in front of a tub, on which bubble bath and shampoo bottles are lined up. On the tile countertop, a couple of toothbrushes are inside a cup shaped like a hippo. Ah, there—a pink princess hairbrush, but it's clean, no hint of any hairs entwined in its teeth. No chance to extract DNA from an obvious source.

But why would I want Mel's DNA, anyway? She's just a girl who resembles someone else, someone I loved more than life, someone who is gone forever.

Phoebe looks up, startled to see herself in the mirror—an unknown woman, her eyes are too bright, too hopeful, her hair wild, tendrils clinging to the sweat on her forehead. Her knit sweater is unraveling, a few strands of yarn hanging from the bottom. She wipes her forehead, finger combs her hair, takes another deep breath, and exhales.

You can do this. She is about to open a drawer, but a door slams downstairs, voices approaching, growing louder. She can't risk staying up here another minute. She turns and runs down the hall toward the landing.

CHAPTER TWENTY

Back outside at the garage sale, Phoebe shows Liv a photograph of Logan with a beard. Before driving here, she took a pair of scissors and carefully excised herself from the picture. "Is this Mr. Favre?" she asks.

"I don't know," Liv says, frowning. "When was this taken?"

"Several years ago," Phoebe lies, the sun in her eyes. Overhead, a bald eagle soars, harassed by smaller birds. The predator trying to evade its prey.

"What makes you think you knew Ben?" Liv says, squinting.

"The name sounded familiar. When you said Ben Favre. We might have worked together. In Bellevue. But he called himself Benjamin back then. It took me a while to make the connection." More lies, her recent trespass infecting her blood.

"You work in software?" Liv says, watching Mel return to the dollhouse.

"Obliquely."

"He did work at Microsoft for a while, I think."

"Microsoft, yes! Does he have a beard and mustache?"

"I wouldn't recognize him without them."

"No, I wouldn't, either. I'm pretty sure I knew him. Isn't it a small world?"

"Completely. I could get your info. Oh, you gave it to me. For the vase."

"I was in management at Microsoft," Phoebe lies again. "Personnel management. I worked with people. Not computers so much."

"Where was it taken?" Liv says, looking at the picture again.

"At a wedding for a friend."

"It could be him. Hard to tell. It's one of those things. Borderline."

"Well, he was a lot younger. Maybe on social media he has a picture of himself without the beard? I knew him that way, too."

"Oh hell no," Liv says, laughing. "He's always telling me not to post my photograph anywhere. You know all that facial-recognition stuff? Our faces are everywhere. The government is watching us, logging all our info. It's totally scary. He says don't do that fingerprint thing on your phone, either. Don't freaking give your info to anyone. And don't buy those home systems. They spy on you. They record your voice. He's so totally not into any of that."

"Wise choice," Phoebe says, pocketing the picture. "I'm sure he knows better than anyone else what could happen . . ."

"Big Brother. That's what. He totally turned me on to protecting my privacy. Resist. Right?"

"Right," Phoebe says faintly, wondering what she will find out when she googles Ben Favre. "Well, I would love to meet him again. To catch up, for old times' sake."

"He's coming back next weekend. He's at the conference in LA. But I'll give him the info when he gets back."

Next weekend.

Phoebe nods, hesitant to leave, but she has no choice. Reluctantly, she goes, but she parks the car a few blocks away, walks back through the streets, ventures close enough on foot to watch from a safe distance, cars coming and going to the garage sale until the sun sinks on the horizon. The day is growing cold, her fingers numb, her breath puffing out in condensed clouds, but she hardly notices. A part of her steps back, alarmed at how obsessed she has become.

Finally, Liv and a friend are closing down, carrying the remaining inventory into the garage. Then the friend leaves, and Liv and Mel go inside the house. The outdoor lights wink off. Phoebe is shivering, her stomach turning inside out from hunger. She forces herself to go back to the car, drives to a Chinese restaurant to order takeout, and while waiting for the food, she googles Ben Favre on her phone. No images come up of the Ben who lives in Wappenish. Mostly, images of Brett Favre, a football player, pop up everywhere.

When she's finally back in her motel room, exhausted, her phone buzzes, lighting up with a call from Renee. She shovels kung pao tofu into her mouth with chopsticks, staring at the screen. She considers not answering, tucking away her phone and forgetting about everyone in Bayport. But she needs to pretend everything is normal.

She hits the "Answer" button. "I'm not up for talking right now. I'm having dinner."

"I swung by your house. Your mailbox was overflowing," Renee says. "It's mostly junk mail, though. A million catalogs."

"I haven't been gone that long, but thank you. My mind isn't where it should be."

"Come home. We should talk about plans. I thought you were going to California with me."

"Did I say that?" Phoebe says sharply. "Are you leaving?"

"I'm still looking for jobs. The sun is always out in California—"

"That's not true. It rains. And there are fires."

"But there are opportunities in California."

"You're trying to distract me."

"What happened at the garage sale? I've been so worried about you. Was it at the house where the girl lives?"

"She is so much like . . . Ava. And her father is into origami. Just like Logan. He uses the same cologne."

"*What?* Phoebe, how do you know that?"

"I asked to use the bathroom, looked around a bit while I was in there."

"You can't do that. This is not a game!"

You used to go along with my games, Phoebe thinks. In first grade, she and Renee made up elaborate stories. They were princesses relying on their wits to escape from a dragon. Sometimes they were mountaineers, astronauts exploring the galaxies, or detectives solving a case.

"I have to investigate." Phoebe paces on the threadbare motel room carpet. Her body buzzes. She can't stop the electric energy coursing through her. "None of this is a coincidence. The note Pauline scrawled on the back of the photograph. The playground. Mel . . . *Origami,* Renee."

"So what? It has to be coincidence, Phoebe."

"I should've taken Mel's DNA—"

"What? *Why* on earth would you do that?"

"Pauline discovered this place, too. But then why did she visit Bayport first? Unless Bayport was her first stop, and she intended to come here next, following a trail of bread crumbs."

"*What* bread crumbs? Leading to whom? You're scaring me. Stop and think about this. Don't forget the way things are. Don't forget who you are. That's what you told me, remember? Not to forget what's real? You need to come back."

Phoebe flops on the bed, gripping the phone close to her ear. She follows the zigzagging cracks on the ceiling. As a college sophomore, Renee moved in with a new boyfriend in Brooklyn. He was often AWOL, and she would call in tears to say he hadn't come home for the umpteenth time. But she loved him. Phoebe told her to cut her losses, pack her bags, and leave. The reality was, he was bad news. *Don't forget who you are and what's real.*

She wired money to help Renee rent her own apartment and start again. Then Renee quit college, met her husband, and had a son. *This is real,* she said. And after the accident, she returned to Bayport to help Phoebe, to keep her grounded.

But now—now, Renee is wrong. She doesn't know what's real. After all, she didn't see what kind of man Darin really was—verbally and possibly physically abusive, from what Phoebe gathers from reading between the lines—until recently. She didn't want to face the truth. She refused to see.

But Phoebe does. She sees all the connections. "Ben Favre is away . . . consulting. I have to talk to him when he gets back."

"Why? You *know* he's not actually Logan."

Do I know? I don't. Phoebe leaps up off the bed and glares at herself in the motel room mirror. Her hair is still a mess, her cheeks still flushed, new dark circles beneath her eyes. *I am not myself.* "You don't believe me. That's okay. But just promise not to tell anyone what I just told you, okay? Nobody."

"Phoebe, I—"

"How long have we known each other? We've been through a lot together, haven't we? We promised to always tell each other the truth, to always ask for help if we needed it."

"I am trying to help you now."

"Remember the blood pact when we were seven?"

"Pricking my finger hurt like hell. And we're not seven anymore."

"Doesn't matter. Cross your heart and hope to die."

"I can't do this, Phoebe."

"Do it! Promise. Swear."

Renee sighs into the phone. "All right, I promise."

"Good, good," Phoebe says, pacing faster. The room is too warm, the heater whooshing. "I'm coming home. I don't have much time to get to the bottom of this."

"You're coming back here. Good," Renee says, her voice relaxing with relief.

"I'm not staying long, though. I've only got a few days, then I have to come back to Wappenish."

CHAPTER TWENTY-ONE

"What makes you think it will help?" Don asks.

Phoebe now interprets his voice as patronizing, not soothing or reassuring. He's been trying to discourage her from acting on her hunches. Why did she not see this before? This cold Monday morning, they are on the coroner's office property, she and Don, walking on a narrow wooded path toward the woods. He met her outside, suggested they get some fresh air. She suspects that he wants to buy time, to convince her that she doesn't need to see the file on Logan and Ava.

"I need the closure," she lies, stopping at a lookout point, where a memorial bench is engraved with a plaque commemorating someone who died, someone who was loved.

Don leans over the railing, resting his forearms on the iron bars. He looks at the locket around her neck. "Don't you have closure already?"

"I have to see for myself." She is calling his bluff.

"The photos are not pretty."

"I know, but I have to see."

"You won't be able to forget. Some images stay with you forever. They haunt the hell out of you."

She watches a junco flutter beneath the bushes. "I know you wanted to spare me pain. You shouldered the trauma for both of us."

"It's my job." He turns his hands palms upward, the lines deep and furrowed, life lines, health lines. His hands are chapped from frequent washing, like hers. "You know, I thought I could handle it, but . . ." He blinks away tears, wipes at the corner of his eye. "He was my friend . . . and Ava was so young."

"I know—don't you think I know? She was my daughter." This all feels like a charade. When she returned to town, Renee came over, tried to dissuade her from visiting the coroner, without success. But at least Renee kept her promise, not saying a word to Don. He does not seem to know where Phoebe has been.

He leans forward, his muscles taut, bending over as if suffering from abdominal cramps. "Sorry, Phoebe. You shouldn't . . ."

"I need to see the file," she says firmly. "I feel like I'm falling into this black place. Ever since Pauline showed up on the table, I've been, I don't know . . . hallucinating."

"Hallucinating what?" He straightens to his full height, looks down at her, his bloodshot eyes wet with tears. He hasn't slept well in a while.

"People I thought were dead. But I don't know if they are."

His eyes widen. Like her, he is surrounded by ghosts. "I know about fucking hallucinations," he says. "When I saw Pauline, I thought she was you. I thought I'd lost you, too, and I could not bear the idea. But when I realized she wasn't you . . . I almost kissed the ground and thanked God. I did—I prayed but under my breath. Because my next thought was, somebody did lose a loved one. Pauline was somebody's daughter, sister, and for all I knew, mother." He chokes on the last word, as if he didn't mean to say it.

"Mother," she echoes. *Can I even call myself that anymore? Mother to a dead child?* But, it seems, Ava may not be dead at all. She looked at Phoebe, and she was about to call her *Mommy.*

No, she wasn't.

Phoebe looks at her hand, and she realizes Don is holding on tightly, the way people do when unbearable grief pulls them down like quicksand, and they need some anchor to the world aboveground. His fingers are heavy, their grip insistent.

"I'll do what you want," he says. "But my advice to you, and I know you're not asking for it, is to leave this alone. It will only lead to heartbreak."

"Yes, I understand." The junco takes off in a flurry of black-and-white wings. Little birds that don't migrate in winter. They stick around, braving inclement weather.

"So you'll try to let this rest. Because I'm the one having a nervous breakdown."

She sets her jaw, focuses her thoughts. "What was it like? I mean, right when they came in?" She watches his face closely for a sign of subterfuge, but he hides deception well.

"I was a medic on scene. You know I was a first responder."

"You had a partner."

"Yeah, Eddie Watters."

"I want to talk to him."

"You can't. He burned out."

"He's not working as a medic anymore? I can still talk to him, can't I?"

Don's jaw twitches. He hangs his head, looks at his polished shoes, not made for these walks on dirt trails. "Eddie is no longer with us."

The words hover in the air, a roadblock sign. *No longer with us.* "He quit?" she says, although she knows this is not what Don means. But she needs to make him say it.

"Eddie took his own life about a year ago."

She draws in a breath. "Oh, how terrible. Why didn't I hear about it? I know about everything that happens in this town."

"It didn't happen here. He moved back to Mississippi to take care of his parents. The guy was already burned out, couldn't take it. Shot himself with a twelve-gauge."

"That's awful." She has seen this before, a handful of times. Restoration is all but impossible in such a case.

"There was no viewing at his funeral down there. His family didn't want all his friends to know."

He's gone now, the only other witness at the scene of the accident. She wonders if Don is telling her the truth. "That is tragic," she says carefully. "I'm sure his family is devastated."

"Yeah, I'm sure," Don says, drawing a deep breath.

"Let's go inside. I need to see the file. Now."

He concedes but drags his feet, slowing as they enter the building. In the conference room, the fluorescent light flickers as if infested with a restless, irritable spirit. Phoebe's hands, resting on the unyielding tabletop, look skeletal.

Don leaves the room and is gone for several minutes, giving him time to doctor the file, to alter its contents to show her what he wants her to see. *Is this what I really think of him? That he is corrupt?*

Outside the window, a rufous hummingbird hovers above a winter-flowering camellia, defying the odds, this little bundle of hyperspeed metabolism, the wings a blur of iridescent purple and green, in such contrast to the motionless gray of the room. The bird buzzes high, seeming to look at Phoebe, and then is gone, just as the door opens and Don comes in holding a manila file folder.

He sits across from her, his tie askew, a slight sheen of sweat on his face.

"Sorry I took so long," he says. "I had to find the file."

"Don't you keep everything organized here?" she asks crossly.

"It was in the archives. In storage."

"Already?"

"It has been three years. Are you sure you want to do this?"

She holds out her hand, and lips pursed, he slides the file across the table. "Text me if you need me," he says. "I have a few calls to make."

After he leaves, she stares at the crisp folder, slightly creased and weathered. She runs her hand along the smooth exterior.

She opens the folder and begins to read Don's report, full of jargon and notes about injuries, contusions, massive and catastrophic. Her hands begin to tremble, the room wavers, the sky darkens. It was worse, much worse than she ever imagined. Skull fractures, severed hands, broken ribs. Logan was thrown clear. This is all they are now, her husband and child, if she is to believe the report. Numbers, statistics. They are two-dimensional, trapped in time, stuck on paper. Don was right: she should not look at this. Should not have opened Pandora's box.

He tucked the photographs behind the other paperwork, at the very bottom, perhaps hoping that she might change her mind and not want to look. At first, she can't comprehend what she's seeing. She scrambles to her feet, gasping, nausea rising in her throat. *Some images stay with you forever,* Don said, and now there is no turning back. She hyperventilates, a high, keening cry erupting from somewhere inside her. The pulverized faces, the blood-caked clothing and hair. The bodies could be Logan and Ava, but they are unrecognizable. They could be anyone at all.

CHAPTER TWENTY-TWO

"I'm not going to tell you it's impossible," Mike says in the afternoon. "It does happen." He looks different today, like a stranger, or perhaps it's the angle of her view through the scrim of fog in the parking lot. He's leaning into the back of the van. She has just asked him if bodies ever get mixed up in transit or have ever been misidentified, in his experience.

When he pulls out the blue cadaver pouch, so small that he can carry it under one arm, he looks like himself again, only slightly more detached than usual. He looks different each time she sees him.

She knows she is not the same person she was yesterday, either, or the day before, before she saw Mel on the playground. Before she saw the photographs in the file this morning. She's more hopeful than she was.

"So if the bodies were unrecognizable, how could you be sure they were who you thought they were?" she says, following him in the back door leading to the refrigeration room. No chance of running into a member of the public, going in this way.

"You could do a DNA test," he says. The cooler is an icebox. There's a sickly-sweet odor in the air, but it's not the smell of death. It's the cleaning solution the janitor uses on the stone floor, installed for the easy flushing away of body fluids.

"What if you can't? What if the bodies were cremated?" The goose bumps rise on her arms. He slides the infant-removal pouch into a small drawer, closes the baby inside. Like he's putting laundry away, cleaned and folded.

"Then you're out of luck," he says.

"Don't tell anyone I'm talking to you about this."

"My lips are sealed."

She reaches up and rubs her throat, tries to loosen up. This shouldn't bother her, being in here. She shouldn't imagine the tiny child opening his or her eyes, seeing only the blackness of the bag.

"Are you okay? Hey, Phoebe," Mike says, tugging her sleeve.

"What happened? Boy or girl?" she says, gesturing to the closed drawer of the cooler.

"It was a girl. SIDS."

Sudden infant death syndrome.

"Oh no," she breathes. She knows what the baby's parents must be feeling. Numbness, disbelief. They probably want to die. "Excuse me, please." She escapes down the hall to her office and locks herself inside.

This is a dead end, Don said. A voice in her head insists on agreeing with him, but she searches the internet again, returns to Pauline's Facebook page.

Help me solve the mystery.

The mystery of Logan's whereabouts, she might've meant, since she did not know his real name. She did not know about the accident. But there it is, the comment from her roommate, Xia Page.

The guy has a habit of disappearing. He's an asshole.

Now Phoebe understands this comment in a new context. She sends Xia a message on Facebook.

I was married to Pauline's disappearing boyfriend.
What did you mean?

The reply comes almost immediately.

You could be anyone. You could even be him.

I'm not, I promise. Could we meet in person?

Phoebe refrains from mentioning Mel or any of her suspicions.

Public place. Meet me at Forever Vegan tonight
at six.

Phoebe logs off. She has five hours to get there. On a Monday evening, the drive takes maybe three. She packs an overnight bag in case she needs to stay in Portland. On the drive south, she tries to prepare questions in her mind, an interrogation that will not seem like one. She can't alienate Xia, but she has no idea what to expect. A glut of traffic slows her down through the state capital in Olympia. The white spire of the capitol building rises on the eastern horizon behind a dense, dark forest. Noisy construction crews have blocked off the right lane. She grips the steering wheel. If she is late, she could miss Xia altogether. The young woman might change her mind about meeting and disappear into the ether.

Finally, the traffic thins, and Phoebe speeds up through the flat, agricultural fields of Centralia, Lacey, past the turnoff to Mount Saint Helens. She imagines Logan driving this route, listening to Miles Davis or Bachman-Turner Overdrive, his two favorites. Stopping every hour for coffee. He was addicted to caffeine. She wonders what he was thinking during those long hours in the car. Maybe he didn't think at all. Perhaps he shifted smoothly from one persona to another.

As she crosses the bridge over the Columbia River, marking the separation between Washington State and Oregon, the traffic slows again. Her back is sore, her vision beginning to blur. She has stopped once for a snack, another time at a rest stop. The farther she drives from home, the more alone she feels. Or perhaps it is only that her aloneness becomes more apparent, more defined. It used to be that when she and Logan traveled, they reveled in their anonymity. Nobody knew them, and they didn't know anyone they encountered, but they always had each other. In hotel rooms at night, they could commiserate, unpack their day, the people they saw, the museums they visited. They could make plans. But now, it is just her.

She follows the GPS directions into an uptown, densely populated Portland neighborhood, the main road lined with quaint boutiques, bookstores, and restaurants. Tall shade trees cast moving shadows, students racing along the sidewalk carrying backpacks, couples strolling arm in arm, families of three or four stopping into toy stores or ice-cream shops. The city feels leafy, erudite, and . . . young.

As Phoebe parks on a side street a block from Forever Vegan, she takes a deep breath, wondering what on earth she is getting herself into here. She is tired, stiff, hungry, and a little shaken from her second long drive in two days. She often found herself sandwiched between big rigs, long-haul drivers careening around curves.

She enters the cozy restaurant, the interior painted in deep, almost neon blue and green, and she feels suddenly old, aware of the streaks of gray in her hair, the lines on her face. Nearly everyone here, huddled at tables, leaning into each other, is young and engaged in earnest intellectual conversation. They take their lives so seriously. They believe anything is possible. She can see on their faces that they have not, for the most part, experienced the pain of grief. They don't think about their mortality.

The waitress is no different. Open faced and friendly, she is smooth in every way. Her skin, her manner, her straight, shiny hair. She places the menu on a glossy wooden table. "Anything to drink?" she says brightly.

"Just water for now," Phoebe says. "I'm expecting a friend." *I hope,* she thinks, sitting with her back to the window, so she can see the doorway. The menu offers a mind-boggling selection of coffee drinks and vegan entrees. Quinoa and edamame bowls drizzled in a house ginger sauce, braised or deep-fried tofu, the Forever Vegan veggie plate. At this point, anything will do. Her hunger has become a gnawing pain. She watches couples milling in and out, small groups of friends, college students, two silver-haired women adorned in flowing, muted clothing, seated at a small table in the back, laughing at some private joke. Phoebe wonders what these women do for a living, why they are meeting here. How they know each other.

She is looking at the menu when she senses Xia coming toward her. The door has swung open and shut, the cool air sweeping in. Xia's energy precedes her. "Hey, you're Phoebe," she says in a throaty, deep voice.

Phoebe looks up into an angular, surprisingly mature face. Xia seems older in person than she did in her Facebook photos. She looks more serious, determined, her hair cropped close to her head, as if she is keeping it under careful control. Her body is lean, athletic. *Like a dancer,* Phoebe thinks. Phoebe flashes back to her own college days, when she could run for miles without breaking a sweat, when she could've made long drives without any aches or fatigue.

"You're Xia," she says, shaking the young woman's hand.

"You're older than I expected," Xia says, whipping off her backpack and throwing it onto a chair.

"Thank you, I think."

"I didn't mean it that way. You're not *old.*"

"It's all right," Phoebe says.

Xia folds into the chair across from her. She is still tall, even when seated. She seems to be all arms and legs. The waitress comes over, and Xia says, "The usual."

"Hey, Xia . . . Cranberry cocktail coming right up." The waitress turns on her heel. She must be a colleague. This is where Xia works, after all.

She places her elbows on the table, hands clasped in front of her, fingernails short and ragged, but she wears numerous thin bracelets that clink on her wrists and slide down her forearms. "So here we are," she says. "I thought you were going to stand me up."

"I thought the same thing, that you might not show," Phoebe says. Her glass of ice water feels cold against her fingers. The waitress brings them two plates, hand-painted in small orange poppies.

"Are you ready to order?" she asks.

"I need a minute," Xia says, opening the menu.

The waitress nods and walks off.

"What do you know about my husband?" Phoebe says. She has already decided to order the Forever Vegan veggie plate.

"You get right to it, don't you?" Xia looks at Phoebe over the top of the menu.

"Don't think me rude, but I don't have the patience for small talk."

"Well, okay," Xia says, "I'll be honest. I can't believe he was married to you. I mean, it's not anything about you—"

"I'm older than you expected, and not his type? Or what?"

"You just look so . . . normal."

Me, normal? Phoebe wants to laugh out loud, but she thinks Xia might mean plain or ordinary or . . . tired and faded. "You're saying Logan wasn't normal."

"Isn't," Xia says. "Isn't normal."

A shiver ripples across Phoebe's skin. *Isn't.* "What exactly do you mean?"

Xia motions to the waitress with a curve of her index finger, which is encased in a thick silver ring. The waitress returns, and Phoebe and Xia order the same thing, but Xia asks for her vegetables without the sauce. The waitress takes the menus. The noise grows too loud. The laughter. If only everyone would be quiet—it's too difficult to hear what Xia says.

"The guy never dies." She clasps her fingers on the table again, then unclasps them and grabs her knife. She turns it around and around between her thumb and forefinger, the shiny metal catching the light.

"So you're saying he's a vampire or something. Everybody dies."

"You sure about that?" Xia lays down the knife, looks up at Phoebe. "Logan, or whatever you call him, does. Not. Die. I know. I looked into it. I look into things. It's what I do because you know what? I'm in grad school. Agora. U of O. Working here is just a part-time gig."

University of Oregon, Phoebe thinks. But she has not heard of Agora.

"School of journalism," Xia explains, probably seeing the confusion on Phoebe's face. "It's my mission in life to report the truth. Investigative journalism."

"That's a good mission," Phoebe says, nodding. "Noble." *What is she getting at?*

"And you know what truth I uncovered? That guy was full of shit." Xia presses her finger into the table for emphasis. "He was full of shit from the time Pauline went gaga for him." Now her hand flutters in the air, like a wayward bird.

"What do you mean, gaga?" Phoebe says, unsure if she wants to know. It occurs to her then that there was a first time for Logan and Pauline. A moment when the two locked gazes, when they first spoke to each other. When they flirted, kissed for the first time. First held hands. First retreated to a rendezvous . . . *Stop,* she tells herself. *Just. Stop.*

"She couldn't stop talking about him. About how kind he was. How romantic. How caring. How attentive. He seemed to know what she wanted before she even wanted it." At this, Xia rolls her eyes, drinks her cranberry juice.

The way he was with me, Phoebe thinks. She keeps a carefully bland expression.

Xia leans forward, looking right and left before skewering Phoebe with her gaze. "You want to know something? She knew him before. They met like, seven, eight years ago. She was living downtown back then, working in the Sasquatch Café. They hit it off, had a good time, and then they were on and off after that."

Nausea rises in Phoebe's throat. "On and off meaning what?" The film of her marriage plays back in her mind—going over the wedding preparations together, honeymoon plans, picking out his tuxedo. Visiting the doctor together when she was pregnant. Trying out new recipes, painting the nursery. He was seeing Pauline, *on and off,* all that time. If what Xia says is correct. Phoebe wants to hurl the silverware against the wall, stand up and scream, tear out all her hair. *Keep it together,* she tells herself, while she feels her insides breaking apart. "So, she knew him as Michael Longman all along." Somehow, against all odds, her voice stays calm.

The waitress brings the steaming vegetable bowls, but now Phoebe has no appetite.

"Yeah, fake name." Xia forks broccoli into her mouth.

"His real name was Logan McClary," Phoebe says, her lips numb. The barista fires up the espresso machine behind the counter, a loud hissing sound nearly drowning her words.

Xia points at her with the fork. "See, I didn't have that information. But I traced him. He talked bullshit, but she didn't see it."

"How serious were they?" Phoebe asks. "Did they talk about marriage, kids?"

Xia keeps shoveling vegetables into her mouth, chewing and swallowing. "She talked about it. I don't know if he did. I felt like there was more. About their history together. Something she didn't tell me."

"Like what? Any idea?" Phoebe sips her water, imagines shattering the glass into a million pieces.

"She said she had been looking at wedding gowns. I thought it was wishful thinking on her part, but maybe he was stringing her along the whole time. Saying he wanted to marry her, but then something happened and he changed his mind."

"He married me, that's what happened," Phoebe says bitterly. She wonders at how he managed to flip back and forth between two separate lives, sustaining his charades without faltering.

"Yeah. Now I know," Xia says. "So how did he die? Supposedly?"

"Car crash," Phoebe says in a clipped voice.

"Like a big fiery wreck? Did you see the body?"

"I saw pictures," Phoebe says distantly. "He was . . . difficult to recognize. The car went off a cliff. It wasn't exactly a big fiery accident."

"Anything like this accident?" Xia unzips her backpack and whips open a file folder. She slides an article, printed from the internet, across the table. "Maine, nine years ago. This guy disappears at sea, out sailing with his wife, leaves her behind to mourn."

Phoebe stares at the article, uncomprehending. "What does this have to do with my husband?"

"Read it," Xia says, pointing at the article. "Go on."

Phoebe reads, a curious ringing in her ears. "You're saying this is . . ."

"Your husband. *Was.* I found a picture of him. Ever wonder why he didn't want to have his picture posted online?"

The ringing grows louder, a shrill hammering at Phoebe's eardrums. "He didn't have a social media presence. He said it was about privacy."

"Yeah, the privacy of his criminal enterprises. He was swindling investors out of their funds as Keith Michaels a year before he ever got to your town," Xia says.

"Wait, *what?*" Cold fingers press into Phoebe's throat. The words stab at her. *Swindling. Investors . . . Keith Michaels. Michael Longman.*

141

"I have a friend who's really good at using facial-recognition software." Xia slaps a picture of Logan on the table, enlarged and unmistakable. "He was sitting in this park, behind the sculpture in this newspaper article. But he's in focus. He doesn't even know he had his picture taken."

Phoebe looks closely at the picture. It's Logan—there is no doubt. "What was he doing?" she says, her mouth parched. Her vegetables are growing cold.

"He set up marathons and other footraces for women, attracting investors who paid him a shitload of money. Then he canceled, ripping off his suppliers and creditors. He never followed through on what he promised the runners, who paid through the nose to sign up." She slaps printed blog posts on the table. "Found these posts about Keith Michaels, from the companies he didn't pay. And then he died on a boat, his body never recovered."

Phoebe's fingers shake, her breathing shallow and ragged as she flips through all the evidence, her vision blurring. "This is . . . I can't believe this. I can't."

"Sorry, it's got to be a shock for you," Xia says softly. "It's not like you could think of all this. You couldn't make this stuff up."

"No, no, you couldn't." It's all Phoebe can do not to rip the articles to shreds, not to set them on fire.

"She didn't listen to me," Xia says, pointing at the papers, then looking up at Phoebe through glassy eyes. "I tried to tell her. But she went up to Bayport anyway. I didn't want her to move out."

"*Why* did she move out?" Phoebe asks.

Xia looks away, wipes her tears. "She said she needed her space. Doesn't matter anymore. She always did stupid things." Her body is trembling.

"I'm sorry you lost your friend," Phoebe says.

"Yeah, well. We're going to have a little candlelight vigil, us friends of hers. Can't get to California for the formal service with her mom. We do our own thing."

"She was lucky to have people who cared so much about her." Phoebe stands stiffly, heavy with the weight of what she has learned. "May I keep these papers?"

Xia shoves the pictures and articles into the file folder and slides it across the table toward Phoebe. "Go ahead, do what you want. He's done it again, hasn't he? Logan the escape artist?"

Is it possible? Phoebe thinks, her mind awhirl. *He could have remade himself all over again.* "I have no idea," she says. "But I'm going to find out."

CHAPTER TWENTY-THREE

On the long drive back to Bayport, Phoebe curses under her breath, her urgency to get home making her drive too fast. She keeps letting up her pressure on the accelerator, trying to stick to the speed limit as the road darkens ahead of her. Trying to keep her eyes open. She should've stayed overnight in Portland to get some rest, but she needs to get home. Her meeting with Xia feels unreal, the outcome a strange nightmare but also a vindication. *Logan could be alive. Ben could be Logan.* She even says this aloud against the noisy vibrations of the car engine. "The bastard tricked me. He's been doing this his whole damned life. He's Ben Favre now."

But even as her own voice reverberates through her head, another one whispers to her, *You know this can't be true.*

"Yes, it is," she says. "I saw the evidence. Mel must be Ava."

You know they are dead.

She pulls off the highway into a rest stop parking lot. She needs some perspective, needs to stop talking to herself. She's losing it. She hits speed dial for Renee's phone, gets voice mail, does not leave a message. *Damn it.* What Xia said, all her research—it's devastating. And too fantastical to believe.

Phoebe takes a deep breath, goes into the women's restroom to splash her face with cold water. Blinks herself awake. She looks up into the mirror, her reflection an impressionistic shadow. The mirror is not really a mirror at all but an opaque, scratched, barely reflective sheet of metal nailed to the tile wall.

She washes her hands, shakes them out, as the blow-dryer is not working, and returns to the car. She must stay awake for the rest of the drive home, another hour. Stay awake and not lose her mind.

She pulls out onto the highway, gripping the steering wheel. Presses her foot to the gas. *I have to get back to Wappenish. I have to know the truth.* Logan got away with starting a new life under a new name, Ben Favre, up in Wappenish, letting everyone in Bayport believe he is dead. *Everyone* meaning her.

Could he have returned to town to kill Pauline? But he would not have even known she was coming to look for him. He's living his life as Ben Favre, unaware that anyone is onto him.

Pauline had a photograph of a house in Wappenish, but not *his* house. Not Mel's house. An empty cottage on Cameo Lane.

Xia did not have that piece of the puzzle. She knew nothing about Wappenish. And she did not know that Michael Longman was Logan McClary. The only trail she could follow belonged to Michael. The voice in Phoebe's head telling her that Logan is dead becomes softer and softer, until the whisper barely registers in her brain.

She could fly back east, talk to people who knew Logan in Maine, try to decipher what happened and who could have helped him escape and establish a new identity. But she's more interested in what happened much later. What happened in Bayport. And how he managed to escape with her daughter.

You know this is not possible.

When Phoebe arrives home, she is exhausted. The house feels stuffy, heavy with secrets and lies. The times Logan locked himself in his office to "catch up on work," the light bleeding out from beneath the closed door, take on an ominous significance now. It must have required an inordinate amount of work to maintain his parallel lives.

The clutter of antiques, books, and other collectibles seems to have gathered more dust. The obstacle course begins to irritate her—there is something tired and threadbare about the entire house, every room oppressive.

She showers, soothing her worries in the hot water, and when she crawls into bed, her phone lights up on the nightstand. Barry left a message while she was in the shower. "Uh, Renee mentioned you've been going places—some town in the mountains? Is that where you were today? I know you called in, but we should talk, Phoebe."

Yes, we should, she thinks, wondering what he might know. She takes Xia's file folder from her purse and lays out the printed papers, the articles, the evidence, on her bed. Reads everything again. Logan managed to fool everyone. It occurs to her that to fake his death, he would've required help. Accomplices. People who could cover his tracks. He could not have done it alone.

CHAPTER TWENTY-FOUR

Early Tuesday morning, Phoebe begins to pack up Ava's room, boxing up the bibs, tiny sweaters and booties, the onesies and rattles, the mobiles and floating bath toys. Ava must have been growing up all this time—she is not gone. Older girls don't like to play with baby things. Ava is no longer an infant.

When Phoebe steps back to survey the room, the walls look bare, the furnishings sterile. But Ava will repopulate the space with her own personality. Books, maybe. Ballet dresses. Or mountaineering gear, an off-road bicycle like the one Phoebe once had.

What are you doing? she asks herself as she leaves the room, closing the door quietly. *Ava is never coming back.*

An hour later, at Fair Winds, Phoebe parks in the empty spot that once belonged to Logan. *Now it's mine,* she thinks, grabbing her purse and striding purposefully into the mortuary. She peels off her coat and gloves in her office. Barry has left a message on her desk, asking her to talk to him and mentioning a restoration in prep room one.

She checks the prep room, where a teenage boy—or what is left of him—lies beneath a sheet. Her heart breaks when she gazes upon his broken remains. The force of something unyielding has nearly sheared him in two.

This has happened once before. A young girl arrived who'd been hit by a train, but there was no viewing. Her friends had seen her deliberately step onto the tracks.

This time, Phoebe will have to perform great feats to create the illusion of normalcy. *How cruel it is to even have a viewing,* she thinks. *Let him go.* But she can't judge others, not when she, herself, is teetering on the edge. She's not sure she can attempt this one.

She rushes down the hall and finds Barry tap-dancing in his office, the blinds closed, the music playing softly. She forgot about his unusual habit. Perhaps these private moments of lively dance keep him from sinking into the death that surrounds him.

He turns off the music when Phoebe walks in, his face flushed from exertion. "Sorry," he says. "I was practicing for a performance at the community theater. Please, sit down. I'm glad you're back. Did you get my message?"

She nods, sitting across from him, the desk between them. "I saw the boy in the prep room."

"The viewing is tomorrow," he says.

She nods again, looking around the otherwise tidy office, the urns and catalogs on the shelves, the plaques on the wall denoting his credentials. "Why don't you keep pictures of your family on the desk anymore? You used to have a whole lot of framed photos in here."

"What can I do for you?" he says, avoiding the question.

"Well, *you* said we should talk."

"About the trips you made—"

"Am I now required to ask your permission?" she snaps.

He gapes, taken aback. "No. I was only worried—you said you weren't feeling well."

"I wasn't. I'm still not. I need to know something. Three years ago, you cremated Logan and Ava. I wasn't in any condition to help. I wasn't paying attention at all. I left everything up to you."

"And I was happy to help," he says, giving her a head tilt in sympathy. "What's bringing this up now? I know the anniversary recently passed."

"Did you lie to me?"

"About what?" His gaze is steady, the blood still in his cheeks from the exertion.

"Did you cremate other people? Two people that were not my husband and daughter?"

"What?" His face is white now, his lips taking on a grayish hue.

She unclasps her necklace and sets it on the desk. The silver metal glints in the light, an accusation. "What the hell is in my locket? I thought it was a mixture of Ava and Logan."

"Then it is. That's exactly what it is." He flinches, as if she has slapped him.

"Did you know for sure what you were doing? Whom you were cremating? Because if you were a part of Logan's deception, so help me . . ."

"What are you talking about?"

"Who were they? The people you cremated?"

"You know who they were. Is this a serious question?"

She slams the flat of her hand on the desk, startling him. She grits her teeth, pain in her temples. "Everything I ask is serious."

He fumbles in his desk drawer for a handkerchief, dabs at his sweaty neck. Pushes his chair back a little, away from her. She has flustered him. Good. "Yes. I cremated Logan and Ava. You've asked me this before. You know the answer."

"I don't," she says curtly, looking at the necklace. "I don't know the answer. You know what I do know? I know my husband was a liar." Her neck feels bare. She picks up the necklace, still warm from her skin.

"I'm sorry about that," Barry says.

"You knew. You don't look surprised."

"I'm not. But what good does it do now? I never was going to take any legal action."

"Legal action. Against whom? For what?"

"Against Logan for embezzling. He's gone. You didn't know."

She grips the arms of the chair, afraid it might take flight, and she will fall hard to the ground. "How much? How much did he take?"

"It doesn't matter now. I think you made the best choice to accept my buyout offer, under the circumstances. And in case you don't remember, we've been through the cremation thing. You asked me before."

"I don't remember. I guess I did. I mean, I think I did."

"Yes, you did. How many more times do we have to go through this?"

"You're right." The past unravels, and she sees herself asking, *You're sure? You saw their faces?* "I mean, did we talk about this? We did?"

"Think," he says, a touch of desperation in his voice. "Just . . . think. Yes, we did."

She gets up, trips over the leg of her chair. Everything gets in the way, the corners of things, legs, tables, piles of books, and memories. "I mean, there was no DNA test done. It was just assumed."

"But it was Logan, and it was Ava." He gets up and opens the door for her. The knob doesn't turn easily. Sometimes the wood expands and sticks. Her lungs tighten. She needs to get out of here. In the hall, she draws a deep breath.

"You okay?" Barry says.

"I will be," she says, forcing a smile.

"Go home and get some rest. Do what makes you happy. Take some more time off. Don't do all this."

"All what? What am I doing?"

"You know what I mean. Let's not tread over the same old ground."

CHAPTER TWENTY-FIVE

Phoebe returns to her office, shaking with anger. This is not the "same old ground." Barry knows it is not. He didn't ask *why* she accused him of lying to her. Because he knows. Of this, she is certain. She didn't tell him about Mel. But maybe he knows everything. And if he does, he is complicit in Logan's criminal deception. *Unforgivable,* she thinks. *Collusion.*

If Logan owed Barry money, why would Barry help him? Unless Logan paid him back in spades, and he's not telling her. *No, you're losing it.* She sits at her desk, opens the drawer, and takes out Dr. Ogawa's business card, her cell phone number scrawled on the back. A number to call in case of a breakdown. *Call me—I'm here for you. Grief is terrible, lonely, isolating,* Dr. Ogawa said. *But it's natural and perfectly, imperfectly human. Everything you're feeling. This is the mind's way of grappling with the unimaginable. The best way past is through.*

The words bounced off Phoebe, but she needs them now. She needs to understand why this is happening—and what is wrong with her. A whisper in her head is still telling her to leave this all behind, to drive away from this place and keep going, to find a better future, a future of forgetting. *He's gone, Ava is gone. Let them go.*

But I can't, she screams inside.

She can't stand to stay here, in this oppressive air, lost in these dark shadows of memory. The boy in the prep room is waiting for her—but he no longer notices the passing of time. He is not the one waiting. His survivors are. Impatience, the need for order and restoration—these are reserved for the living.

Phoebe throws on her coat. She is gathering her purse and gloves when she glances out the window. Barry's Lexus is just leaving the parking lot. He's taking off early.

She dashes out to her car, screeches out of the parking lot, drives in the direction he usually goes, toward his home in the heart of town. She and Logan once visited Barry and his family for a company dinner. The modest two-story was well appointed, the garden manicured to a fault, as she recalls. *I should've stayed in touch with his wife,* she thinks absentmindedly. She has lost track of her former acquaintances, even the ones who live close by.

There he is, the Lexus two cars ahead of her. She grips the steering wheel, stays far enough behind, she hopes, that he doesn't glance in the rearview mirror and recognize her car. Instead of turning up into a residential neighborhood, Barry drives through downtown and all the way out of Bayport, on and on along the winding waterfront road. *Where the hell is he going?* Maybe he has an appointment somewhere. The commercial buildings and dense neighborhoods fall away, expanding into meadows and forests and occasional farms, and still he drives on, leading her fifteen miles out into the suburbs.

Finally, he turns onto a street populated by newly constructed mansions, stops below a curved, steep driveway to check the mailbox. The house, built in a modern northwest style with large windows, towers above the ground in nearly three stories. Perhaps twice the size of his previous home. For this must be where he lives now if he's checking the mail. She had no idea the family had moved. She should have known—Bayport is not a huge town—but Barry keeps to himself. And she has been hiding out, lost in her own mind.

There is no sign of Barry's kids. She recalls bicycles, a trampoline, a portable basketball net in the driveway of the family's previous home. She parks at the curb behind a buffer of trees. Barry's car idles in the driveway, then the garage door whirs upward, and he drives inside. The garage closes again.

She considers her options. *Go home,* the voice of reason tells her. *Forget all this.* But Mel dances into her mind. And Xia's bright, glinting eyes, her determined expression as she slides the printed articles across the table. *This is him. This is Logan.*

Phoebe rolls down the window, glances up at the mansion in which Barry now lives. She could knock on his door and ask how the hell he could afford this place. His wife is a stay-at-home mom. Unless she has suddenly acquired a lucrative profession.

If Logan paid him off, and if Barry shortchanged her on buying out Logan's part of the business, he could live this way, far from the clients who have made him rich through their losses, through their grief. She watches as a light goes on, his shadow appearing behind a bay window.

She waits to see if anyone else appears—his wife, kids—but only one light is on, no others, no sign of activity. A few minutes later, a car races up the driveway, a deliveryman in uniform balancing a pizza box in hand as he rushes up to the front door.

She slides down in her seat. Barry answers the door, hands cash to the deliveryman, looks out toward the road. The delivery car leaves, speeding away in a cloud of exhaust, and the house once again swallows Barry. Still no sign of his family.

A dark SUV turns the corner and pulls into Barry's driveway. The motion-sensor lights wink on above the garage. Someone gets out and strides up the walkway. The front door opens, a shadow appears, and

Barry admits his visitor. The door closes again. The light soon goes on in the living room.

Phoebe gets out of the car, glances up and down the road, then sneaks through the trees, slinking through the grass at an angle toward the house, out of view of the living room window. If Barry has cameras, a surveillance system, she's out of luck. But no alarms go off.

Leaving a trail of shoe imprints in the soggy grass, she crouches beneath the bay window. She peers up through the glass, and she can see Barry at an angle, pouring a drink—looks like a whiskey—from a bottle at the bar near a fireplace. The room is tastefully, expensively furnished. He's in a T-shirt and jeans—she has never seen him dressed this way, never so relaxed. And seated on the couch, turned away from the window, is a woman half in shadow. There's a pizza box on the coffee table.

Phoebe watches for a bit, trying to wrap her mind around the surreal tableau, the woman leaning forward to accept a drink from Barry. His mouth is curled up into a half smile. The woman holds her glass in both hands, appears to look down into the amber liquid. She shakes her head and sighs.

Barry sits beside her, rests his arm over the back of the couch. They are talking, but the woman's shoulders are tense, her face still turned away from the window. She puts her glass on the table, gesticulates. She and Barry appear to be arguing, or perhaps they're simply engaged in an animated, intense conversation. Then he pulls her close and kisses her. The woman turns partway toward the window, so that her face is lit up in profile.

Phoebe gasps, drops out of sight. Her nerve endings are shredding, the night bleak and unyielding. She squeezes her eyes shut, tries to dispel the image. *Let it go, leave,* Phoebe thinks. *You're trespassing.* But she can't help herself. She peeks through the window again. The lovers are holding hands, walking out of the living room. *What the hell?*

Her heart bursting, Phoebe runs back through the grass, staying low. When she reaches her car, she is sweating, out of breath. She looks back up at the house. A dim hallway light winks on upstairs. Two shadows pass beneath its illumination, the silhouettes of Barry and Renee. And then the light goes out.

CHAPTER TWENTY-SIX

"What is this all about?" Renee says at seven in the morning, seated across from Phoebe in the Bayport Bakery. The sun is rising across the Puget Sound, lighting the water in a pink glow. Renee seems to glow, too. But then again, she would, considering what she has been up to. The nerve of her. Her mascara is smudged beneath her eyes. She looks as if she just woke up in someone else's bed. She's wearing the same clothes she wore yesterday, the mustard-yellow blouse and jeans. She hasn't been home. And who was taking care of Vik? If Phoebe still had Ava, if her daughter were home again, she would never be left alone or with a babysitter, ever again. *You don't even know what you still have, and yet you squander it and lie and sneak around.* She is trying hard not to hate her friend, not to reach across the table and strangle her right now.

"You remember high school, when you told me to be your alibi?" she says instead, keeping her voice on an even keel. She sips her mocha, swallows the hot, chocolatey liquid. *Stay calm.* The café is filling with the morning crowd of commuters on their way to the ferry landing. Nobody works in Bayport anymore, it seems. They mostly take off for the city.

"What about it?" Renee glances down at the phone in her lap, pushes her hair behind her ear. She looks up again, shifting in her seat, her gaze darting around the café. "I need to get going. We have to be at work soon, and—"

"Not for an hour," Phoebe cuts in. "It's only seven."

"Way too early," Renee says.

"Oh, that's right. You have to stop at home first. Maybe take a shower, change your clothes?" Phoebe can't keep the hostility out of her voice.

Renee's face flushes, the pink traveling down to her neck. "Excuse me? I've got errands to run."

"Maybe pick up breakfast for your son? I know you're so busy."

"What's wrong, Phoebe? Why the insults? Is this urgent, or can we meet some other time?" She won't look Phoebe in the eye. Typical, when she has something to hide.

"Your boyfriend in high school, what was his name, Arthur Wight? I remember because it was an unusual name, and he was such a nice guy. Honest. Moral. He trusted you."

Renee swallows, puts her phone on the table, straps her purse over the arm of the chair. She looks shell-shocked. "He was one of my regrets. You texted me at oh zero thirty to talk about Arthur? He's history. What's going on? You look like you haven't slept. Is something going on with you?"

"Funny, I was going to say the same about you." Phoebe sips her mocha. "You look like you haven't slept, but for an entirely different reason, I imagine. I never told you this. But when Arthur found out you were fucking that jock, whatever his name was, he came crying to my house. Arthur was so sad. He felt betrayed. I talked him down. Right down from the ledge. As I recall, I talked you down numerous times, too, back when our lives were pretty normal. But Arthur. He was a nice guy, and you broke his heart. Not only was he nice and loyal, but he was good looking, too. That was a plus. I developed this . . . horrible crush on him, but he never saw me in the same way. Never even saw me at all. He was so into you. He just wanted to cry on my shoulder.

About you. He would've gone to the ends of the earth for you, and you lied to him. You made me lie for you, too. And I went along with it. I regret doing that."

Renee's jaw goes slack. The blood drains from her face. She plays with the ring on her right pinkie finger, turning it around with her thumb. "I'm sorry. I apologized a million times. Why are you bringing this up now? We were teenagers."

"But you're not a teenager anymore. You have a son, and Barry has a wife."

Renee's face goes completely white. Her lips tremble. "You brought me here to accuse me of sleeping with Barry?"

"I'm not accusing you. I saw you. That's different."

"You saw us where, doing what? We work together." Renee stands, snatches up her purse and phone, recomposes her face. She looks haughty now, her features turning to stone. Phoebe wonders if her ex-husband, Darin, is really such a bad guy. Phoebe doesn't know him. She flew to New York to attend the wedding but stayed only a couple of days.

The truth is, she doesn't know Renee anymore, either. After high school, thousands of miles stretched between them. They spoke on the phone, held on to a thread connecting them, but what was really going on in Renee's life? When she returned for Logan's funeral, and even when she stayed a few extra weeks, Phoebe was far away, stranded in her sorrow. Maybe the smooth egg of their friendship was always cracked, and now it has split open.

"What about Vik?" Phoebe says, wiping whipped cream off her upper lip. "Did he stay with the babysitter all night? Did you ask her to make up an alibi for you?"

"You were spying on me," Renee says softly, her voice shaking. "Like you're still in high school yourself. No, elementary school. What the hell do you think you were doing?"

"I was going to ask you the same question," Phoebe says through gritted teeth. "I've met Barry's wife. Have you? She's a lovely person. I wish I'd stayed in touch with her. She and Barry have two sons. The boys are, oh, thirteen and fourteen now, I'm guessing."

"No, I haven't met her," Renee says, sweat breaking out on her brow. She sits again, playing with her ring. "Were you following me last night?" Her brow furrows, a hurt expression on her face. "Why would you do that?"

"I was following Barry, and there you were. It made me think about the time Logan went to New York on business, remember? And he met up with you for dinner. Your husband was gone. You called me to tell me all about how you showed Logan around the sights. The Empire State Building and now I'm thinking, you know, I wonder what other sights you showed him?" Phoebe glares at Renee, and the table seems to expand between them, to become an uncrossable ocean.

Renee straightens in her chair. "You think Logan and I . . . You can't be serious."

Phoebe taps the table, taps and taps. "You two must've had so much fun in New York. When he got home, he couldn't stop talking about you. He said you and Darin were having problems. He said he was impressed with you, that I'd picked a great best friend. He suggested we visit New York more often. You know what? I didn't realize it then, but when I looked up 'signs that your spouse is cheating,' one of those signs is the spouse talking about another woman, a 'friend' too much. Why didn't I see it? I trusted Logan. I trusted you. But that was a mistake." The words are tumbling out of her now.

"You've got this all wrong," Renee says, lowering her voice to an almost-whispered urgency. "I don't know where you're getting all this, but I did not sleep with him. I would never do that to you."

"But you would do it to Barry's wife. Why? Because you don't actually know her? So what does it matter, right? Out of sight, out of mind?"

"She left him," Renee blurts, sitting up straight. "She took the boys and walked out. Or didn't you know?"

"No," Phoebe says, frowning. "I thought she was just too busy to stop by."

"I can't believe you didn't know."

"I don't listen to gossip. I'm out of the loop."

"His wife worked in the city, hardly ever showed up at the mortuary. Barry said she was queasy around the dead. But she was having an affair with her physical therapist in Seattle. She and Barry had this big blowup about it a few months ago. She took the boys and moved in with her parents. How could you not know this?"

"I don't pry into other people's lives—into their misery!" Phoebe finishes her mocha. Now she understands why he removed the photos of his wife and sons from his office. She thought he did not want to taunt grieving customers with images of his own happy family, but obviously, something entirely different was going on.

"You know how the rumors go," Renee says. "People talk."

"I didn't hear it," she snaps. "Barry keeps his private life . . . private at work."

"And work has been your whole life," Renee says. "Just because you want to be miserable all the time doesn't mean I have to be."

A stunned silence follows, the ocean between the two of them growing wider. "Shit, sorry," Renee says, shaking her head. "I didn't mean that—it's just, sometimes you seem so out of touch. The boys are still going to the same school. Barry's wife is supposedly 'visiting' her parents to help take care of her dad. He was sick for a while."

"But you knew the truth. And you saw your opportunity." The coldness Phoebe feels toward Renee is becoming ice.

"It wasn't my fault."

"So you did sleep with him," Phoebe says.

Renee gapes, her face flushing again, a deeper red. "I did go over there. Obviously, you know that, since you have nothing better to do than spy."

"You slept with him. I saw you both go upstairs."

"You were trespassing."

"Because of Logan. Were you involved in helping him disappear?"

"What?" Renee shouts. The couple at the next table looks over. She waves at them, lowers her voice again. "Stop talking about Logan . . . disappearing. You're scaring me."

"*I'm* scaring *you*?" Phoebe breaks into laughter that sounds unhinged, even to herself. If she weren't in a public place, she doesn't know what she would do. Upend the table, throw Renee's drink in her face.

"He remade himself again, but he couldn't get rid of the things he loved, traits that he carried with him. He can't help himself. He still loves antiques, origami. And what better place than Wappenish to hide away, to start a new life?"

"Omigod, you are serious." Renee's mouth drops open. She gives Phoebe a searching look. "If some guy in Wappenish is Logan, then you must believe that girl could be—"

"Ava," Phoebe breathes.

"And what, your dead husband kidnapped her? You really believe this."

Believe what? In hope? Phoebe wants to scream. "What do you know about Barry? Look at where he's living. In opulence. No wife anymore, no kids."

"He's a funeral director, what do you expect?" Renee says. "Business is booming. People keep dying. I'm not having this conversation with you anymore." She gets up and strides out the door. People turn to look.

Phoebe, paralyzed, stares at her empty mug. Then she gets up, grabs her purse, stumbles her way toward the door, following Renee outside into the biting air.

"You're not listening to me," she says, grabbing Renee's arm. "I have every reason to believe Logan deceived not only me but other women before me. He not only had affairs, but he swindled people, changed his identity."

"What the hell? Now you've really lost your mind." Renee yanks her arm away. "Let go of me. Do not touch me again."

"It wasn't a coincidence that I saw my daughter in Wappenish. And the only way that can be true is if Logan is there, too. And he needed help to get there."

"You think I helped your dead husband start a new life in some town in the middle of nowhere. You need—"

"What? What do I need?" Phoebe steps close to her friend. She can smell sweat and stale perfume.

"You need . . ." Renee lifts her arms and drops them in a gesture of despair. "You need help. You're seeing things. You're seeing connections that aren't there. People who aren't there."

Phoebe steps back, as if she has been punched. She narrows her gaze. "I know what I saw. I have pictures of what I saw. I spoke to the nanny, and I spoke to Mel. She could be my daughter."

"You spoke to the dead."

"She has so many mannerisms that are exactly like Ava, the way she was, the way she would be now. I am not imagining this."

"Look, I can't explain why you think Mel is Ava, except that you glommed on to Pauline, your doppelgänger or whatever, and a wire got tripped in your brain. But either way, I had nothing to do with this. Nothing to do with your delusion."

"This is not a delusion."

"Whatever. I'm allowed to live my life without you spying on me. You're sick, Phoebe. You need to talk to your therapist, maybe check yourself into a—"

"What, a psych ward?" Phoebe shouts so loudly, so forcefully, that she spits in Renee's face.

Renee wipes her cheek. "I can't convince you. But your therapist can."

"Just tell me if you are covering for Logan and Barry."

"No, I'm not," Renee says. "If you hadn't saved my ass my whole life, if you were not once an amazing, caring person, the most centered person I know—if you weren't my best friend . . ."

"Then what? What?" Phoebe feels each word like a stab in the stomach.

Renee steps closer, her eyes dark with sadness and frustration. "Then I wouldn't have tried so hard to pull you back into reality. I tried. So hard. But I can't do anything more, Phoebe. I can't." She turns away and strides briskly to her car.

Phoebe follows her, rage rising inside her. "I can't believe I thought you had matured after all these years. What do you know about what happened to Ava?"

Renee presses the button on her key ring. Her car chirps, the lights blinking. She opens the driver's-side door. "All of this is in your imagination," she says, getting into her car. "Because that is the only possible place where Ava is still alive."

CHAPTER TWENTY-SEVEN

"Don isn't home," Wendy says Wednesday evening. Phoebe spent all day working on the boy in prep room one, stewing all the while about Logan and Ava, Ben and Mel Favre, exploring all the angles. Now she is here, watching Don's wife carry groceries up the walkway toward the house, a reusable canvas bag under each arm. On the front step, Wendy puts down a bag and fumbles with her house keys. "Did you try him at work?"

"He's avoiding me again," Phoebe says. A BMW sits in the driveway. Shiny, pristine. "When did you buy that car? Wasn't it about three years ago?"

"Sometime around then. Don bought it."

"A few months after Logan died."

"Maybe. I don't remember." Wendy forces a tight, fake smile, and Phoebe wonders if the woman ever smiles for real. Her hand shakes. She drops the keys on the entry mat, picks them up. Normally she's so confident, a multitalented superwoman. High school science teacher, marathon runner, mom to three young children. But today she is anything but sure of herself.

"Nice playground setup," Phoebe says, pointing to the custom-made wooden climbing bars, slides, and swing set in the yard.

"The kids like it," Wendy says. "Why are you here?"

"Three years ago, how much did Logan pay Don, and you, maybe, to keep your mouths shut?"

"Excuse me?" Wendy opens the front door, throws the bags into the foyer, and steps inside. Then she turns toward Phoebe while closing the front door. Phoebe is already there, pushing the door open. Wendy's eyes widen in alarm.

"How much? Or did Don not tell you?"

"I don't know what you're talking about." Wendy's face is tight with fear.

"Maybe you don't," Phoebe says, wondering how Wendy can afford to stay home from her teaching job when she complained about the need for two incomes the last time Phoebe and Logan came over. "Or maybe you do know . . . I can't tell."

Wendy's face goes cold, so unlike the warm, welcoming expression she offered Logan the first time he and Phoebe came here for dinner. "What is this all about?" she snaps. "I have somewhere I need to be."

"You mean you're not going to invite me in?"

"I don't think that's a good idea."

Don's car pulls into the driveway. He gets out and sprints to the porch, a look of alarm on his face. "Hey, Phoebe, is everything okay?"

She backs down the steps and turns to face him. "I want to know whose bodies you sent to Fair Winds three years ago. There were other accidents during that storm."

He and his wife exchange looks. Wendy shuts the door. Phoebe can hear the dead bolt clicking into place. As if *she* is the threat and not the criminals who colluded to steal her daughter.

"Let's talk in the car," Don says.

"Why not out here?" she says loudly, looking around at the neighborhood. "New BMW, yard toys. New roof, too, looks like. But you stayed in the same house. Why not just buy a bigger house? Barry did."

"What are you talking about? Come on." He steers her toward the car, opens the passenger door, practically shoves her inside. He gets into the driver's seat, and she has barely fastened her seat belt before he's screeching out of the driveway and careening around the corner, out of the neighborhood.

"Oh, are you going to kill me and dump my body now?" Phoebe says, only half joking. She grips the door handle. Automatic locks, childproof. He won't let her out. *Don't panic, he won't do anything,* she thinks. He knows the neighbors must have been peering out their windows. He wouldn't be that stupid. The Don Westfield she thought she knew, the Don who supported her after the accident, who watched over her—he wouldn't harm her. Or maybe he would, to protect his family, to protect his chances for reelection as coroner next year.

"The kids will be home soon," he says. "You can't be there when they get back."

"Can't have them knowing where their designer play set came from, can we?"

He pulls over into a gravel turnout. "What the hell are you talking about?"

"Do you know where Logan is now? I'm taking a risk, talking to you. If you tip him off, well, he won't be able to set up a whole new life that fast, will he?"

"Tip him off? New life? Where is this coming from? What were you doing scaring Wendy?"

"I went to Wappenish, and I saw Ava." She shows him the photographs on her phone of the little girl and her own sculptures. She can tell by the way he sucks in his breath that he can see the resemblance between Mel and the face she created in clay. "That child lives in Wappenish."

He lets out his breath. "Did you approach the kid? Did you say anything to her?"

"Why do you care?"

"I care about you getting arrested."

"How much did Logan pay you to help him and Ava disappear? Did you know where they were? Did you even think about what you were doing, or did he give you some story? You were helping to separate a mother from her child!"

He rubs his chin, his movements jerky, frenetic. "What is the name of this child?"

"Why should I tell you? Don't you already know?"

"What's her name? Who are her parents?"

"Her mother is supposedly dead. But I know her mother is not dead! I am her mother!" She's shouting in his ear, making him wince.

"I saw their bodies. So did you. That child is not Ava. I guarantee it."

"I followed Barry home to his new mansion in the boondocks, where he is now living alone and wining and dining my dear friend Renee."

Don's brows furrow. If she didn't know better, she would think he was genuinely surprised. "Barry and . . . He's seeing Renee?"

"Sleeping with her, apparently."

"And you know this how?"

"I spied on them. I confronted her. She lied to me."

"She has the right to do what she wants."

"She was my best friend—"

"Maybe she wants to keep her relationship with Barry a secret."

"He's married with kids!"

"That is not our concern. And Logan didn't pay me, okay? My dad died and left me an inheritance. But it's none of your damn business."

A fracture forms in her certainty. Or maybe it was always there. "Oh, Don . . . I'm . . . sorry about your dad. You didn't tell me. I didn't know."

"Yeah, well. My dad and I never got along. He wanted me to become an attorney like him. He didn't want me to marry Wendy. He called her 'white trash.' But she worked her way through college. Worked her whole life."

Phoebe looks at his gaunt profile, the shadows like bruises on his face. "Why didn't you follow in your father's footsteps? Why are you working at the morgue?"

"I didn't start that way. I was a paramedic. I care about helping people. I like to be of service. I give families closure."

"Well, you don't have to pretend with me. I know Logan and Ava are still around."

Don straightens in his seat, nods, and rubs his chin. "You mean their spirits are around. Yeah, I feel them, too."

Her grip tightens on the door handle. "No, I mean they are around."

"You mean alive." He looks at her sidelong—a touch of fear in his eyes. "You think they're around in person. Shit, Phoebe. They are not still alive."

Her self-assurance breaks apart, her confidence floating away on the wind. "There is one thing I know for sure," she says. "That child looks exactly like the girl I've been sculpting—"

"There's a resemblance," he says. "But the likeness is open to interpretation. Many girls could look like the face you made out of clay."

"You know that's not true. The nose. The eyes."

"Okay, look. I wasn't going to mention this to you, but the child you saw *could* be Pauline's."

"Renee suggested the same thing. I'm not buying it."

He turns in his seat, rests a hand on her shoulder. "I examined Pauline's body, okay? Maybe you don't want to hear this, but she was, at one time, definitely pregnant."

CHAPTER TWENTY-EIGHT

Phoebe drives home in a daze. If she had examined Pauline closely, if she had pulled down the sheet all the way, Don said, she would have seen the faint, dark line of pigment traveling down from the navel, a vertical discoloration on the abdomen. The line is darker on some women than on others but is present on any woman who has ever been pregnant.

Don could be lying, she thinks. What if there was no pigment line? But he allowed the body to come to Fair Winds. He knows she could've seen the body. But he instructed Barry to keep her out of the loop. Maybe he hoped Barry would cremate Pauline immediately, and Barry certainly sped up the job.

But if Don wanted to hide the truth about Pauline, he could have insisted on waiting for Haven of Repose to reopen. He would've needed only a few days. But maybe he couldn't justify the delay.

If Pauline gave up her baby for adoption and then changed her mind, she might have gone in search of her child. Maybe this was why she looked at the house in Wappenish. The address was a vacant home for sale. But she was also looking for work, which made it unlikely that she could have received a mortgage loan. Maybe she had an inheritance socked away somewhere.

Phoebe calls Darlene Steele, explaining that the coroner had found evidence of a pregnancy, pretending to have seen it herself. "It's been nagging at me. I mean, I know it's none of my business, but I've been wondering what happened to the baby."

"She never had a baby," Darlene says, her voice thick with emotion. "Don't you think I would know?"

"Maybe she kept it from you?"

"She couldn't have kept such a thing from me. I stayed with her for a year after Michael disappeared. She was so depressed. I had to watch her. She might have kept secrets from me, but she could not have kept one so big."

"You're sure." *Then Don was lying—and so smoothly, so well.*

"I do have a thought," Darlene says. "I think I can explain. She was pregnant once, but . . . she suffered a miscarriage, I'm afraid."

"I'm so sorry," Phoebe says, exhaling. So, Don was not lying. At least not about this one point.

"It happened a long time ago, before she ever met your husband. She was young. I haven't thought about it in years."

"There was never another time?"

"No, there wasn't . . . there was no baby. No baby, okay? Let's put this to rest. I can't talk about it anymore." Her voice rises, her tone insistent.

"Thank you. I'm sorry to have bothered you." Phoebe hangs up, smiles out into the sunshine, even as a dark undercurrent runs through her. *Vindicated. Don is wrong—he doesn't know what he's talking about.* Of course Pauline did not have a child. She wasn't the type to become a mother—the miscarriage was for the best.

Mel is my Ava. I always knew it.

CHAPTER TWENTY-NINE

When she arrives in Wappenish Thursday afternoon, the sun is high, thawing the frozen ground, the moisture rising as steam, as if the earth is bubbling below. She drives straight to the playground. An icy wind seems to keep most people away, except for a couple of brave souls. She does not see Liv or Mel. She drives on, her heart pounding with fear. *What if someone tipped off Logan? What if he and Mel are gone?* She parks down the road from the Favre house, out of sight, and waits as the slanted light fades into sunset.

From the passenger seat, she grabs a small backpack in which she has stowed a few important items. Then she gets out of the car, straps the pack over her shoulders, and steals up the driveway, her hoodie pulled up against the cold. The house looms into view. Around back, she crouches outside the kitchen window. *I've become a spy, unpredictable and erratic.*

She peers in at Liv and Mel seated at the dinner table. Mel is laughing. Liv reaches over to push Mel's hair out of her face. Phoebe aches to do the same, to share these mundane moments with her child. A half-eaten piece of apple pie sits on a plate in front of Mel, her glass half-filled with pink liquid, maybe strawberry lemonade. Oh, to cuddle her, to know her favorite food, her favorite drink. To witness every milestone in her life. Not long ago, Phoebe would've thought her voyeurism irrational, even fanatical, and yet, this all feels normal now, peering in upon other people's lives.

Her pocket vibrates and she pulls out her mobile phone. Renee sent a text. Phoebe quickly deletes the message. No time for a lecture now, and the risk of being discovered is too great. She cranes her neck to see inside the kitchen. Mel is putting on her coat. Phoebe runs to hide behind a bush just as Mel emerges from the back door.

"Stay in the yard," Liv calls out. "Just a few minutes, then you have to come in."

"Why?" Mel whines.

"It's getting dark. No arguing."

"O-kay," Mel says, skipping toward the swing set. Liv goes inside and shuts the door.

Mel stops and looks toward the bushes, as if she might sense someone nearby.

What is my plan? Phoebe asks herself. *How do I reach her?*

Liv is watching Mel through the window.

Phoebe works her way around to the side of the house, in a blind spot. She sidles along, approaches Mel, staying up against the house, out of Liv's view. Music pounds out from the kitchen, way too loud, and the neighbors are too far away. If Mel were to hurt herself and cry out, Liv would not hear.

Mel heads toward Phoebe and smiles. Phoebe shakes her head, presses her finger to her lips. Mel grins at her. Ava always loved to play peekaboo, even at two.

"Do you remember me?" Phoebe asks. There is music playing inside, Liv singing along loudly, off-key.

Mel nods. "You came to the garage sale."

"Do you know who I am?"

Mel gives Phoebe a long look, then runs to the swing set and gets on, pumping her legs, her hair flying. "Could you push me?"

Phoebe wants to so badly. She has pictured this moment in her mind. "Why don't you come back here for a minute? I have pictures to show you. From when you were little."

"Am I in them?" She jumps off the swing and skips toward Phoebe.

"I think so," Phoebe says, trying to rein in her excitement. She sits cross-legged on the cold concrete, takes a deep breath. *Don't panic— you're here, she's here.*

"Are you a stranger?" Mel says.

"No, remember? I'm a mom. I'm pretty sure I knew your dad."

"Are you best friends?"

"Yes. Your dad and I were best friends."

"My dad is coming home soon."

"I know! This weekend? I want to surprise him. He'll be so happy to see me."

"But you're not my friend."

"I am your friend. I'm just a new friend."

"My best friend is Brittany."

"That's a lovely name. But not as lovely as yours."

"I have the best name." Mel gets up and swings her arms. "I'm not supposed to talk to strangers. You're a stranger."

"No, I'm not. I know your dad. So I'm not a stranger, right?"

"Okay."

"I won't hurt you. I can show you for sure that I was a friend of your dad's. Want to see?" Phoebe holds out her phone like an offering.

Mel sidles up, looks closely at the picture, and Phoebe can smell baby powder, shampoo, something gentle and innocent. There is a pulsing in her veins, a force of energy.

"That's you," Mel says, pointing at the smiling woman in Seattle.

"And that's your dad," Phoebe says, pointing at Logan. She holds her breath.

"That's my dad?" Mel says tentatively, bringing the picture close to her face.

"Yes, you recognize him, don't you? It's from before you were born. You were only a twinkle in his eye."

Mel hands the phone back, her expression unreadable. "I miss my dad. He brings me presents."

"What kinds of presents?"

"Like, a toy," she says, sticking out her bottom lip. "Tiny soaps."

Phoebe laughs. She loves this girl. She wants to whisk her away. But Mel is returning to the swing set in the waning light.

"Don't you want to see yourself?" Phoebe says. "I have pictures of you, too. As a baby. Baby Mel!"

Mel whips around and runs back toward Phoebe, bouncing on the balls of her feet, as if an invisible puppeteer is holding the strings above, about to lift her into the sky. She looks at the phone again and shakes her head. "That's a cute baby." She kicks at the ground with her shoe. The music shifts to another song with a deeper bass sound, a faster beat. Liv could come outside at any moment. She's still in the kitchen singing off-key.

"It is you. I was holding you." Phoebe watches for a sign of recognition in the child's eyes. "This teddy in the picture once belonged to you. Do you remember? You cuddled him all the time."

"It's a girl teddy."

"You're right, okay. It's a girl. And that's you." *I must slow down. I can't scare her off. She is still too young to understand.*

"That's really me?" Mel narrows her gaze, mild suspicion and confusion in her eyes.

"Yes, it's really you." Phoebe takes a deep breath. She is pushing too hard again. A car rumbles in the distance. The music ends. Silence. She longs to ask Mel, *Do you remember reaching up your arms and calling me "Mama"? Don't you know in your heart that I am your mother?*

"You left the teddy behind," she says instead. "Do you remember? You left it at home."

Mel shakes her head vigorously, hesitation in her eyes. Maybe she's beginning to remember.

"Do you know your room? You had the moon and stars above your bed, the whole solar system. And all your stuffed animals in bed with you. An elephant. A turtle. A girl turtle you loved."

Mel looks up toward the clouds flitting across the sky. "I had a turtle. The stars and the moon!"

"Yes, yes," Phoebe says. *I am her mother.* A mother knows her daughter. The accident . . . it could not have played out as everyone thought it did. "Your hair is so pretty," Phoebe says, "almost the color of mine." She holds up strands of her own hair.

"I have princess hair," Mel says, and when she smiles, there's a small gap between two front teeth.

"Did the tooth fairy come?" Phoebe asks. "You lost a baby tooth."

"My dad helped me pull it out," Mel says, her tongue pushing through her teeth.

"My dad used to help me, too," Phoebe says. "I got scared when he tied my tooth to the doorknob and then shut the door. Sometimes it hurt."

"Mine didn't hurt."

"Well, that is lucky," Phoebe says. "You have a good dad."

"He's the best daddy in the world." Mel spreads her arms, then claps her hands.

Phoebe takes off the backpack, pulls out a blue hairbrush. "This was yours, do you remember?" She's lying—the hairbrush is new, unused. "I used to brush your hair."

"I brush my own hair."

"Right, you're a big girl now," Phoebe says. "But may I?"

Mel nods, pouting a little. "Okay."

Phoebe holds her breath, brushes Mel's hair. Brushes and brushes. The child's hair is already tangled in the brush, so easily. "Now you're spiffy. You look like a special princess." She tucks the brush back into her backpack. *DNA, finally. I will have proof.*

Mel shakes her head and pats her hair, smiling.

"I'll have to come back to surprise your dad," Phoebe says. "Don't tell. It's our secret, okay?"

Inside the house, the music has stopped. Mel nods as Liv calls out, "Mel! Where are you? Get back here, okay?"

Mel places her finger to her lips. "It's a secret," she says, and then she turns and runs back into the house.

CHAPTER THIRTY

Friday afternoon, Phoebe pulls up in front of Mike's house, a log cabin nestled in the woods, a slate pathway leading to a covered porch, on which two Adirondack chairs are arranged on either side of a small table. She didn't know what to expect—maybe a ramshackle bachelor pad, an unkempt yard, a truck in the driveway. But he takes great care with his front garden, and the cabin appears newly constructed, pristine.

He must have seen her coming, as he opens the door before she even knocks. He's in jeans and slippers; his hair is sticking up on one side, a soft plaid shirt buttoned up only halfway, as if he yanked on his clothes in haste.

"I'm sorry to bother you," she says, trying not to show her urgency. "But may I come in?"

"Oh, uh, yeah—sorry, I'm off today. I was taking a nap."

"I can come back another time." *No, I can't,* she thinks. To hell with being polite. "Actually, it feels urgent. I looked you up. It was easy to find your address on the internet. But I'm not a stalker."

He laughs and steps back, holding the door wide open. *"Mi casa es tu casa,"* he says.

So this is what his home looks like, wide open and airy, so unlike her closed-in house, which cringes from the world. Mike's log cabin says, *I have nothing to hide, hang out for a while,* and smells faintly of woodsmoke, perhaps from the woodstove in the corner of the living room, which opens into a rear dining area, a kitchen to the right, a large back window overlooking the forest.

The bright sunlight illuminates the hardwood floor, rustic furnishings, pictures on the wall, which must be his beloved family, so many of them, men and women who look like him, and she feels a stab of envy. What she wouldn't give for family, for a sense of being enveloped in love and connection.

And he loves books—they're neatly arranged on shelves, on the coffee table, in the windowsill next to a pair of binoculars. He's tidy, which makes her even more mortified that he stayed over in her messy, cluttered house.

She reaches down to take off her shoes.

"No need," Mike says, but she lines her shoes up next to his boots anyway. "Coffee? Beer? Water?" He looks flustered, which is unlike him. He strides into the kitchen and opens the fridge. "I would offer you juice, but I need to go shopping, too."

"Thanks—I don't have time for a drink," she says, standing awkwardly.

"Have a seat," he says, gesturing to the living room.

She picks the armchair. On the shelf, a white ceramic sculpture catches the light, a bowl shaped into the face of a young girl. "That's one of mine," Phoebe says, drawing in a sharp breath. "Is that the one you bought at the studio in town?"

"Yeah, I love her expression. I know it's a bowl, but I can't put food in it. It seems more like art, you know?"

"Thank you for buying the piece," she says. "But you can use it. It's not that fragile."

"Maybe I'll give it a try." He sits on the couch, rests his elbows on his knees. It's strange to see him here, stripped of his uniform and so clearly just up from sleep. "Barry says you called in the rest of this week. He finished the restoration on that poor kid."

"I've had things to do."

"You okay? Are you sick?"

"I know this is going to sound strange, but remember in the Rusty Salmon, when you said you used to work in a lab?"

"My sister does."

"Is it a lab that could do a DNA test?"

He sits back, rubs his hands down along his thighs. "If you're doing your family tree, you could use one of those kits."

"I need to compare my DNA to someone else's."

"The plot thickens." He rubs the palms of his hands together. "You're not talking about that woman, Pauline."

"No, no," she says quickly. She bites her lip, knowing that if she tells him everything in her mind, all the dots she has connected, he might call her certifiable. He would be perfectly within reason. She's not sure she can trust him—but she doesn't know anyone else who could help her with the test. "If I give you some hair and a scraping from inside my cheek, could you, you know, find a way to get them to a lab to compare the two? There's so much to the story—I don't want to bore you with it."

"Sounds the opposite of boring," he says. "Did you ask Don? He's got access to a lab—"

"I can't ask him, and you can't tell him. Please." Her throat tightens.

"Why? Is the hair his?" Mike laughs.

"No . . . Um, maybe it was a mistake to come here." *What was I thinking, expecting a stranger to help me?* She gets up, heads for the door, but Mike is up in an instant, his hands resting on her shoulders.

"Hey, it was a joke, okay?" He lets his hands drop, and she can't help it, she bursts into tears. He hands her a tissue.

"I'm losing my mind," she says, blowing her nose.

"No, you're not. Where's the DNA?"

She takes the baggie of Mel's hair out of her pocket and hands it to him. Pulls out another baggie with cotton swabs inside. "I took cells from the inside of my cheek, to compare to the hair. Please keep this confidential. Don't tell anyone."

He nods, holds up the baggie. "So whose hair is this?"

"It belongs to a little girl."

"You think she's related to you."

She closes her eyes and takes a deep breath. Opens them again. "Yes, and my ex-husband might not be dead."

He doesn't blink. "Are you sure it's him? Did you see him?"

"Not yet. But I will. I think he somehow survived. I don't know. I need to find out more."

Mike nods, not looking surprised. Down the hall, there is the muted ringing of the telephone. "You talked to the guy?"

"I haven't seen him. But I'm going back there."

"Whoa, this is—wow. Okay." He touches her necklace, lifts the locket gently to hold in the palm of his hand.

"Someone else must be in there." She snatches back the locket. "Barry cremated the bodies. He insisted they were Logan and Ava, but I don't trust him. I went to see Don for the file on the accident. The bodies were unrecognizable."

"Okay." Mike's eyes betray no skepticism.

"You don't believe me."

"It's what you believe that matters."

"My ex . . . he might've altered his appearance. He could've changed the way he walks and talks."

Mike glances out the window, then at her. "Is this guy dangerous? I mean, will he come after you?"

"He doesn't have any reason to suspect me. He thinks I'm a collector interested in glass vases."

"Have you thought of bringing in the police?"

"I need proof. The DNA test results. I can't go to the police with what I have."

He pockets the samples she has given him. "I'll have the samples tested for you, but it could take a while—like a few days or weeks. I don't know."

"I'll pay whatever the cost."

"We'll cross that bridge when we come to it," he says. "Don't worry about the money."

She touches his arm gently. "You don't know how much this means to me. I know you have to go out of your way."

"No, I don't. This is something you need, and DNA doesn't lie. So I'm happy to do it."

CHAPTER THIRTY-ONE

The dream comes to her again, sharp and clear. A screaming wind, the car sliding around the bend, the wheel spinning. Splatters of snow on the windshield, the rushing and cracking, going airborne, her stomach plummeting. And then . . . she jolts awake, bathed in sweat, her heart pounding, her nervous system raw, as if all her skin has been peeled away. A distant voice reverberates, a smell of disinfectant. *Blue walls, the desk with the built-in lamp above in the recessed ceiling.* She is there, seeing everything through her lashes, the boundaries of the room circumscribed. *No, I'm not there. Where am I?*

She opens her eyes, sits up, and shakes her head. The pad of paper on the table next to the Wi-Fi USB port reads Mountainside Motel, Wappenish, Washington, with the address printed below. She checked in last night, avoiding the last place she stayed. Trying to regroup, to figure out what to do, she paced, jotted notes to herself.

Talk to Ben Favre. Meet him.

He will have altered his appearance, his voice, and he will deny ever knowing her. *Be prepared.*

Ava is starting to remember.

The turtle, the stars and moon. Her teddy bear. The recognition in the little girl's eyes was unmistakable.

Figure out how Barry and Don were involved—confront Logan.

Nobody will admit any wrongdoing—nobody has.

She did not imagine Mel. Mel is real. Alive.

And so am I. More alive than I've been in three years.

All sounds are magnified, from the rush of the wind and the hiss of the heater to the murmur of conversation in the room next door. She reaches across the bed to slide open the window, inhaling the smells of morning—fallen leaves, fresh air. Freedom.

Perhaps talking to Mel was a mistake. Mel could tell Liv about Phoebe's visit. A child can keep a secret for only so long. It's time to go back there, damn the consequences.

Someone's knocking on the door. It's still early, the sunrise awash in pinkish blue. "I put a 'Do Not Disturb' sign on the door!" she calls out through the window, craning her neck to see who it is. But it's not the motel cleaning service. It's Mike Rivera, lifting his hand to knock again. She pulls back away from the window, patting down her hair. Looking around in a panic. The only way out of this room is through the door. It's too late to pretend she's not here.

The stuffed animals and toys peek from an unzipped bag on the luggage rack. She rushes to zip up the bag, hiding the toys, then answers the door. "What are you doing here?" She yawns and squints in the bright sunlight. "How did you know where I was? They're not supposed to give out my name at the front desk, or what room I'm in!"

"They didn't," he says, jabbing his thumb backward toward the parking lot. "I checked two other motels before I came here. Your car is parked right in front of your room."

"Crap." She wasn't careful, but she didn't expect Mike—or any-one—to drive all the way here. She didn't even tell anyone she was returning to Wappenish.

"May I come in?" he says, glancing over her shoulder into the room. "I drove a long way to find you."

"I didn't ask you to come here."

"Hospitality becomes you," he says.

"Sorry—I'm not feeling very social. I have things I need to do here. Alone."

"Like what?" He looks around, points at the coffee maker on the desk by the television. "Do you mind? I could use a cup."

"They have coffee in the lobby."

"Yeah, but I'm not a guest."

"No, you aren't," she says, then gestures to the coffeepot in resignation. "Whatever, go ahead. I need to . . ." She points toward the bathroom.

"Take your time," he says as he steps inside.

In the bathroom, she locks the door, draws a deep breath. She wonders how much Mike knows. *What is he doing here?* Barry could have sent him. Or Don. It's too late now to ask for the DNA back.

Think, don't panic. She takes a deep breath, imagines a calm lake—*I am that serene person. He can't stop me, no matter who he is.*

When she comes out, Mike is sitting in the empty chair. How presumptuous of him to make himself at home. His hands, resting on the arms of the chair, feel like a violation, and she can smell the mortuary on him, not death exactly, but something sterile and sharp, like alcohol, like disinfectant, or maybe the smell is a remnant of the dream.

"You should come back," he says, looking at the peeling wallpaper. "We've got a restoration."

"There's always a restoration." She perches on the edge of the bed. "It's the weekend, and Barry can do everything I can do."

"You're the best," he says. "Barry makes dead people look like . . . clowns. Too much lipstick. He colors outside the lines."

She laughs. "Flattery will get you nowhere."

He shifts in the chair. "You don't think anyone cares about you or appreciates your work, but they do. They want you there. You're an artist."

"They want me there because every time they see me, they can thank their lucky stars that I was the unlucky one. They get to live happier lives."

"No, it's because you know what you're doing. There was an elderly decedent yesterday . . . Her family wanted her to fit into this small blue dress for the viewing. No way could she fit. She was like size sixteen and the dress was size four."

"And?" Phoebe says, crossing her arms over her chest.

"Barry cut the damn thing . . ."

"That's what I would've done. Cut the dress down the back."

"He got the front and the back mixed up. Cut it down the front. We were in trouble."

"I'm sorry to hear that," Phoebe says, feeling a twinge. "But I can't come back."

"Yes, you can," he says. "I want to help you."

"I don't need any help," she says, getting up. "And you smell like cigarettes, which will get me in trouble. The rooms here are nonsmoking."

"Then let's get out of here. Come back with me."

"I'm not going back." A current of energy courses through her. "I have to stay. I saw Ava. I talked to her."

"I get it. I talk to my brother all the time."

"Your brother," she says, looking at him.

"Yeah, he was eighteen. I was seventeen. We were surfing out near Westport. It's fucking cold out there. But we were both into it."

"Why are you telling me this?" She grabs her coat. "I don't have time for stories."

"We spent our summers surfing. Jim—that was his name—wanted to be a surgeon so he could make enough money to keep surfing. His board hit him in the head. He went under. I swam out to him, but I couldn't save him. I tried."

She stops with one arm halfway into her sleeve. "Oh, Mike. I'm so sorry."

"I didn't surf again after that. I thought it was all my fault. I wanted to go out that day, wanted to ride into the strong currents. Took a lot of years for me to realize he would've gone out that day anyway. All on his own. He was more of a surfing fanatic than I was. He knew the risks."

"That must have been awful," she says.

"It was an accident," he says. "You get that?"

"And you saw him, talked to him like what, a ghost?"

"Oh, he's still with me. I sense him. But I don't talk to him anymore."

"I'm sorry for your loss. But I really have to go."

"You don't have to."

"Yes, I do. There's something between a mother and her child."

"I know." Mike gets up, pulls a folded newspaper article from his pocket. Yellowed, cut from the original issue with scissors. "I brought this for you to look at."

"You want me to read some old newspaper article."

"It's the only way I can convince you."

"Convince me of what? What is this?" Her voice is nasal, high pitched. Her vision blurs. Now she hates him and wants him to leave, because if he stays, she might crumble into dust. Or she might kill him.

"Take a look." He reaches out to give her the article, but she makes a strangling noise and slaps his hand away.

"Where did you find that? Why did you bring that here?"

"Because I know what you think you're going to do," he says.

"What, you can read my mind?"

"I can guess. Don't do it."

"You can't stop me."

"I have to try—"

"Did you test the DNA? Did you?"

"I sent it away. It will take some time."

"I'll wait for it."

"Then wait in Bayport."

"I'm staying here." She won't take the folded newspaper. He leaves it on the dresser.

The disappointment digs at her throat. She thought his compassion and understanding made him different. His lack of judgment, the way he seems not to care what kind of mess she lives in, the kind of mess she is. But she is truly alone—she knows that now. He won't help her, won't back her up.

"You should leave," she says. "Please go. I don't want you here."

"You don't really mean that."

"Yes, I do. Go. Now. Before I call the management."

"I'm only asking you to think about what you're doing."

"I've thought about it a lot. I know exactly what I'm doing."

He looks down at his hands, shakes his head, and when he looks up at her again, his eyes are dark and sad, full of worry and regret. "Be careful, Phoebe. Please, okay?"

She does not reply. He strides past her, hesitates in the doorway, then leaves. Choking back tears, she reaches for the newspaper article so neatly folded on the dresser. Her hand shakes. She turns away. *I won't read it. I won't look. It's nothing.* Mike should not have brought it here, should not have challenged her resolve. Good thing he is gone. Yet he was the only person who did not question her, and now she feels his absence, a cold, solitary wind blowing through her. But sometimes truth is lonely. Sometimes only one person knows it. Sometimes you have to hold on all by yourself.

CHAPTER THIRTY-TWO

She loads the car with her luggage, including Ava's belongings in the backpack. Maybe Mike had a point: she could call the police. It would all be simple, but she has no proof. Only she should, shouldn't she, demand that the police be the ones to determine that Ben is Logan, that Mel is Ava?

Ben would not be arrested, not at first. Maybe the police would accompany Phoebe to knock on the door, and Ben—*Logan*—might answer, smile pleasantly, and pretend not to know her. He would say the child is not Ava, the woman must be a lunatic, keep her away from us for the sake of Mel. And Phoebe would scream at him, would lose her cool, which would suit him just fine. You know, the hysterical woman, she doesn't know what she's talking about. And then the cops would run a background check on Phoebe, and they would agree with Logan. Her husband and child are dead, cremated—there are records.

The police would not, in the end, believe her. She is alone in this. Part of her does not want to go through with the plan. Part of her insists on letting things be. But her more optimistic self, the Phoebe everyone thinks is out of touch with reality, is her hopeful self, the one who drives back to the Favre house. On the way, she sees Liv and Ava—no, she must still call the child Mel—playing in the park, the dappled sunlight filtering through the trees. The day is unseasonably warm, and when

Phoebe parks at the curb and gets out of the car, the breeze feels soft, almost like springtime. She sits on a distant bench, sunglasses on, coat collar turned up. She hopes not to be recognized in her hat, far from the central play area. But from here, she can watch Mel and her nanny through the trees, and she wonders if the child told Liv about what happened, if she mentioned that her mother came over and showed her pictures.

When Liv and Mel finally leave for home, Phoebe has not had a chance to talk to Mel alone. It was excruciating to watch the poor child fall, and the stupid nanny—she should have been watching—and now Mel has a small cut on the palm of her left hand, from the sharp gravel. Phoebe had to resist the urge to run over and scoop the little girl into her arms.

Phoebe returns to her car, drives cautiously down the road, and parks a few doors from the Favre house, but then an elderly gentleman shuffles past with his tiny terrier, giving her a long look through the passenger-side window, and she pulls away from the curb and parks closer to the Favres' driveway and gets out.

This time, it's easy to get Mel to come to her in the backyard. Phoebe and Mel know each other now. It's evening again, not yet dusk, and Mel's elusive father is not yet home. But he's expected back today.

"You know what?" Phoebe says. "I have some of your things with me. Stuff you left behind at my house when you were little."

"What kinds of things?" Mel's face perks up.

"Oh, things like toys and books. *Curious George*, which used to be your favorite. You weren't reading yet, but you liked the yellow book covers . . ."

"My dad reads me those." Mel looks at Phoebe with curiosity and a deeper sense of knowing. She gazes down the driveway toward Phoebe's car, parked at the curb, half-hidden by trees at the bottom of the driveway. "Do you have toys in your car?"

"Yes, I have some! You loved stuffed animals."

"I used to. I have lots of them already."

"But there's the turtle you loved, and a spider."

"A spider!" she exclaims, her mouth dropping open.

"Are you afraid of them?"

"No, I love bugs."

"I know you do. So do I." Ava loved bugs, even at age two. She was never scared. Phoebe begins to sing "Itsy Bitsy Spider," and Mel sings along with her, as if they have always done this, since the beginning of time. *Down came the rain and washed the spider out* . . .

"You loved that song when you were a baby, even though you couldn't sing it yet," Phoebe says. "It put you to sleep."

"My dad sings to me! He said my mommy did, too."

Phoebe fights back tears. *Yes, your mommy did. I did.* "Do you remember being in an accident?"

"I fell off the swing." Mel points at her right knee. "I almost needed stitches. Almost."

"That must've hurt."

"Yeah, but I put a Band-Aid on it."

"And it was all better," Phoebe says, reaching for Mel's hand. She doesn't take it. "What I meant was, do you remember a car accident?"

"No," Mel says. "I wear my seat belt."

"Of course you do. You're safe." *As Ava was. Until the car flew off the road. Or maybe it never did. The accident never happened.*

"My daddy is a good driver."

Phoebe nods, biting her lip. "Well, we should look at the toys, before you have to go in."

"Is there something for my dollhouse?"

"I don't know—there might be."

"I can't wait to see." Mel skips along next to Phoebe down the driveway.

They are almost to the car when Liv calls out from behind them, "Hey, what are you doing? Where are you going? Hey, Mel, get back here!"

No, damn it, you should've stayed in the house. Phoebe grabs Ava's hand. Her fingers are warm and so small. "Come on, we have to hurry."

"Why?" Ava tries to squirm away. "Liv is calling me."

Phoebe holds on tighter. "We have to get you home. To your room. Do you remember?"

"No, you're hurting my hand!"

"But you must remember."

"I don't—"

"I'm your mom. Don't you remember, honey?" Phoebe grips Mel's hand—*Ava's hand.* "Don't you know your name?"

"Hey, let go of her!" Liv races down the driveway in her slippers, her voice frantic.

But she needn't worry, Phoebe thinks. *I'm not going to hurt Ava. You're the ones who hurt her, who hurt me.*

"Ow!" Ava shouts. "Liv!"

"Don't worry about Liv," Phoebe says to Ava.

"It's okay, honey," Liv yells. "I'm here."

"She's mine," Phoebe shouts. "She's my daughter."

"My God, what are you saying?" Liv's mouth drops open. "Mel, run away from her. Come back here!"

The child tries to twist out of Phoebe's grip. But she must know that Liv is brainwashed.

"I'm her mother!" Phoebe shouts.

"No, you're not," Liv shouts back. "Mel, that lady is not your mother. Get away from her right now."

"You're not my mom!" Ava cries, emitting a high-pitched scream. Phoebe has to drag her now—this is not what she planned, having to force her own child to come home.

Liv yells into her cell phone. She must've called 911. "Someone is trying to kidnap a child. Yes, I'm the nanny. Oh God, please hurry!"

"I'm not kidnapping her!" As she drags Ava toward the car, a part of Phoebe separates from herself and watches, frantic. *What are you doing? You know this isn't right—this is all wrong. It always was.* She must be crying, too—she can hear herself sobbing as she yanks the screaming child toward her car.

An SUV comes around the bend, then speeds up and screeches to a halt at an angle across the road. Phoebe is gripping Ava's arm. "I'm your mom. Everything is going to be okay. Just wait."

"You're crazy!" Liv grabs Ava's other arm. "Let go! The police will be here in a minute."

"She needs to come home," Phoebe shouts. "She knows who I am. I've been trying to find her for three years. You have no idea!"

"You're completely insane!" Liv shoves Phoebe in the chest, knocking the wind out of her.

Phoebe stumbles backward, loosens her grip on Ava. "They took her away from me. Where is Logan?"

"Who? What are you talking about?" Liv screams.

"He needs to answer for this! He kidnapped our daughter."

"Who is Logan?" Liv shouts. "Let go of Mel! The police will arrest you!"

Ava is crying.

A man emerges from the SUV and sprints toward them, yelling, "What the hell is going on here?" He separates Liv from Phoebe, wedges himself between. He grabs Ava's hand, yanks her away. "Liv! Get in the house. Now! I'll take care of this."

Liv looks at him blankly, in shock, and she goes in the back door.

"What the hell are you doing?" the man booms, whisking Ava away, sweeping her into the house and locking her inside.

"Don't take my daughter!" Phoebe shouts, sobbing and falling to her knees. "Give her to me!"

He yells through the door, "Get the hell away from here. I don't know who you think you are."

Ava is yelling and crying, too. "Daddy, Daddy!"

Phoebe hears her voice from far away. *Don't take her, please. Don't. She is all that I have left.* The man inside is talking to her, but his voice is too deep. Even with the beard and mustache, he is all wrong. He's too thin. He's not supposed to have that nose or that chin. Or the wrong color eyes. He shouldn't be here, calling Ava his daughter. Ava should not be crying for him. This man who is not Logan, who is somebody else.

CHAPTER THIRTY-THREE

Phoebe's room has calming, pale-blue walls, wooden shelves for her clothes. A wicker basket, a turquoise bath towel, frayed at the ends, threads coming loose. A potted ficus plant, its waxy leaves flourishing while she withers in her soft pajamas. Nothing sharp in the room, nothing that could pierce the skin. Nothing she could use to hurt herself. No ropes or string.

She remembers the place well from the first time she stayed here, but the room she had before, nearly three years ago, was painted in a lighter hue. Next to the shelves, a wooden table is set into a recess in the wall, a fluorescent tube light built into the ceiling. She could sit there to write, but to whom? To her mother? Lidia can't visit her, doesn't even know she's here. Doesn't know her own daughter. *Better not to alarm my mother,* Phoebe said to Dr. Ogawa. *I don't want to upset her.*

Next to the table, a window with slat blinds overlooks an interior courtyard, where patients wander, bodies bent at strange angles, some of them mumbling. Laughing, yelling. One man with a ruddy face keeps shuffling back and forth, dropping his pants to reveal colorful underwear, then pulling up his pants again, lifting and dropping.

She turns away, swallowing the lump welling in her throat. She is one of them, delusional, like the elderly woman hunched over a table in the common room, talking to the voices in her head, painting her nails in silver polish to match her large silver wig made of gigantic curls.

Phoebe's tongue is dry, her thoughts drifting to her sessions with Dr. Ogawa and her attorney. Mel's father, Ben Favre, will not press charges. He understood when they explained her loss. He won't seek a restraining order unless she returns to Wappenish. She must stay off the property, away from Mel.

But she can't go anywhere right now, anyway. She won't. She will get past this. She has all the help in the world. What she almost did . . . horrifies her. She is sorry. Sorry for Mel, for what she put the child through. The poor little girl.

She told Dr. Ogawa everything from start to finish, about the remarkable doppelgänger on the mortuary table, the picture she found in the property room, her visit with Pauline's mother, the tortuous thread of hope that launched her trips to Wappenish. Her descent into delusion.

But now, gradually, she has begun to remember the truth in bits and pieces. She once held a small urn in her hands. She waded into the icy sea, her teeth chattering, her legs numb, sobbing as she let go of the receptacle, watching her daughter float away.

In her sessions, she speaks about her grief. She brings Ava back to life through her spoken memories. And she realizes that Logan did love his child. Sometimes Phoebe would wake and find him watching over Ava. He would say she was so beautiful, and he needed to make sure she was real, he felt so lucky to have her, he didn't deserve her, and sometimes he worried it was all a dream.

Phoebe sits by the window in her room, all painted in blue, and remembers the first time she thought she heard Ava crying, several days after the accident. Phoebe jolted awake, mumbled to Logan to go. She was too tired. But his side of the bed was flat, empty. She tumbled into a chasm. *Logan is gone,* she thought. *Forever.* But the clock kept ticking too loudly, the damned relic.

She could barely swing her legs over the side of the bed. *Why am I still here?* she thought. *I should have died, if not that night, then afterward in my sleep.* She thought she should step off the curb in front of a moving bus. Or take the entire bottle of sleeping pills.

She emptied the bottle onto the nightstand next to a book Renee had given her: *Sacred Spaces.* The book was supposed to help her heal, to work through grief. But there was no working through this.

Renee clanged around in the kitchen, running the faucet, turning on the coffee maker. She had been sleeping on the couch, had left Vik in New York with his father.

The crying, there it was again. Distant but unmistakable. Phoebe threw on her robe and stumbled down the hall, flung open the door to Ava's room. The bed was still made, the plush animals lined up. But the crying. *Ma! Mama!*

"I'm coming, Ava, honey!" she shouted, yanking open the closet door. Ava wasn't there, but she had hidden somewhere. She was trapped. She liked to wedge herself into small spaces. Under the ottoman in the living room, beneath the bathroom cabinet. *Come and find me!* Why did she keep hiding? Because she was afraid to be forgotten, to go missing forever.

"What's going on?" Renee said, rushing in. "Are you okay? I heard you shouting."

"Ava was calling me," Phoebe said, looking around. But how could that be? She could vaguely remember the memorial service in the chapel, the large portraits of Logan and Ava that Renee had ordered from the Bayport Photography Studio. In vibrant color. But that must've been a dream.

"Not again," Renee said, taking Phoebe's hand. "Let's go to the kitchen."

Phoebe wrestled her hand away. "I heard her in here—she was here."

"She's not here," Renee said gently. "I wish she were here, but she is gone. She died in the accident."

Phoebe collapsed into her friend's arms, as the antique clock in the hall chimed the hour. How she had come to despise that sound.

She spent the next week—or was it a month or a year or a lifetime?—in bed, occasionally rushing down the hall when Ava called out to her.

Renee stayed a few more days, her voice muffled, from far away, asking if Phoebe would like breakfast, if she could run the shower, do the laundry.

"I can't stay," Renee said one day. "I've been gone too long. I have to go back to New York. Vik needs me."

"Of course, you need to go," Phoebe said vaguely, looking out the window. The spindly trees swayed in the dry winter wind. She knew she was not much of a friend to Renee anymore, not a friend at all, really. She was hollow, needy. No use to anyone.

"Someone should be here with you," Renee said. "You can't stay here alone like this."

"I'm all right," Phoebe said, knowing she was not, but not caring at all.

"Will you call your therapist? May I call her for you?"

Phoebe nodded absentmindedly. Her therapist, the queen, the pope, the president of the free world, it didn't matter. Call them all. Nothing mattered, that was the thing. The world was keeping Ava from her. Hiding her child. No, Logan was keeping Ava from her. She could hear Renee speaking in low tones to someone in another room. On the phone.

She stared at the television screen, and there she was. Ava, masquerading as a little girl on the local news. Her mom—not really her mother, obviously—was profiled as a local lavender farmer in Sequim, and there was this toddler in her arms. Ava. Same dark hair, different style. And the child was a little older, but Ava would be a little older now, too.

"Your therapist is going to stop by," Renee said, standing in the doorway, her hand pressed to the doorjamb, as if she could hold up the house all by herself. "It's not the usual thing, but you need some help. Don't you agree?"

Phoebe nodded, her mind hurtling toward Sequim, to the lavender farm, which was buried under frost in winter.

"I'm going to pack now, okay?" Renee said. "I've got a flight—"

"That's fine," Phoebe said.

"I want to stay. I miss you," Renee said. "I miss the way things were, I mean. But I worry about leaving Vik with his dad. Darin and I are having some issues. Well, I won't bore you with that now. But Vik misses me, and he's only five . . . Sorry. I just—"

"It's okay," Phoebe said. "You go ahead and pack."

"You're strong, Phoebe. You always were. Underneath, that strength is still there." Renee hugged her, then left the room.

Phoebe grabbed her purse, jumped into her car, and escaped, driving a little crazily all the way to Sequim. She found the lavender farm, wandered through the icy fields looking for Ava. At the main house, the big cedar structure in which Ava's kidnappers lived, she pounded on the door. The woman answered, the one who claimed to be the mother. "Are you all right? Can we help you?"

Phoebe looked down at herself and gasped at her pajama bottoms, the wet cuffs. Her feet were numb. She had driven all this way in slippers, all the way west across the Hood Canal Bridge and around Discovery Bay. She could not pinch herself and wake up. She was already awake, already in hell.

The police came. Somehow, Phoebe ended up back at home, not in jail. People were compassionate when they learned that you had lost a child. But she knew what they thought inside: they were glad to have their own children. They considered themselves lucky. *There but for the grace of God go I.*

Dr. Ogawa helped. They sat in a softly lit office made to look like a living room, full of plush pillows and lamps and neutral colors. Phoebe talked about her feelings, her inability to sleep, her desire to stop living. She agreed to more sessions, to more drugs to carry her in their pharmaceutical arms.

Don't feel you are weak, Dr. Ogawa said. *Everyone needs help. Antidepressants can keep you going for a while. They're temporary.*

The chemicals dulled Phoebe's mind, made her sluggish. Made her see things, weird shapes. Stole her appetite, brought it back, and still she kept on talking in therapy, drumming her fingers on the arms of the plush chairs in her therapist's office.

Dr. Ogawa smiled benevolently and made soft, sympathetic noises at the right intervals, rearranging her face into careful expressions of compassion. She sat on the other side of the universe, the happy side.

Phoebe came to realize that there were two kinds of people in the world: those who had lost a child and those who hadn't. Those who hadn't, well, they lived in another dimension. They were a different species. They thought they understood loss, but they had no idea. It would have been better for them not to pretend, not to say they knew "how she must be feeling." They had no clue.

But the drugs, the sessions in cognitive therapy, allowed her to get up in the morning and say to herself, *I will stay alive today, just until bedtime.* She could scoop coffee grounds into the coffee maker, check the mail, walk around the block. Brush her teeth. Put one foot in front of the other.

And after a while, she returned to work. *Are you sure the mortuary is where you want to be?* Dr. Ogawa asked.

I'm good at my job, Phoebe said. *It's an art.*

But you're working with the dead every day.

You get used to it, Phoebe said. *I'm helping people find closure.*

But was she? Was there ever such a thing as closure?

She kept seeing things. Once, when a customer walked up through the trail into the burial forest, she thought the man was Logan. She followed, and she saw a woman holding Ava's hand. But she could never catch up.

As she worked in the preparation rooms, she talked to the dead, restoring them uninterrupted. While aggrieved families sobbed down the hall, she could keep her distance. *Nobody is ever truly gone,* she wanted to say. *They are here if you pay attention.*

She stopped answering her cell phone, decided to take a break from therapy. It all felt so fake, while Logan and Ava had become so real. She had to concentrate, notice where they were. Sometimes, they hid behind a tree, playing hide-and-seek or peekaboo. Sometimes, they peered in the window at her, daring her to go outside and follow them into the woods.

It was Barry who called her therapist again, when Phoebe had been hiding in the preparation room well into the evening. Only later, after Dr. Ogawa convinced her to check herself into the psychiatric facility, into the blue room, only after weeks of grief counseling and weaning herself off the medications, did Phoebe understand how dire her situation had been. She had been barely functional, her mail piled up, her house a mess, rotting food in her refrigerator. The electricity had been turned off, her mortgage in arrears.

But slowly, surely, she straightened out the wrinkles, and by the time she left the blue room that first time, she no longer heard the voices of Logan and Ava, no longer saw them disappearing around corners or summoning her.

She closed Ava's room, never went in there, lost herself in her artwork in her studio. Ava came back to life in clay.

"But this time it all felt different," Phoebe tells Dr. Ogawa now.

"How so?"

"I think I knew what was happening three years ago. I knew they weren't really there. I had just lost them, and the medications clouded my mind. I had strange dreams. I saw things and people that seemed only halfway real."

"How is it different now?"

"This time, Mel was real. Pauline was real. The resemblance between Mel and Ava was real."

"You mean Ava the way she would look now, if she had lived."

"Yes," Phoebe says, irritated. As if she needs to be reminded. She knows how to imagine what the dead might look like still alive, without bacteria creeping across their bloated faces. She learned how to imagine age progression, similar to facial reconstruction. For a reconstruction, one must imagine a missing chin. For an age progression, one imagines an older chin. She could do both. "What I'm saying is, this time, Pauline came to me," she goes on. "She was real. I didn't imagine her. I didn't imagine Mel."

"No, you didn't. And that makes the loss so much more difficult, doesn't it? Because the similarities are uncanny, drawing you back in."

"Yes," Phoebe says, looking out the window into the stark brightness. "Like a temptation to madness."

Here in the blue room that first time, she got better and got back to her life, or so she thought, until she saw Pauline on the table. And then she saw Mel, a child who resembled her own. She thought she had worked through her sorrow—but grief is never finished. It just becomes a part of you. She knows that now.

CHAPTER THIRTY-FOUR

When Phoebe emerges from the clinic, the brightness hurts her eyes. Not that she has been imprisoned in darkness these past several weeks—she has walked the manicured grounds every day—but the quality of sunlight has changed, growing more penetrating as winter recedes and springtime takes hold.

She's unsure if she's ready to return to the world, to the noise of traffic, crowds, the endless danger—a child running out into the road, a meteor falling from the sky. A nuclear attack, a pandemic, but also . . . freedom. Possibility.

After her days in the blue room, her life is hers and hers alone. She looks down at her hands, plain and worn, the skin still chapped from too much washing. But they feel real, alive, the air blowing over them. She will do her best to make them useful again.

How can she face the people who know her? The incident in Wappenish brings her shame, and she can't imagine who she was. The memory of it all—the police arriving, Ben Favre whisking his daughter away, everyone treating her like she had a horribly contagious disease—is still too embarrassing. Her interior world, the mirage she created, burst into a million pieces. She can no longer return to magical thinking.

But maybe she would rather exist in that fantasy world. There's nothing so great about knowing, finally, that your child is truly gone, that you will not see her anywhere ever again. No matter where you look, no matter what you hear or smell or touch, she will never be there. Her atoms have scattered into the universe.

Phoebe wonders how she is still alive, walking, breathing. Her body feels fragile, as if her bones might crumble, and she will break apart and dissipate into thin air. If only she were made of sturdier stuff.

A pink-breasted Anna's hummingbird buzzes in the air above a fuchsia plant, then zigzags off into the sky. Phoebe marvels at the tiny creature's ability to survive against all odds, to fly backward and forward and even to hover upside down. She learned all this from books she read while in the blue room, from the library down the hall. *How amazing,* she thinks, that the hummingbird can also fly at thirty miles per hour; its heart beats hundreds of times per minute. But when hummingbirds sleep—in a state called *torpor*—they might seem to be dead. Their heart rate drops, and they nearly stop breathing. But they always come back to life.

Phoebe exhales, a soft breeze playing with the budding leaves of an oak tree. Everywhere, new blooms appear on the colorful rhododendron plants. Sunlight dances in the grass, through the fluttering alder leaves.

She descends the steps, drops her heavy suitcase on the sidewalk, shields her eyes to scan the parking lot. A family spills from an SUV; maybe they're here to visit someone. The little boy bounces off, his older sister running to grab his hand, and the family heads toward the main building.

Mike should've been here by now. There he is, parked at the far corner of the lot. He gets out of his car and strides over to grab her suitcase. He's a whirlwind in a green windbreaker, jeans, and sneakers. The spring sunlight reflects off his hair. He seems to have added more bulk to his frame. Over the past weeks, Phoebe hasn't seen him. She refused all visitors. Now here he is, grinning at her.

"Good to see you," he says. He puts the suitcase in the trunk, envelops her in a tight, firm hug, lifting her off her feet.

She can't help but smile. "It's good to see you, too. It really is."

In the car, she leans back in the passenger seat, happy to let him take the wheel and steer her away from the clinic.

"Where would you like to go?" he says. "I mean, I'm assuming you want to go home first—"

"No, let's go to Fair Winds."

"Your wish is my command."

At the mortuary, her office feels smaller, stuffier than before. There's no mail on her desk. She sits in her chair, unsure if she belongs here anymore. Outside in the parking lot, Mike is waiting for her, pacing, looking up at the trees.

Footsteps clop down the hall, there's a knock on the half-open door, then Barry rushes in, not waiting for her reply. "It's Phoebe in the flesh!" he says, smiling. "We've missed you. All of us. Me especially." He has that slightly sweaty look, as if he has been privately tap-dancing in his office again. He's in a button-down white dress shirt, probably for a memorial service.

"I missed you, too," she says, a lie, but sometimes, she knows, a small fib is kinder than the truth. She does like Barry, but she does not miss being here, and he is part of the fabric of Fair Winds, part of what is beginning to feel like her past. She can't shake the image of him resting his arm around her best friend's shoulders, leaning in to kiss her. "I'm sorry . . . for everything," she goes on. "I trespassed on your property. I spied on you."

"It's water under the bridge," he says. "We know you were going through something . . . We understand."

Do you? she wants to say. *Can anyone ever truly understand?* But she knows he means well. "Thank you, Barry. Again, I'm so sorry."

"It could happen to anyone," he says, and he sounds sympathetic. He sits in the chair across from her desk. "There's something I need to tell you," he says, looking down at his fingernails, then up at her again, a pained expression in his eyes.

"I'm fired," she says, almost with relief. "I understand. I would fire me, too."

"No, no—not at all. You always have a place here. Your skills are exemplary. It's about Logan." He looks behind her, at the books on her shelves, and his eyes fill with tears. In all the years Phoebe has known him, she has never seen him cry. His face has always been carefully configured to provide sympathy for others.

"What about him?" she says, bracing herself for another shocking revelation. "I'm not sure I want to know. I've put all that behind me now."

"I didn't tell you before. I thought it would only make things worse for you. But now I think it might help."

You—and everyone else—made decisions for me, as though people who grieve become childlike, she thinks, but she keeps her expression neutral. "Go on."

He gets up, walks to the window, and looks out at Mike, who is talking to another removal technician at the far corner of the parking lot. "Logan came to me a couple of weeks before the accident. He was distraught. He said that he had made a lot of mistakes in his life. He'd done things that could never be forgiven."

"That's true," Phoebe says. "How perceptive of him."

"He begged me to forgive him for stealing from the business, and . . . he wanted to pay me back."

"That's good—maybe he went only halfway to hell instead of all the way," she says distantly.

"I refused the payback," Barry says, turning to face her. "Because of you and Ava. You needed the money. He said he didn't deserve you."

"That's true," she says, but the iceberg inside her begins to thaw just a little. So the buyout was more than generous.

"He said Ava was the love of his life—he was leaving behind everything he had done, and he hoped you would forgive him. He was going to tell you everything."

Tell you everything . . . the last words she heard from Logan. Words he utters in her dreams that later melt away.

"And what is everything?" she says.

"I don't know," Barry says. "I was his friend, but I couldn't be his confidant. I told him that. I stopped him from confessing his sins, because of my friendship with you. Because if he didn't want me to tell you, I couldn't keep a secret from you."

Phoebe swallows, fatigue spreading through her. "It doesn't matter anymore," she says, getting up. "I know all the secrets about him that I'm ever going to know."

Barry follows her to the door. "Whatever else he did, he loved you and Ava. He planned to stay. He wanted to be different, and you know what? I believed him."

CHAPTER THIRTY-FIVE

She wipes tears from her cheeks, pulls on her protective gear, and heads down the hall into the prep room. The faint smell of putrescine wafts into her nose, the sickly odor of decay mixed with disinfectant, the tools laid out. The man on the table is young, maybe in his twenties. Dark haired, sporting a goatee. She imagines him trimming his nose hairs, the handlebars on his mustache.

The paperwork sits on the countertop, waiting for her to flip through the details of his life and death. If she learns who he was and how he lived, she might do a better job of restoring his face. She will be able to imagine him in life. In death, so little is left of him. Half of his skull is missing, but she can use hardening compounds, adhesives, wax, and putty to replace what has been lost—create a new cheek, fill in the missing eye, build out the imploded forehead. She can fill the cranial cavity with cotton to create the illusion of wholeness.

Biker tattoos that once gave him character now resemble misshapen, forgotten graffiti on the side of an abandoned building. On his left forearm, an outlaw in dark sunglasses races on a Harley-Davidson. On his right forearm, a skeletal figure, the skull empty eyed, rides a motorcycle through fire.

"What will I find on your back?" she asks. "How fast were you going?" His injuries suggest impact at high velocity. She can tell these things. He was likely wearing a helmet, or the damage would've been worse.

She flips through the paperwork. There's a photograph of him on the bottom page. Good-looking guy, amiable smile, his eyes full of life. She doesn't recognize him as anyone she knows from town.

She takes inventory of her supplies, including a glass eye. A marble catching the light, beautiful and grotesque. This task will take some time.

"I can fix you," she says, looking at him. "I can give you eyebrows. But that cheek is pretty messed up, and your forehead is . . . concave."

His loved ones will see what they want to see, disregarding her small mistakes, ignoring any hint of skin slippage. They will accept the makeup as his true skin color in their desperation to believe he died at peace. No suffering, no pain.

She picks up a brush, puts it down. Her senses are magnified. Static crackles in the dry air, a machine whirs in a nearby room, the telephone rings, and Barry's distant voice drones on. She can feel the disturbance of the air, catches the scent of alpine soap, the whiff of cigarette smoke. Mike is standing behind her. The door is slightly ajar—he did not make a sound. "Bad one," he says, coming up beside her.

"Yes," she says. "Did you know him?"

Mike shakes his head. "I can't even say he looks familiar. He doesn't look like anyone."

"He's not anyone anymore. But his spirit is free."

"Yeah, there's that. They're having a viewing, seriously? They should just bury the guy. Why wax him up?"

"My job is not to ask why," she says, although she has never understood why Fair Winds, with its wild burial forest on a hillside, still clings to some traditional practices. *We're a mix,* Barry tells customers. *We offer a variety of choices, but we're leaning toward the green options.* He can't seem to make up his mind, like he couldn't make up his mind about Renee, about his family.

"So you're going to work on him?" Mike asks.

"I don't know. I don't think so." She puts down the makeup brush. "I need to get out of here."

CHAPTER THIRTY-SIX

"Stop here," she says as Mike drives her to the top of the winding road, just before the pavement levels out and then descends the hill again on the way out of town. On both sides, spindly madrone trees reach for the sun, interspersed with cedars extending their branches across the road, forming a cathedral of shade.

Phoebe forces herself to take deep breaths. She has not driven this way since the accident. She has always left town on an alternate, less-scenic route. But today, she has asked Mike to bring her to the top of this hill. She feels somehow stronger, knowing he is with her.

He pulls to the right, parks on the gravelly shoulder at a wide turnout. "Scenic spot," he says. The ocean glimmers through the trees, winking in and out of view in the distance. A car passes in the opposite direction, heading into town.

She nods, takes another deep breath. He's right. This turnout would be romantic if you hadn't lost anyone here. There is no evidence of the accident, no memorial cross or stones, no heaps of flowers. No broken trees, no obvious damage to the landscape. Cars pass every day, coming and going, their occupants unaware of what happened here.

"You sure this is the place?" he asks, looking at her.

"I think so—I don't know for sure. But in the pictures, there's a twisty madrone. That one." She points to the tree corkscrewing upward, its red bark peeling. A breeze gently rustles the leaves.

"Hey." Mike reaches across the seat to rest his hand on hers, his warmth and strength seeping into her. "You sure you want to do this? You seem tense."

"I am," she says, gripping the door handle.

"We don't have to be here. We can go."

"No, this is something I need to do." She gets out shakily, closes the door. Walks across the gravel to the soft grass leading to the ragged edge of the cliff. She has always thought of this drop-off as a sharp descent into an abyss, or a plunge into hell. But in fact she is gazing down a gentle slope thick with growth, leading to the bottom of the ravine. Where the hillside was once snowy, thick bushes and trees have cropped up. She thinks she should feel something, but there's nothing, only the sound of the wind in the trees.

Mike comes up next to her and looks out, too, as if there is something important to be watching for. "Thank you for driving me," she says.

"It's what I do," he says. "It's no trouble."

She turns to look at his profile, his hair lit by the sun. He has grown on her—at this moment, she thinks he's the most beautiful man she has ever seen. She can't explain why. "When you drove to Wappenish, you went there just to check on me. To bring me back to reality. Why? You barely even knew me."

"Doesn't matter," he says, looking at her. "You needed someone."

She understands, now, that it's really that simple for him. "I blew you off and sent you all the way back here. I suspected you of collusion with Logan. But inside"—and here she presses her fist to her chest—"I knew they were gone."

"You don't have to apologize," he says.

"No, I do. You're a nice person. You're decent to the core. I'm not sure I understand people like you."

"There's nothing to understand. I'm not a saint. I have my selfish reasons for doing things."

"Like what?" She smiles at him, and he grins back, kicks at the ground with his boot.

"I think you're cute, and weird. I like weird."

"Thanks a lot."

"Hey, I'm weird, too."

"Yeah, you are, kind of."

A gray squirrel scampers across the road, right past them and down through the brush. Phoebe points down into the ravine. "That's where the car landed. Upside down. It was totaled."

"You don't have to talk about it."

"Yes, I do," she says. The dream is always the same. It always happens here, where the tall madrone tree leans over, tall and spindly. The car is airborne, and the snow pelts the windshield, the wipers still going and going. She turns to Mike and says, "At the motel in Wappenish, I know why you wanted me to read the newspaper article."

"I was worried about you, that's all."

"I know that now. I knew it then, too. I couldn't handle it, though."

"Yeah. I figured that out. Didn't want to press you."

"I knew what was in the article. I always did."

"I figured that was the case, too," he says, watching the squirrel scamper up a cedar tree.

"I want to tell you what happened."

"Like I said, you don't have to."

"I do. I need to tell you. I have to say the words, or it will never be real. I want to tell you everything."

CHAPTER THIRTY-SEVEN

The forecast called for high winds that night, strong enough to topple trees, especially under the weight of snow. Visibility only a few feet. *Best not to drive if you can help it,* the forecasters said. A strong storm was set to roar down from Canada.

"I bought gas for the generator," Logan said. He swiveled in his office chair, and Phoebe noticed that he had hastily turned on the screensaver, so she could not see what he'd been typing on his computer. Her gaze shifted to his cell phone on the desk, the screen glowing in the faraway springtime color of the garden.

In the master bedroom, Ava had just woken, her voice still dim, sleepy, fussy. Phoebe turned and hurried to her daughter, her own brain moving in slow motion. Ava had been sick twice this winter with strong viruses, both of which Phoebe had promptly caught. Her sense of smell had fled for most of the winter, as had any promise of a full night's sleep. She wanted to stride back into Logan's office, slam her fist on the keyboard, light the screen to reveal whatever message he'd been typing, but she needed to care for their daughter, something he had neglected to do far too often in the past three months.

"Mama," Ava said, holding out her arms. Her cheeks were smudged with tears. "Mama gone . . ."

"I'm not gone," Phoebe said. "I was talking to Daddy." She scooped up Ava, tried to tamp down her rage. He was too focused on whatever damned business idea he'd come up with. He discarded them as fast as he could conjure them.

But then she felt his arms encircling her waist, and he bent his head over her shoulder to make a funny face at his daughter. Ava grinned, and then she laughed. The sound of her giggles, unstoppable, made Phoebe smile, too, filling her heart.

"I'll take her," he said, reaching around to pick up Ava, swinging her above his head. "Who's Daddy's brave girl, intrepid adventurer, future president of the world?" He trotted down the hall, Ava laughing on his shoulders, her tears forgotten. He ran into her room and Phoebe followed, her misgivings dissolving in a flood of relief.

But halfway down the hall, she pivoted and backtracked, slipping into his office instead. He was good at this, shifting instantly from distant to eminently present, 100 percent a daddy, which was what spun her head around. She loved him for sweeping their daughter out of her arms, but she sensed a deeper layer of deception, as though he were playing a role.

She found his computer turned off, another origami crane on the mouse pad. The folded paper shapes were multiplying all over the room. She counted twenty of them. This meant he was restless.

She sat at his desk, staring at her own reflection in his computer monitor, a virtual ghost of herself. His elusiveness exhausted her. Or perhaps it was motherhood that had worn her down, turned her into a faded, threadbare rug, too often trodden upon.

She went back down the hall and stood outside Ava's room, listening to the deep and soothing cadence of his voice. He was reading *Curious George* again. Next it would be *Goodnight Moon*. How could she fault an attentive dad?

She retreated into the kitchen, surveyed the nearly empty refrigerator. There was nothing for dinner. She hadn't had time for shopping.

"Let's pick up pizza," Logan said behind her. He held Ava in his arms. She was asleep again with her cheek pressed to his shoulder. Phoebe felt simultaneously moved and slighted. Ava never fell asleep on her shoulder, but then Phoebe's shoulders were bony, not broad like Logan's.

"You'll wake her," she whispered.

"She sleeps in the car—you know that."

Phoebe looked out the window. Snowflakes swirled in the air, still benign. The drive could give her a chance to talk to Logan, to get some real answers. But even as she said, "Pizza sounds good," a cold front passed through her like a premonition.

She called in the order of a Greek and a Mediterranean. The side salad and drinks. Logan walked down the hall while she was placing the order so that her voice would not wake Ava. As she watched him recede into the shadows, she had a strange feeling that he was receding into the past.

They bundled up Ava, who woke a little when they strapped her into her car seat but dropped again into a slumber. On the drive down the road, Phoebe glanced at Logan in profile, took in his handsome features, which she had come to take for granted, and a deep ache pressed into her, a fear that she was losing him. Part of her said, *Let him go. If he is lying to you, if he is having affairs, why do you want him?* She wanted him to be a better man. She wanted to believe in the man she thought she had married.

She could see him in Ava's expressions, in her temperament. Sometimes, Ava was patient, allowing him to turn pages in a book, staring at rain or a butterfly or her own shadow with intense concentration. She could shut out the world, but at other times, she became restless. Just like him.

Now he was silent, brooding. As the car hummed down the road in the softly falling snow, Phoebe turned to Logan and asked, "Who is it?"

"Who is what?" he said, glancing over at her. She could see in his eyes that he was somewhere else.

"Who is the other woman?" She knew he had one, although she wasn't sure she cared much who it was. She just wanted him to admit to an affair. But instead, he laughed.

"What are you talking about?"

"How long has it been going on?"

"Shit, not again," he muttered. "You keep bringing this up."

"Because it keeps happening." But she could not remember bringing it up recently, except as a joke when they'd seen a tattooed woman in a local café. She'd asked if the woman was his girlfriend, knowing it was not likely, as the woman was pushing eighty. She wore her tattoos well.

He'd frowned, ordered his latte, and stomped out. When she had asked him what was wrong, he'd said, "I can't believe you're so paranoid. Just leave it alone."

She'd found herself apologizing, as if she were the one to blame. She had dropped the matter, and he had succeeded in planting doubt in her head again. Perhaps she had overreacted. Perhaps her insecurity had come from her childhood, since her mother had been away so much, leaving her husband and daughter to fend for themselves.

"You received mixed signals from her, for sure," Logan had often said.

He always implied that she was asking too much of him when all she sought was honesty.

"I don't always bring this up," she said, reaching forward to wipe condensation off the interior of the windshield. "I'm just asking you to tell me the truth."

"We're on this nice family outing," he said in an irritated voice. "The three of us going out for pizza. Why do you have to ruin it?"

For a nanosecond, she thought she *was* ruining it. "We're picking up pizza," she said. "And Ava's asleep."

"It's cozy, fun, all of us together, but you want to make it a fight. Can't we just enjoy this evening?"

"I'm not fighting. I'm asking. Why aren't you answering?" He was winding her up all over again. "Are you about to take another trip somewhere? Are you?"

"Why are you guilting me? I go to conferences for us, for our future. You know we can't do this forever."

"I thought you loved Fair Winds. You were all about the funeral business when I met you."

"Things change. I'm always looking ahead—you know that."

"Are you having an affair?" she repeated, her voice rising. The snow thickened, clinging to the windshield. "Yes or no. Are you sleeping with someone else?"

"Are *you*? Because that would be your reason for asking, wouldn't it?" His phone lit up. He glanced down at the screen. She reached over and slapped it out of his hand.

"When would I have time?" she shouted. "I take care of Ava, drive her to day care, and then I go to work. I'm up all night with her while you're off gallivanting. Need I go on?"

"I'm working, not gallivanting. I'm here now, aren't I? I'm here. Why do you want to bring up the past?"

"I'm not bringing up the past. This is right now."

"You're shouting. You'll wake her."

"Now you're worried about waking her?"

"Our daughter needs to sleep. She's exhausted." He looked at Phoebe, and she saw something in his eyes—fear and anxiety. And she knew then that he was afraid of losing her. "Let's talk when we get home," he said. "Later, I promise. I'll tell you everything."

Phoebe wanted to shout at him, *Tell me now!* But she bit her lip, saying nothing so as not to disturb Ava's slumber. "I don't know how you do this," she muttered instead. She reached through the sound of the rising wind, into the past, rummaged for a memory of the Logan she had once known. Honest, attentive, romantic. Flowers, candlelit dinners, long talks late into the night, discussions about future plans, leisurely strolls through antiques shops, the accumulation of beloved vintage furniture.

Even as visibility dropped to zero, she was trying to pinpoint the exact moment when he'd begun to drift. But then Logan was shouting something at her, his voice coming from far away.

It's as if she can see them now, the tawny doe and two fawns bounding in front of the car. The steering wheel turned sharply to the right to avoid them, as the deer leaped to the left, and miraculously the car missed them. They were safe, but the car hit a patch of ice and violently skidded. No matter how the wheel turned, the car had a force of its own, the laws of physics spinning it around and around. Her stomach lurched as they went airborne, and she saw her own hands on the steering wheel, the car weightless as a feather before plummeting into the ravine.

CHAPTER THIRTY-EIGHT

She looks over at Mike, who has been patiently listening to her story without interrupting. "You already knew," she says. "You were waiting for me to admit it."

He takes her hand. His fingers are a lifeline. She senses no judgment in him, no expectation. "I wasn't waiting for you to say it. That was for you to decide. But I was waiting for you, Phoebe. Just. You."

She squeezes his hand, the breeze drifting up from the ravine, sweetened with scents of the forest. "I believe you. Isn't that strange? After all the lies Logan told me. After everything."

"This drop-off is steep. Miracle you got out alive."

A miracle or a curse, she thinks, and she still cannot decide which. "My punishment was surviving. I have some scars on my legs—I don't even know what cut me. And I had a concussion, apparently. A few fractured ribs." *And a broken mind.*

"I wish I could've been here for you. To help you."

"You are a helper, aren't you?" she says, looking at him.

"Yeah, it's in my nature, I guess."

"I probably wouldn't have even noticed you. I wasn't myself. Pretty much ever again."

"Understandable," he says.

"Renee came back to take care of me. I owe her my life . . ."

"She told me she owes you hers, too—multiple times when you were growing up."

"You spoke to her?" Phoebe says sharply.

"A few times at work. She misses you, and your friendship."

Phoebe falls silent, unsure which is truer, that she took her friend for granted, or that Renee betrayed her trust. Perhaps both are true.

"Let's go down there," Mike says, gesturing into the ravine.

She hesitates, watching him venture down a narrow dirt trail along the hillside. Then she follows him, the way unfamiliar to her, along the winding route to the bottom of the ravine, where a meandering stream is now running, gurgling along, unaware of the tragedy that occurred here. No trace of the car remains, no point of impact. Salal bushes, blackberry vines, and small alder trees have grown up around the site of the accident.

Phoebe can't remember what happened after the car hit the ground. The truth is, she can't remember swerving off the road. The images come to her only in dreams. She does not remember Don showing up, although he must've been here—she was unconscious. She only remembers waking in the hospital, the beeping of monitors, white walls, the doctor's face like a mirage above her. She does not remember her reaction to the devastating news about the deaths of Logan and Ava, which must've been imparted with care, lest she lose her mind.

Then she was sedated, but she tipped over the edge all the same. For there is no way to tell a person that they have lost everything without throwing them into an abyss. She has been here, trapped in this ravine, in the dream, for three years.

She crouches, reaches her hand into the stream, the cold current pushing through her fingers, racing down from snowmelt in the mountains toward the vast Pacific Ocean. She imagines herself a molecule inside the water.

Mike crouches beside her. "It's okay," he says. "It was an accident. It wasn't your fault. You did what anyone would have done. Anyone would've swerved to avoid a doe and her babies."

She nods, clinging to his words because she needs them. She needs to believe them. She can feel the tears, lets them fall into the stream, and then she and Mike climb the trail out of the ravine and back toward the sunlight.

CHAPTER THIRTY-NINE

As Mike drives her to the Willows, she looks out at the waning light. She feels weightless, as if her troubles floated downstream. "I've never told anyone about that night," she says to Mike. "I mean the part about Logan and me arguing."

"Then I'm honored that you told me." At the Willows, he parks beneath a shady cedar tree. "I'll just . . . wait out here."

"Why don't you come in with me? I'd like you to meet my mom."

"You really want me to?"

"Yeah, I think she'll like you. But I should warn you. My mom is . . . unpredictable. She's not violent or anything. She's just . . . in and out."

"I can handle it," he says.

"I know you can."

They find Phoebe's mother in a rocking chair facing the sliding glass doors in her room. Her silver hair is lit by the sun, and when she turns around to look at them, she smiles, radiant and beautiful. *She did fine without me,* Phoebe thinks. Her mother is knitting again, a square of pale-blue wool in her lap and two white knitting needles. She calls this pastime a meditation.

Phoebe pulls up a chair and sits beside her. A forest breeze wafts in through the screen door. "Mom—how are you?" She holds her breath, unsure what today will bring, whether her mother will be here or somewhere far away.

Lidia looks at Phoebe with warmth and kindness in her eyes. *Thank you*, Phoebe thinks, exhaling. Her mother does not remember the accident, has no idea that Phoebe was driving, and she does not seem to remember her granddaughter. But perhaps this is a way to block out the pain, to simply forget. "How was your drive to that town, Wappenish?" Her mother places her knitting on a side table.

Phoebe smiles, relieved, although she knows her mother's lucidity is temporary. "It was enlightening. I'm sorry I haven't come to see you in a while."

Her mother looks up at Mike, who is standing next to Phoebe. "Who is the young man?"

"This is Mike Rivera, Mom. I work with him at—he's a colleague."

"Pleased to meet you, Mrs. Glassman," he says, reaching out to take her hand.

"What a nice young man," Lidia says, shaking his hand. "You have honesty in your eyes."

"Never heard that one," he says, smiling. "But I'll take it."

"Phoebe found a good one this time," her mother says, letting go of his hand. "Finally." Lidia picks up her knitting again.

"Mom?"

No answer. Just knitting.

Phoebe fights back tears. Mike pats her shoulder. "Nice picture there," he says, pointing to the photograph of Phoebe at her tenth birthday party in the park. "That's you, isn't it?"

"And that's my dad," she says, feeling the pressure of grief on her chest. "And that's Renee."

"You were all so young. I mean, you still are. Your dad was a good-looking guy."

"He didn't much know it, though," she says. The day was bright, sunlight glinting off their hair, out on the grassy field, tall oaks and cherry trees in the background. But there is something else, something that nagged at her before. No, *someone*, also in the background. The face is slightly fuzzy but clear enough to make her draw in a sharp breath.

She picks up the picture, shows it to her mother. "Mom, you said something to me a while ago: 'He's Professor Glassman to you.' What did you mean? Did you think I was someone else?"

Her mother looks away, staring outside, her knitting resting in her lap now.

"Mom," Phoebe says, trying to keep her voice calm. She places the photograph right in front of her mother's face.

Her mother frowns, her eyes filling with tears. But she does not say a word.

"Why did you say, *He's Professor Glassman to you?*"

"Phoebe," Mike says.

Phoebe backs up. "Sorry. It's just . . ."

"We've all moved on," her mother says. "I gave him an ultimatum. I had no choice."

"Moved on from what, Mom?"

"I told him it was either her or me."

"What? Told whom?" Phoebe says, unable to catch her breath. Her mother's words are sucking the air from the room. "You had to tell whom?"

"Your father," Lidia says, looking at the picture. "I wasn't there for your birthday. I'm sorry."

"You weren't there, no. You were in France."

"I started it. You know, he was a good man. I pushed him to it."

"You pushed Dad? How did you push him?"

"I was always the one to stray. He was loyal until that day."

"You had an affair?" Phoebe says, her voice high pitched. *How can this be true? My own mother?*

Lidia does not reply, but she seems to shrink.

"Dad used to brood in front of the fireplace." Phoebe always thought he was thinking of his lectures or the book lying open on his lap, but perhaps he was fretting about his broken marriage.

Sometimes, when her mother came home from a trip, Phoebe heard her parents arguing in hushed tones, hurling barbs at each other. *You never want to come with me,* her mother hissed at him. *You both could come.* And her father: *Phoebe has school. You think you can do anything you want.*

I'm a career woman, this is important to me.

I know what's important to you, her father replied. *You've got no impulse control. You have a daughter to raise.*

Phoebe blocked out those arguments. They made her tense, made her hide her head under the pillow, singing to herself to tune out the bickering. In the morning, her parents always feigned normalcy, kissing each other goodbye, but only a peck on the cheek.

"I had to come home early," her mother says now. "I had to be here. I couldn't let it go on."

Phoebe is hyperventilating, the room spinning, the colors leaching away. She sits with her head between her knees until the blood flows back into her brain. "You couldn't let what go on? Your affair or his?"

"Well, both," her mother says, sighing.

"You're not remembering correctly," Phoebe says. She looks at Mike in desperation.

His brows rise as he points to the photograph. The person in the background looks familiar. The same woman was in a picture in Darlene Steele's house. At Phoebe's birthday party, the woman stands in the background, touching the arm of Phoebe's father. She is Pauline's birth mother, Marianne Tyler.

CHAPTER FORTY

Lidia returns to knitting with shaky fingers. The scarf she is spinning, a rectangular strip of wool, glimmers with a hint of cobalt blue.

"Why didn't you tell me?" Phoebe says. "How long have you known?" Her voice rises, the hurt curdling inside her.

Mike takes Phoebe's hand, squeezes, but she hardly notices.

"I knew from the beginning," Lidia says, looping the wool furiously. "But I didn't know there was a child. Your dad never said a word. And then he got sick, his heart began to fail. Still, he said nothing until he called Logan into his room, the day before he died, and I heard what he said. He said there was a child, and Logan needed to go to her and tell her. Pauline never knew, you see. Marianne never told her."

"Logan was supposed to tell Pauline that she had a half sister. That Dad had an affair with her mother. With Marianne." Phoebe is shaking all over. "But instead Logan ended up sleeping with Pauline and lying about his identity."

Mike lets out a low whistle. "Wait, your husband slept with Pauline?"

"Instead of telling her about me," Phoebe goes on, her voice edgy with impatience. "If she had known about me back then, she would've come to see me, don't you think?"

"And," Mike says, "he was supposed to tell you that the two of you were sisters because—"

"Because Marianne and my dad had an affair," Phoebe says impatiently. "He was Pauline's biological father. He kept that secret for years. And then, I don't know, he was dying and wanted to make sure Pauline and I knew each other. He waited long enough."

Mike laughs, shaking his head. "You married a winner. Someone exactly like your dad."

"No," Phoebe says quickly. "Dad was different. Dad . . . didn't lie about everything. He wasn't a grifter. He had one affair. Just one. Right, Mom?" *And you drove him to it. It wasn't in his nature. He was a homebody, a nerd!* But no, he was a grown-up. He made his choices.

Lidia nods slightly, looking out at a robin alighting on a high branch, belting out a loud, cacophonous song. "When Logan came back," she says, "I asked him about Pauline, and he said he looked for her but never found her. I should've questioned him further, but your dad had just passed away. I was in no condition . . ."

"Why didn't Dad tell me?" Phoebe shouts. "He knew that Pauline and I were half sisters the whole time!"

"It's my fault," her mother says. "When I returned from France, our agreement was that he would not see Marianne again, that he would have nothing to do with her if he wanted to stay with us. With you and me. He had to choose. He chose us."

Dad chose us, Phoebe thinks, *and I'm supposed to be grateful?* She scrutinizes her mother's face, the lucid expression in her eyes. There had always been truth in her words, despite her recent lapses of memory. "Dad must've known that Marianne married," Phoebe says, "and that another man was raising his child."

"Your dad kept his promise," Lidia says. "He never looked back."

"Because of you."

"He made his choice. He loved us."

Mike keeps squeezing Phoebe's hand. "Nobody ever told Pauline the truth about her father," she says.

Lidia looks up at Phoebe. "You should go now. I've got a date. My daughter will be here soon."

No, don't disappear again. Phoebe wants to shake her mother's shoulders but tamps down her desperation. "Okay, Mom," she says, wiping her tears. Mike steers her out to the car. She sits in the passenger seat, stunned.

"Well, that was a lot," he says. "You okay?"

"Not at all," she says. "Logan must have started sleeping with Pauline back then. He and I . . . we were barely married."

"Don't go there," Mike says.

"I got pregnant with Ava soon after that." She can't seem to buckle her seat belt. "And Darlene, she must've known. She must have. She was Marianne's best friend. She had to know about Pauline."

"You sure about that?"

"Not completely," she says, twisting her hands in her lap. "But I suspect Darlene knows more than she told me. I have to talk to her. If she knew Marianne well enough to adopt her daughter, she has to know more."

Phoebe dials Darlene's number. The phone rings, then a recorded message blares in her ear. *The number you have reached has been disconnected or is no longer in service.* She tries again, same message. Looks up Darlene Steele online, no listed number. "I don't get it. Looked like she'd been living in that house in Modesto forever," Phoebe says. "Now she's gone?"

"Maybe she died," Mike says. "As we both know too well, it happens."

Phoebe searches online but can't find any record of Darlene's death, no mention of her name on any mortuary website, no obituary.

"She could be in the hospital," Mike says.

"And her phone is disconnected?"

"Maybe she forgot to pay the bill."

Exasperated, Phoebe calls the surrounding hospitals, but they are all dead ends. Then an idea dawns on her, the pieces falling into place—fantastic, improbable, but she can't shake the thought. "I know where she might be."

"I have a shift in an hour," Mike says. "But I could take you after that."

"No, take me home, I'll drive my own car. Don't look at me like that. I'll be all right."

"I know you will, but before you go." He reaches across her lap to open the glove compartment, brings out a sealed, official-looking envelope addressed to him.

"The DNA test results for Mel," she says, sucking in her breath, careful not to say *Ava*.

"I haven't opened it yet. I thought you would want to read it first."

CHAPTER FORTY-ONE

When Phoebe pulls up in front of the house on Cameo Lane in Wappenish, the sun is falling, but dusk has not yet overtaken the sky. The For Sale sign is gone, as she knew it would be. The grass has been cut, new shrubs planted. The siding has been painted sunshine yellow. There is a freshness about the place.

She is taking a risk, showing up in town. If Ben Favre sees her here, he could file a restraining order. He has already shown so much compassion by not filing charges against her. But she'll take her chances. She gets out of the car, strides through the landscaped garden to the front door, rings the doorbell. The sound echoes through the house. No answer. The curtains are drawn. Laughter, voices emanate from the backyard. A pleasant mountain breeze wafts in, the sun bright, redolent of springtime. A neighbor is outside weeding the garden, eyeing her with curiosity. Phoebe waves. He waves back.

She grips the envelope in one hand, the mail that Mike gave to her. She read the message inside. Again and again. On the drive up to Wappenish, she assembled the puzzle pieces in her mind. The address on the back of a photograph, left in a pile of magazines in a bathroom, had been her only real connection to this place. A slender thread. She thought the handwriting was Pauline's, but she is certain now that it wasn't.

She walks around to the back of the house, her heartbeat fast, sees what she expected to see. The home's new owner, Darlene Steele, pushing a child on the swing set. Pushing Mel Favre. Mel is facing the other way, toward the woods, pumping her legs. She does not see Phoebe, but Darlene turns to look, and the color drains from her face. "What are you doing here?"

"I could ask you the same question." Phoebe strides toward her, shaking with anger, holding the envelope in her hand. "You lied to me," she says through gritted teeth. "You knew that Pauline was my half sister."

Darlene stops pushing the swing, her shoulders square, and juts out her chin, defiant. "I don't know what you're talking about."

"Yes, you do!" Phoebe shouts. "The proof is right here. Not that I needed it. My mother told me enough. But this adds a missing piece. And you. You knew, but you didn't tell me."

"You need to get off my property. I'll call the police."

"Call them," Phoebe says, a challenge. "I'd be happy to talk to them."

Mel slows on the swing set, turns to look at Phoebe, and her eyes widen. She leaps off the swing set. She runs to Darlene, grips her hand, and hides behind her.

It's all Phoebe can do not to run to Mel, scoop her up, and hold her tight. "I'm not going to hurt you," she says, backing up.

"You need to go," Darlene says, a glint in her eye. "Go in the house, Mel. Go on inside and have some lemonade. Now. Right now."

Mel lets go of Darlene's hand and dashes into the house. The door slams behind her.

"You didn't tell me the truth," Phoebe says. "But you knew. You should've told me. I deserved to know."

"Do you have any idea what it's like to lose everyone you love?" Darlene asks.

"As a matter of fact, I do," Phoebe says. "How could you be okay with me in a psychiatric ward knowing what you did? I was not imagining the resemblance—"

"Mel, honey! Ready to come home?" a man calls out, coming around the corner into the backyard. Mel's father, Ben, dressed in a bespoke suit, holding car keys in his hand. He looks at Phoebe and frowns, shocked. "What's going on? What the hell are you doing here? I'm calling the police." He whips out his phone.

"Please, wait!" Phoebe shouts. "Hear me out. I mean no harm."

Ben hesitates, and Phoebe knows why. He is the good man who adopted Mel. He did not press charges against her. He had sympathy for her. But he could change his mind in a minute. Time is short. She is pressing her luck.

"Read this—it's important. Then I'll go." She hands the envelope to him. He reads the letter inside, frowns, and looks up at Phoebe. "Is this true? How did you . . . ?"

"Yes," Phoebe says. "We sent away a few strands of Mel's hair for a DNA test."

"You *what*?"

"Don't ask," she says.

"How the hell did you get my daughter's hair? Oh, you were in the house—Jesus."

"It's not what you think," she says.

Darlene's face is ashen. "You will not take Mel from me," she says, her voice hard.

"How long have you known?" Phoebe asks. "About Pauline, about Mel?"

Darlene is shaking. She sits in a patio chair, holds on to the edge of the patio table. "Pauline told me after she found the cards that Michael—I mean Logan—dropped behind her bureau. She told me she had given up her baby for adoption, that he was the father. He didn't want a child with her. Now I know why. *You* were having a kid, too. His wife, at the same time."

"What are you talking about?" Ben shouts.

"You lied about Pauline's miscarriage," Phoebe goes on. "It wasn't a miscarriage, was it? Mel is hers."

"She was going to Washington to look for Michael," Darlene says. "She was more concerned about finding him than finding her own child. She didn't care about Mel, but I did. I cared. I hired a private investigator to find her."

Pauline must've loved her child, Phoebe thinks. *But perhaps her feelings were complicated.* "You knew all of this, but you said nothing."

"Mel is my granddaughter," Darlene says in a brittle voice. "She is all that I have left. She's all that I have, all that I want."

Phoebe glares at Darlene. "When I visited you in Modesto, I noticed some photographs were missing from the wall, but the hooks were still there. You took down pictures of Mel so I wouldn't see them, didn't you?"

"That's ridiculous," Darlene says, but she won't look Phoebe in the eyes.

"You had no right to keep the truth from me!"

Ben is still looking at the paper, shaking his head. "I don't understand. This indicates that—"

"Yes," Phoebe says. "Mel is my niece, my blood."

CHAPTER FORTY-TWO

This April day is full of springtime, rhododendrons in bright white and purple blooms. Puffs of whimsical clouds skid across the sky. When Mike and Phoebe arrive at Renee's place, the moving van is already there. The movers are carting a couch out the front door. Renee is standing in the garden in a jacket and jeans, directing them.

"Where's Vik?" Phoebe says, getting out of the car.

"He's already in California with my sister," Renee says. "She has a daughter about his age."

"How nice," Phoebe says, glancing in the front door at the piles of moving boxes in the hall. Mike is leaning against his car. "Congratulations on the new job."

"Hey, it's not my dream job, but I can move up. The company makes outdoor gear—so, you know, it's in my wheelhouse."

"I'm going to miss you," Phoebe says.

"What about you?" Renee moves closer, lowers her voice, nods toward Mike. "You and that guy?"

Phoebe laughs. "I'm taking things slow. But I know he won't get into weird moneymaking schemes and deceptions like Logan did. Mike is . . . what you see is what you get."

"You think Logan was up to a new swindle when he died?" Renee says.

"There wasn't any evidence of one," Phoebe says, sighing. "I think he was actually trying to disentangle himself from his past, looking for something legit."

Renee nods, squinting into the sun. "His secrets died with him then."

"Not all of them," Phoebe says.

"I know. I apologize for not believing you, when you said Mel looked like Ava. I had no idea."

"It's okay," Phoebe says.

"You will be a good auntie."

"When they let me into her life. I need to prove myself."

"You will," Renee says. "We don't know what we would have done. Any of us." She looks down at her manicured fingernails and repeats softly, "We don't know what we would do."

Phoebe takes her hand and squeezes it briefly, then lets it go. "Thank you for always being there for me." She glances at Mike, who is now walking down the street for a smoke. He's trying to quit. She'll give him that. Then she looks at Renee again. "When I saw you and Barry through the window of his house—"

"I went over there to talk to him. I was worried about you. I really was. We both were, Barry and I . . . because of what happened before. And one thing led to another. It was a mistake."

"I shouldn't have spied on you. But I was so sure."

"It's okay," Renee says. "Anyway, he's still in love with his wife."

"Is that good or bad?" Phoebe says.

"Well, they have kids together. The drama was hard on the boys. They're talking to each other again. That's a good thing."

"So you two . . ."

"We're not compatible. But Barry is a kind man. With interesting hobbies. He helped me to feel hopeful again."

"I know that feeling," Phoebe says, waving at Mike. He stamps out the cigarette, picks it up. He is on his way back.

EPILOGUE

Two Years Later

Second Chance Antiques nestles in a cedar forest overlooking the sea, catching sunlight through the large bay windows for much of the day. When customers enter through the antique front door, they gasp in delight at the summertime displays, which Renee helped to artfully arrange for Phoebe. Renee and Vik often visit from California.

Business is brisk during these lazy, balmy days. Already this morning, dozens of customers have wandered in, and Phoebe has sold two clocks, several vinyl records, two vintage teapots, books, a Tiffany lamp, and an antique display cabinet.

"Where do you want this?" Mike says, emerging from the storage room with a large, colorful *matryoshka* doll in hand. "Nine nesting dolls in this one!" He is tanned from sunny mornings spent walking the beach, his blond hair even lighter.

"Front display case next to the other ones," she says, ringing up a set of silver napkin holders. She keeps eyeing the door, jumping at every squeak of the hinges. The anticipation is almost unbearable, but she tells herself to be patient, everything in its time.

When she woke to the melody of a song sparrow, and Mike tightened his arm around her waist, she lingered in lazy pleasure, watching the sunrise. Today started as a good day after a night without dreams. Such nights are to be savored, she knows, such calm mornings a blessing. *There will be good days,* Dr. Ogawa once told her. *And maybe, eventually, the good days will outnumber the bad ones.*

This is a good day.

Mike came downstairs first to make breakfast, a tofu scramble this time. Each morning is different, beautifully unpredictable. Phoebe sat up in bed against the pillows and listened to him clanking around, listened to the meows of Mr. Tibbles the cat, who had slept on her feet most of the night before wandering downstairs to tend to business in the shop. A loving and friendly gray tabby, he had been left behind when the neighbors moved, and he needed a home. She adopted Mr. Tibbles without a moment's hesitation, and now the furball is snoring in his plush bed on a top shelf. Customers coo at him, asking to pet him, and he always agrees without complaint. He soaks up the attention.

She has no idea why anyone in their right mind would leave behind such a loving creature or any living being, for that matter, abandoning them to a sad fate. But then, Logan was that kind of person in the beginning. He left behind those he was supposed to love, over and over again.

But then he came back.

Barry was right—I believe now, too, Logan would've stayed. The origami cranes did not mean he was leaving her for good. They were a symbol of hope and renewal—for their marriage, perhaps, for their family, but she can't dwell on what might have been. She has been too busy mending her proverbial fences, gluing together her relationships, building Mel's trust in her again. Ben's trust in her. Two years of therapy, hard work, transformation—it has all been exhausting and exhilarating.

After breakfast, she showered, pulled on jeans and a soft sweater, knit by her mother, and came downstairs to the shop.

She glances at her watch. Any minute now . . . There it is, the bell ringing above the door, and Mel bursts in and runs toward Phoebe at top speed, managing to avoid knocking over anything on the way, but it wouldn't matter if she did.

"Aunt Phoebe, Aunt Phoebe, look what I found!" Mel is holding a large hardcover book with a princess on the cover.

"Where did you find that?" Phoebe says, grinning. In the last few months, Mel seems to have shot up a couple of inches. What a gift it is that she has forgotten to be afraid of her aunt. Little by little, she came around, but it took months for her to take Phoebe's hand again without fear. And it took many playdates with Ben as chaperone before he invited Phoebe into their lives.

"I found it in a bookstore," Mel says. "It has all the fairy tales."

"We could read them together," Phoebe says.

The cat has jumped down off his bed and leaps into Mel's arms. She cradles him and buries her face in his fur. "Mr. Tibbles, I missed you. I love you, Mr. Tibbles."

Ben Favre walks in, lugging not one large suitcase, but two.

"Can I see my room?" Mel says, putting the cat down. He rubs around her legs. "I missed my room."

"Go on up," Phoebe says. "The bed's made." Mel is already running toward the stairs, completely at home, Mr. Tibbles trotting after her.

"I'll take these up," Ben says, following her.

"I hope the drive was okay?" Phoebe says.

"Smooth sailing, except for the kid in the back seat, asking, 'Are we there yet?' every five minutes," Ben says. They speak on the phone a couple of times a month, Ben relating Mel's latest escapades and milestones.

Phoebe laughs. "I'm glad you made it safely."

"Go on up with them," Mike says to Phoebe. "I'll hold down the fort for a bit."

She smiles at him, follows Mel up the stairs, Ben right behind her. At the top of the steps, he puts down the suitcases and pulls her aside. "Thanks for keeping her for two months this time. I couldn't get out of the conferences—"

"Oh, it's no trouble at all," she says, smiling. "All summer vacation, no problem. We planned for this." *I've been looking forward to it for weeks.* "Thank you for trusting me."

"You've earned it." He brings out his phone. Swipes through to a photo. Then he hands her the phone. "Darlene wanted me to show this to you."

She takes the phone from him, looks at the image. It's of a crumpled piece of paper, on which someone has written, *Tell my mom I love her. I always did.*

"What is this?" she says, handing back the phone, but she can feel the certainty, the sadness swirling through her.

"Pauline left it behind in the car, in the glove compartment with the vehicle registration."

"Nobody was in the car with her. That's what you're saying. She made her own decision."

He nods sadly. "It does appear that way."

She wipes tears in her eyes. "Poor Darlene."

"She's finding her way," he says. "At least she knows the truth."

They're both silent a moment, then he heads down the hall to hug Mel goodbye in her room, all painted in yellow and decorated with butterfly murals. Nose in her book, she does not seem at all worried about his departure.

Phoebe sees him off, then heads back upstairs, stopping in her studio. Her sculptures and supplies are lined up on the shelves, her newest project on the table. The lips, the forehead, and the hair need adjustment to capture the spirit of Ava the way she would be now, at nearly eight years old. She will keep growing older in Phoebe's studio, year after year, her ceramic eyes gazing out through the bay window, where a shimmering hummingbird hovers in the air, then swoops down and disappears into the glimmering green of the forest.

ACKNOWLEDGMENTS

This book—and, indeed, my entire writing career—would not be possible without the support of my friends, family, and writing colleagues. Deepest thanks to my intrepid, perceptive literary agent, Paige Wheeler; my brilliant editor at Lake Union Publishing, Danielle Marshall; production manager, Nicole Burns-Ascue; and the entire Amazon Publishing team. I appreciate my writing peeps who provided valuable feedback on the manuscript: Jana Bourne, Joe Ponepinto, Susan Wiggs, Sheila Roberts, Lois Dyer, Kate Breslin, Anne Clermont, Leigh Hearon, and Sandy Dengler. I'm grateful to Randall Platt, Patricia M. Stricklin, Dianne Gardner, and Janine Donoho for great brainstorming. Thank you to David Downing for valuable editorial feedback. Elizabeth Corcoran Murray, thank you for touring the Kitsap County coroner's office with me. I'm grateful to the Kitsap County coroner, Mr. Jeff Wallis, for giving us the tour and so much valuable information and expertise. My hat is off to skilled copyeditor James Gallagher, and astute readers Andrea Moran and Kellie Osborne. Thank you, Anthony Estrella, for checking my green-burial facts. Thank you to Gregg Olsen for your support and for putting me in touch with Matthew P. Glass, who shared his fascinating experiences growing up in a family-owned funeral home. His untimely passing shocked and saddened me. My condolences and heartfelt thoughts are with his family.

I wrote the first draft of this novel on my collection of vintage manual typewriters manufactured in the 1930s to 1960s. I'm indebted to typewriter collector and salesperson Robert Donald Feldman, owner of Typewriter Fever in Bremerton, Washington; typewriter repairman Paul Lundy, owner of Bremerton Office Machine Company; Matthew McCormack, typewriter repairman and owner of Ace Typewriter & Equipment in Portland, Oregon; Chris Mullen of Acme Type Machines in Wassenaar, Netherlands; and Richard Polt, author of *The Typewriter Revolution*.

My readers, reviewers, and Bookstagrammers are close to my heart. I can't possibly name everyone, but you are my lifeline along with booksellers and librarians. You make the world go round. Thank you. Special shout-out to Suzanne Droppert, Nathaniel Hattrick, and Markie Rustad of my local bookstore, Ballast Book Company in Bremerton, Washington. Many thanks to my family far and wide, to my husband and our rescued felines—you are the best.

ABOUT THE AUTHOR

Photo © 2015 Carol Ann Morris

Born in India and raised in North America, A. J. Banner received degrees from the University of California, Berkeley. Banner grew up sneaking books from her parents' library, reading Agatha Christie, Daphne du Maurier, and other masters of mystery. Her previous best-selling novels of psychological suspense include *The Good Neighbor*, *The Twilight Wife*, *After Nightfall*, and *The Poison Garden*. She lives in the Pacific Northwest with her husband and five rescued cats. For more information, visit www.ajbanner.com.